Love for a
Vampire

Reviews from the website ...

"I just love this book ... read it three times now. Love it!"
Cassey 05/10/2011

"Just finished reading *Love for a Vampire*. It was far better than I thought it would be. I've read *Twilight* and *True Blood* [series] but this is now my fav book and I can't wait for the next one to come out ... Get this book readers you will not regret it."
Amanda (lover of books) 04/10/2011

"Wicked book! Can't wait for book two ..."
Abbie 30/09/2011

"Thrilling stuff filled with passion, torment and twists that you would never have seen coming ... a perfect balance that keeps you on edge. Wendy has created extraordinary characters that are strong throughout the story, compelling you to reach out to them. This is a stunning non-stop action book that will keep you reading and wanting more."
Tracey 29/09/2011

"Got this book for my daughter after I read it ... will make a great Xmas gift. Well done Wendy Huchison, I really enjoyed your book."
Ebony Jones 28/09/2011

"Wow!!! I loved it. When is the next one out because I so want it?"
Alison 28/09/2011

"Forget *Twilight* and *Vampire Diaries*. This book is spellbinding I just couldn't put it down. Wendy Huchison is a fresh new author that has you lost in her book filled with action, romance and even a dark nature to it ... you just want to read more. Well done and I can't wait for the next book to follow."
Christine 28/09/2011

Read more at: www.wendyhuchison.com

Love for a
Vampire

by
WENDY HUCHISON

Thank you

The Angel-May Saga

W. Huchison Publications

Published by

W. Huchison Publications
5 Wooton Court,
Scunthorpe, DN17 1XU

www.wendyhuchison.com

In association with Hague Publishing Services

© Wendy Huchison 2011
Reprinted 2011

ISBN 978-0-9570580-0-2

Cover & typesetting by Hague Publishing Services,
Doncaster, South Yorkshire

Printed and bound by Bell & Bain Ltd., Glasgow

In memory of Dean Huchison
... we all love you.

LOVE FOR A VAMPIRE is the first book in *The Angel-May Saga* trilogy.

Contents

Prologue

"Angel-May this spell must be cast tonight, or your future won't exist; your life will no longer be on this track," Jurisa advised her as they walked side by side, heading through the corridor towards the old hall. "Why tonight? Why can't it wait till I return from Molax?" Angel asked; her emerald eyes studied the old woman as she waited for the response.

"It's a waning moon on the Night of Hulda, you must do it tonight, your past is reaching that time when *she* first meets Zared, Angel, *please,* it cannot be missed."

Jurisa Sand is a witch born into a long line of powerful women. Her long hair had turned silver and was worn tied in a bun, held tightly in place with pins. She had young brown eyes, wise beyond her years, and skin that had worn with time. Over the years she had shrunk and begun

1

to hunch. At sixty-five years of age she had saved many in their fight to save good from being extinguished.

Jurisa had a daughter in her thirties. She had been captured by Leeda and held in a cell, drained and close to death. She was the next in line to take over the coven and the guidance of Angel's daughter, keeping her safe from those that would attack by the use of spells and psychic abilities that threatened her life, while Angel was away fighting demons by her warrior's and her husband's sides.

"OK, I shall be there in five minutes. Is Zared prepared for his role in this?" Angel asked as they entered the hall. There was a table surrounded by people ready for her to arrive. They rose to their feet when she entered. "Yes my Queen," she bowed. Angel stopped in the doorway and turned to her. "Good because without him doing what we asked of him, then this is all for nothing. Remember I will be asleep when he first comes. I will not recognise this place, but Zared will have to be with me when we do this so she …, so *I*," Angel corrected herself, "know who he is." Angel paused remembering the past. "I dream of him standing in front of me holding my hand. You need to make sure he speaks to me as a friend. He will have to teach me how to read and write. He will have to teach me how to *speak*." Angel turned to the waiting group, feeling their urgency to talk. "Jurisa, it's important he does that. He won't remember what he has said or done, so make sure you don't let him forget."

"Would it be a wiser choice for you to do this, so there are no mistakes?" the old witch enquired. "No I can't be near him right now. You will have to do this," Angel said, looking away momentarily. She didn't want to acknowledge the pain in her chest, or feel another tear on her face. Her throat was tight; clearing it she looked into Jurisa's eyes. "You will do this and I will see you in five minutes outside in the courtyard. Now if that's all, I have things to see to."

"Yes of course." She bowed again, as Angel closed the door on her.

Angel's time in the meeting was longer than expected. They had decided on a plan of action: a group would attack from the south and the east, while the warriors would attack from above. They had discovered that the demons had gathered on the north docks, preparing to open the doorway to Arico. Arico lay just beyond this world. A place of pure evil, with creatures that were strong and hard to kill. They were more dangerous than anything that this world had ever seen before. They would strike on the night after her daughter's fifth birthday; the day of her change, when Isis would become as her father.

"Jurisa, I'm ready to summon her." Angel was dressed in a ceremonial robe given to her after her cleansing from the coven. "Angel, please step this way." Jurisa took her outside to an altar filled with candles and a large bowl centred in a circle of salt. Jurisa handed her a half-closed red rose.

Zared was there already waiting for her. He was dressed in black, looking as handsome as ever. Angel felt her heart almost stop. Her chest began to hurt as she got closer to him. She begged silently not to let the tears appear as she took a deep breath.

Zared's golden eyes followed her every move, their tints of green invisible until he was inches away. He had protected her many times over the years, but she still found it unbearable to be near him at times. He was her first love and would always be her first.

"Please, both of you step inside the circle." Angel nodded. Zared held out his hand allowing her to take it. She took another deep breath before placing her hand into his. Zared smiled at her softly. Her pulse spiked. He had always given her this reaction. They stepped into the circle. "In this bowl we have crushed willow bark and sandalwood powder. This will summon your past to find you safely and protect you on your journey. This rose is to allow you to see your future and what you will become. This is the start of your journey and the time to open your heart to find your mate." Angel shifted, removing her hand from Zared's. She found it incomprehensible whenever anyone mentioned that word, 'mate'. After all, her mate was lost to her and his daughter didn't exist to him. Their future had changed because of Leeda and now it was not yet known who would come out of this war as victor.

"Now, Angel. You must take the rose and prick your finger." Angel did as instructed, stabbing a thin green thorn into her finger, feeling it sting as blood bubbled up on its removal. "Now, close your eyes and place a drop of blood on each eyelid." Angel did. "Zared, take Angel's finger and taste her blood."

Angel felt nerves twisting inside her. Zared lifted her hand. She watched, her breath frozen, as he bent down, placed her bloody finger to his lips and sucked on it lightly. Her breath rushed out; she fought her impulse to groan, a secret delight they once shared.

"This act must be sealed with a kiss." Angel went to protest, but her words froze in her throat. She wanted him every day; to feel his lips again. But she was afraid she couldn't handle it, not now. Zared moved closer, cupping her face in his hands. She could feel the warmth from his skin. He kissed her. A tear fell from Angel's eye; she could feel it gliding down her right cheek. He wasn't Zared of then; it was just a memory hidden deep in her heart. His kiss was cold and numb. His passion was gone, along with everything else they had once had.

"Hulda, Queen of Witches, mother to Diana and Lilly, sister to Freya. I ask of thee that you give safe journey to your chosen child, and allow her to receive hope in a future that's to come. Blessed be."

"Blessed be," Angel repeated, her voice just a whisper. Suddenly everything spun. Angel was falling; her body felt like it was no longer hers. Strong arms caught her before she went limp. Silence. She could hear nothing; she could see only darkness ... but she could feel pain.

Then she felt the pull.

Again she was back. She was highly aware of everything around her.

"It worked," Angel whispered, opening her eyes to see Zared inches from her, staring into her eyes. His fingers pushed hair from her face, tucking it back behind her ear. "Your journey has started. She will go to different times in your life, so if you feel strange then it may be her coming through." Jurisa was pleased. Smiling, she waved Angel to leave the circle.

"If I act differently, make sure you ask me how old I am. Then you will know which of us it is." Angel began to remember the different times she had visited her future self. How different she was back then; how vulnerable she had been.

Zared looked at Angel and smiled. It was an old smile. "There's my lover," he whispered, stepping closer and reaching for her hair. Angel's heart stopped. She suddenly felt faint again; a light of pure gold started to fill her body.

No it can't be! She started to back away from Zared. She remembered the words she had said to him a long time ago. "I have to go. Madoc and I are going over Isis's birthday celebrations plan. There isn't long and she will be celebrating." Angel felt shock; why had things turned out this way? Why did everything have to change again when she had finally come to terms with losing him and starting afresh?

Chapter One

Angel-May's face was numb and covered in bruises like giant plums. Her eyes were swollen purple, making it even harder to see as the burning pain made her eyes water. She blinked frantically to help them clear, feeling cool droplets on her cheeks.

Leaning against the far wall was a long pine mirror covered in dust and surrounded in a frame of cracked wood. It warped her reflection; Angel could see, in its false image of herself, patches of skin untouched, still free from him, from scars and colouring.

Angel wondered if she could change her face, her hair, her voice. Would she still have this life she has now if she were born in a different time and place? Would she live this closed off? Angel wondered many times over what her life would be like if things had been different. If her mother had stayed at home with her instead of going to the corner shop? If her father had grieved over her mother's death without hatred? If she had had sisters or brothers, someone to tell all her secrets to? But everything was ifs and wondering.

Angel sat staring around at her room. This had been her existence for sixteen years: four walls covered in peeling yellow paint. Two had signs of flowered paper that used to hang there many years ago. There was a small old broken single bed, with a badly-stained mattress that dipped from her weight when lying down. Her father had allowed her to change her bedding once a month to keep it from smelling, but dried blood still lingered, embedded in the fibres; evidence of her repeated beatings, and a smell she had become accustomed to.

Across from her bed was a pine bookcase, with six books all for children under ten years of age. She had memorised their words, looking at them over and over, their pages now worn and creased. Her father had also allowed her to have a handful of toys and games, but nothing more. They too sat neatly on the shelf, each having its own place.

At the foot of the bed was a large pink linen box containing clothes that he no longer wanted, passing them on to her. Some stained; others with holes from wear. A few she never wore; the fabric hurt her skin. She guessed that was why she had them.

Angel didn't really know what had happened to her mother, only pieces of information that came from her father as he beat her with his fists – unusual for him; an object was always in his hand. For his last visit it was a cane, long pale wood with notches. He used it on her legs and arms bringing up large, long bruises. He had said many times how it was her fault that her mother had been shot because she was protecting her, and that was all Angel would know. One day, her father had announced that she would die by his hands, and when that day came he would take great pleasure in it. Angel believed him. She often wished that day was soon.

She sat on the painted white peeling window ledge – bruised legs tucked up close to her chest, yellowed arms wrapped around them – looking at the tree that had become thicker and taller with the years; its leaves lush with green now hiding her away from view. But she still remembered when it had been small. How clearly she could see; how everything in the distance had been in view for her. Her window was old-fashioned: a large pane of glass in a chipped wooden frame, and a smaller one above it with a metal latch that had holes. He wasn't worried about her escaping; she would never fit through its small window, and bars had been fixed, bolted through the walls giving just enough room to reach an arm through, abolishing any idea of freedom.

Angel's father's house was surrounded by woodland, creeks, and fields with grass that grew tall and thick, with bright yellow flowers in summer that scented the air in their rich familiar way. She watched as clouds drifted slowly by, tinted with pinks, golds and purples as the sun began to set.

Sadness ached away at her dark empty hole, overpowering her need to cry. Depression had clung to her heart with a vice-like grip, squeezing it slowly with every passing day, tightening until it almost split her in two. It stabbed below her rib line; stabbing through the numbness that she had held in place for so long; awakening her senses to the bitter pain. She was alone, always alone.

She had fought against feeling for so long that it scared her to even try to hope for feel happiness, or just a little peace; afraid that if she did, she wouldn't really know what it was? Closing her eyes, Angel rested her head against cold steel, forgetting the world, listening to the wind passing her by, inviting her to come out, to leave her prison. Her tears returned.

Movement came from the branches in front of her. Her head springing up to get a better look, she felt a surge of excitement followed by trepidation. She knew there was something there; she saw it out of the corner of her eye. She could feel its presence, hear it move.

"I know you're out there," she said softly. "If you've come to take me, make it soon," she begged, staring into the tree in front of her, but there was no answer. She wondered if it was all in her head like so many other things. "I want to die!" It was barely a whisper, but deep inside her darkness was growing, she could feel its change growing stronger, calling to her, seducing her many times with its stillness. "I want to feel free!" her broken voice spoke to the leaves that danced in the wind.

"She won't allow you to die. He will pay dearly if you go." It was a whisper carried on the breeze, making her heart jump with hope. "Who is *she*?" Angel asked into night-filled sky. No one answered. *I must be going mad.* "If she's real then send me help. Break me free. Give me someone who'll stop this! Bring me him!" Her throat tightened. I'm losing it. *Stupid girl! I'm going to rot in this room!* Angel felt the urge to cry again; shifting, she jumped off the ledge. *Think of something else*, her mind told her, blocking her tears, forgetting her darkness – the monster that calls to her offering her peace. Angel's legs went limp, tingling with pins and needles as they slowly came back to life. She yawned with exhaustion.

Next day, Angel woke; her body screamed out with less pain: her bruises had darkened, ready to turn mucky brown before yellow, and her swelling seemed less vicious. Her father entered her room. She rushed to one corner, far away from him, her hands starting to shake with panic at her side. He was dressed in a grey striped suit and a silver–blue tie that showed off his tanned skin and dark hair; his shoes had been polished, shining in the light, and he smelled strong having covered himself in aftershave.

"I'll be back tonight, so don't eat it all at once." His tone was cold, disgusted, as he looked at her; the sheer bitterness of his presence raked at her, almost daring her to speak. He placed a tray of food piled high onto the box at the end of her bed. Angel nodded trembled, afraid to speak, biting her bottom lip to stop it from quivering whenever he moved near. Her eyes glazed, she blinked them hard, forcing herself not to cry. "Good" he responded to her acknowledgement, before letting the door slam shut behind him.

Angel stood, frozen, staring at the door, hearing a click as he pulled a bolt across. She let out her breath in a sigh. It must be important, she thought, he never stays away that long. A car door opened outside. Angel ran across her small room to look outside; she watched as her father came out of the house greeting a woman with long dark hair with a hug and smiles. Angel wondered who she was and how long she had known him.

Her day passed slowly. She played with picture cards and ragged dolls to make the time go by, imagining she could see the people from her dreams and wondering what they were doing right now. She took naps when she felt tired, and ate small amounts when she was hungry, hiding the food that would keep in the bottom of her chest, just in case.

Night was setting in again when he returned. She heard the car door opening and closing, then its engine roar as it drove away. Angel heard heavy footsteps coming up the stairs and stopping on the landing in front of her door. Sounds of something ringing got louder and louder until she heard his voice. She strained to listen; her ears pulsing with every sound that was made. Holding her breath to hear better, she wondered if he was going to enter her room.

"Hello," he said pausing. "Yes, she told me what you want me to do," he replied, then paused. "Soon." Another pause. "Yes." He paused. "When?" Pause. "It will be done then." Angel could hear him shuffling his feet. "No not yet. I will let you know if she does," he replied; his tone didn't sound too happy. "OK, bye," he said quickly, snapping something shut. Angel's heart instantly stopped; she held her breath waiting in fear for him to enter, but instead he walked past into another room, closing the door behind him. Relief flooded her.

I wonder what that was about, she thought, lying down, staring into shadows until her eyes became heavy.

Chapter Two

Morning rose; sun shining bright. She could hear birds chirping outside her window and voices, new voices. Sprinting out of bed, she dashed to the window and looked out to see the same woman as yesterday greeting her father, only she had brought with her another man.

He looked a lot younger than her father and the woman. Maybe her age? He was dressed in a black hooded top with dark blue designer jeans that had holes in the legs. She could see his hair was cut short and close to his head, smoothed down and with spikes across his tanned forehead; its colour was pure black with a hint of blue in the sunlight. His eyebrows seemed oddly shaped to Angel, pointed, with the same richness of colour as his hair. Angel only barely got a look at his hazel eyes, which were dark, confident, and surrounded in thick long black lashes – lashes any woman would die to have. His skin was the colour of caramel, tanned from years of being in the sun. She could hear his voice, deep, lazy, cold, with a hint of danger that made others feel like his prey.

"I'll be in soon. I have to make a call," he told the woman with long dark hair, who was leading Angel's father to the door. Angel watched as he leaned against the house wall, barely able to see him as he pulled something out of his pocket. "Hi, we're here," he said in a careless tone, then he paused. "I'll make sure … If I call him in, he can heal her before we arrive, then after that he can leave." Pause. "Fine, what if she becomes attached?" He paused again. "Yes, but she is vulnerable at this stage." He paused. "Yes." Pause again. Angel saw him rocking himself with his left foot against the wall. "When she is ready, I'll make sure he will no longer be an obstacle. And what do you want me to do with …?" He never finished. "OK, I'll have a place ready." He then ended his conversation, put his phone back into his pocket, pushed himself away from the wall in one fluid motion, and entered the house.

Confused and frustrated, Angel returned to sit on her bed, sinking down with a sigh. *What was he talking about? Never mind that, who are they? How long had her father known them? Do they know I exist? Will he get*

17

rid of me now he has them? Will he forget to bring me food? Thoughts and questions plagued her mind.

Angel realised she was a forgotten child, that her world was lost within these four walls, hidden by the solitary tree – nature's gift. If she were to die here, who would know? Who would mourn her? There was no one to witness her existence; she suddenly felt that reality's cold impact, shivering her to the bone.

She heard the sounds of her father's company leaving. She heard doors slamming. *He's mad; they must have had a fight.* She began to feel fear; her hands started to sweat; her breathing was shallow and rapid; her body tensed. She knew what was coming, she always knew. Thuds of footsteps echoed in her room; the door exploded off its hinges making her jump. Running for a corner and cowering into its walls, Angel's tears flooded her eyes as he stood staring at her, rage burning in his face, blindness in his cold eyes.

In his right hand he grasped a thick leather belt with a large gold heavy buckle. His left hand gripped the peeling doorframe, turning the skin white as it tightened, showing knuckle.

Angel's heart pounded; her body telling her to run. But she was frozen by his presence. She kept on swallowing, feeling a large lump in her throat trying to make her gag, to smother her before he did. Her fear was making her hysterical. The terror had taken hold as her chest tightened; her muscles were shaking, vibrating through her bones; she was trying to back away without realising it; her eyes fixed on him as her back pressed against the wall. Her lungs stopped. She was shaking so much that she stumbled, her legs giving way, her hands up pleading with him not to do it.

He stormed over, overwhelming her view. She gasped as he grabbed her arms yanking her to him, lifting her from the ground momentarily. Turning slightly, he threw her across the empty room. She hit the wall hard; pain exploded in her skull as the back of her head bounced, her spine raging at her, wanting to shatter after its impact. She landed against her old cracked mirror, which shattered as she hit the floor. Shards of glass sliced her skin, embedding in her legs. Her face stung; she felt wet, hot liquid dripping into her eyes. She touched it, automatically wiping the tears so she could see. Angel couldn't stop her eyes from stinging. Pulling her hand away, she saw thick rich red blood covering her left hand. Her cuts were large and deep. To pour so quickly?

She was stunned, wheezing as she picked herself up, hands shaking as she touched the ground. Sharp shards dug into her skin, slicing her easily. Her body pounding and twitching with pain, she managed to lift herself up enough to crawl a couple of steps before he kicked her with such force that it spun her around so she landed heavily on her back. She turned quickly onto her side, feeling pain so powerful that it stopped her breath. She wrapped her arms around her stomach, trying to ease it. She felt as though he had ripped her insides in half. Tears flooded from her eyes; she felt coldness travel through her body.

Angel threw up. She coughed the last of it out, spitting its foul taste on the floor, trying to ignore the sickening stench that lingered around her. He grabbed a handful of wild hair, nearly ripping it out from the roots. Angel screamed in agony, grabbing at his wrist, pulling it down to release some of the strain.

Everywhere was raw. She was hyperventilating from his torture. She could see from out of the corner of her tear-stained eye that he was enjoying it – his mouth curved up slightly.

Then she saw his fist. He moved quickly, hitting her hard, putting his full weight behind it, connecting with her jaw, splitting her lip and gum, making her woozy. Blood filled her mouth. It tasted metallic. It had taken a day for it to stop bleeding and now he had split it again. She could feel the blood trickling out from between the corner of her lips, descending down her bruised chin. She couldn't swallow; her throat was closing. She was tired, so tired.

Angel felt weak, sleepy. Darkness wanted to take her; she wanted it to take her. Her eyes rolled back. She was falling.

When she opened her eyes she was surrounded by light. Pure white calming light. She could feel its healing power as it caressed her soul. *Is this heaven?* she thought, *no it can't be, it must be that place I dreamt of before.*

Looking down, she could see long grass – grass she once could see from her window before the tree blocked all view. She bent down to run her fingers through the blades of grass, wondering what it felt like: *was it rough or smooth?* But all that happened was that her fingers passed through the blades, as though she was just a thought on a breeze.

Angel kept walking, passing tall strong trees bathed in light. She could hear water flowing. Following its soothing sound, she came upon a creek, its rushing water swirled, hitting stone and mud islands. She sat on its grassy bank. She could smell its freshness and hints of flowers floating around her, mixed with an earthy smell from damp soil and wet bark.

Angel heard a noise behind her. Jumping to her feet and turning quickly, she saw a large beautiful black animal stalking through tall grass – its tail swaying in a frantic rhythm – looking at her like she was prey; its lips peeled back revealing sharp yellowed teeth and pink gums.

"What are you?" she whispered. It slowly crept towards her. Angel saw its teeth long and sharp. Shocked, this wasn't in her dream last time. Suddenly, she felt herself falling again. She felt it too soon; she tried desperately to hang on, to stay by her creek, but all she could do was follow. It was unstoppable. She woke up in her own body, covered in dried blood, on the cold dusty floor by herself.

Angel ran herself a hot bath. She entered it gently, every movement was cut with pain. She took quick breaths as she lowered her damaged body. She lay there with a wet cloth over her face, cooling the burning. The warmth of the water numbed her body briefly. *I wonder if I'll ever be free, s*he thought, tears seeping into the cloth. *I wonder if ... he will come. S*he was hoping more than ever that her dreams would become real. She wished she could return to that place near the creek and find out more about the thing she had seen. She wished for her future to come and save her.

Angel's skin was wrinkled. Blood tainted the water and the smell of vomit had gone for now. She left the bathroom, grabbing an old shirt and shorts that felt loose around her skin, and right now even that was hard to bear. She grabbed an old top, which was now too small for her, out of the drawer, and used it to mop the vomit into a pile. Wrapping the old top around the mess, she picked it up, returning to the bathroom and flushing it away. She had to repeat this four times. Then, rinsing the top through and returning to the same spot, she began to wash the floor, trying to get rid of the hideous smell that lingered, mingled with blood and dirt.

She opened her window. Outside she heard his voice again – the stranger. Again she wanted to shout to let him know she was here, to ask him for help, but something inside her held her back. "Yes I'm sure," he said, before pausing. "I'll let him know, if that will make you happy!" he said, before a door opened. The sound of her father's voice forced her to back away, to forget any hope of help.

Angel yawned feeling tired, very tired. She climbed into bed, closing her eyes, passing into sleep.

Chapter Three

Angel dreamed of a different life. Like always, she was free, running across grass. She realised someone was at her side; she could see his jet-black hair lying straight and messy around his face. She could hear his rich laughter that made her feel warm and safe, as if it were only for her. She saw glimpses of gold in his eyes, tinted with green as bright as hers. His face was paler than hers, and wings as black as night lay flat against his back.

But there was something unusual about him; she could feel a bond between them.

Then she remembered him from before. He was the one that came to her in her dreams. He had visited her ever since she was young, saying he was a friend. There were many times when he had a woman called Isis with him, standing as a guard, and she called Angel 'mum' – a greeting that was always given to her with a warm smile or loving embrace. Isis spoke to her as a friend. Angel had known for a long time that she was cherished by this person.

On his first visit, he'd told her that she would see them often, and that she didn't need to be afraid; that he would protect her; that she was meant to be here, and her life would change on the day they'd meet again; that there were others who would always protect her; that she had family and was important to everyone here, and loved, loved by many. They would teach her what she needed to know. As she got older, she felt a complete trust in him, and their nightly visits were always longed for.

As she became a teenager, their relationship changed. She wanted more. She wanted him more. To feel him closer to her; to have him kiss her. He was her protector, and she loved him for it.

"Zared?" It was a whisper that stopped her heart. "Come on Angel, we have to hurry. We can't be late." He grabbed her hand in a steel grip, running for the woods while she dragged behind. His skin was cold in her hand, yet she felt heat from him. When he moved, she felt out of place by his side, stumbling along to his graceful strides. Out of breath, her attention was brought back to their surroundings. She saw thick woodlands, with the setting sun gliding across the tops of the trees, turning them to shades of gold. She heard distant voices laughing as they waited.

"Late?" she wondered, eyes wide, seeing bodies of all sizes gather in groups; some leaned against trees, some sat against the trees, some rested next to creatures that lay in the cool long grass, feeling the heat from the last of the sunlight, smelling familiar scents drifting in the breeze.

"You're OK, aren't you? I know you're a bit off, I can feel it." He came to a stop turning to look at her face. She had changed only slightly. Her eyes had softened, becoming vulnerable; the fear in them from her tortured life had been replaced by a hardness that had come gradually over time. But in this moment, the look of a child's innocence replaced the bitter hardness, reminding him of a time he missed in so many ways. Now he realised who she was. "Angel, how old are you right now?" This was not his Angel, but the Angel of past. "Seventeen," she replied as they headed into the crowd, which automatically parted as they passed. "Where am I?" She scanned the people. She didn't recognise them. Then again, why would she? All she had known was a caged life, and only what her dreams had shown her.

"Mummy you just made it!" The small girl with rose-coloured lips smiled, jumping up and down before bounding right for them. "Daddy said you would make it!" She smiled happily, her cheeks glowing. "Of course she would. Do you really think anything is going to keep her from her daughter's fifth birthday? I don't think so, not if we have anything to do with it!" Zared's smile touched his eyes as he picked her up in his arms, holding her close, squeezing her tight. He planted a big kiss on her cheek, tipping her back at the same time. Angel watched as the child giggled and held him tightly as she wiping her face with one of her delicate little hands. "Yuk!" She carried on giggling, her voice filled with love.

This is how it should be, Angel thought, seeing how close they were and smiling at their interaction as he began blowing raspberries on Isis's face, making her laugh louder. "Mummy, it's starting, look you were right!" she said, breathless from giggling, her arms reaching for Angel. Angel took the girl from him, both still smiling.

This little girl was beautiful. Her hair of golden ringlets flowed down her back, the colour of autumn leaves. Her creamy skin was flawless, with cheeks turning pink when she smiled, reaching her golden eyes with their rings of bright green surrounded by long lashes. "Mummy isn't herself at the moment Isis." Zared gently placed a warm protective arm around Isis's back. "Remember, we spoke about mummy. That her old self from before would come to the future and see us," he said, stroking a hand over her golden hair, bouncing her curls. "Yes," she replied – they could see her thinking – "that's how she knew about today and my change, and what happens when I'm older," she said matter-of-fact, looking so proud of herself.

Angel couldn't take her eyes off the little girl in her arms. *Isis!* She still couldn't believe it. Angel studied the little girl's face to see if she could glimpse the young woman from her dreams that she knew was hidden there. "That's right princess," Zared said, pleased. "She hasn't discovered about the other kinds yet, so we can't tell her," he continued, putting a finger to his lips. "She needs to follow her own path on that, so we have to keep quiet, just in case it changes our future like the witches said it might, and we don't want that do we?" His warm smile brought hers out again. "Mummy you won't be scared of them will you? You're stronger than them. You can stop anything. That's why they follow you and daddy," she whispered loudly towards Angel's ear, looking around to see if anyone had noticed.

Isis's faith flooded over Angel, making her feel immortal, just as she seemed to be in the little girl's eyes; she was a hero. Isis's face glowed. Her smile widened, showing her white fangs. They were small and delicate making her look very cute. Angel couldn't help but smile back, she was so infectious! "I have to go back now mummy, you will watch won't you, before you go back?" she asked, fidgeting in her arms. "I will, I wouldn't miss it for the world," Angel replied, putting the child down. Happiness flooded her; she was meant to see this. "Good," she laughed, giving her a quick kiss. "I love you mummy!" she said, excited as she ran back to what looked like a table made of stone.

"I don't want to leave," Angel whispered, watching her daughter standing tall and fearless for such a small child. "You have to, otherwise this will never happen and we will never meet. The fight that you face will never be fought and they will win without a soul trying. Your daughter will not be born and you will never marry… And, I would not be what I am today," he whispered in her ear, pulling her close to him, wrapping his arms around her tightly. "You are more important than you realise, this will not exist without you, and without you my existence will be meaningless," he said and kissed her hair. Angel realised that they had been close. When she saw him, she dreamed of her first kiss with him. She knew his face by heart: every curve, every scar. She pictured his lips on hers many times; his strong arms around her. She wished for it every night, that one day she would be with him, even if it was just a dream.

"Your Majesty, the time has come for your daughter to evolve, taking her place as our protector, our warrior and our future ruler, just like her father." An old man smiled in her direction then continued, "With this our lives are pledged to her. We will die for her, all of our kind and others will know this, and those that are against this will meet their death." The old man spoke to them and all those that had gathered. His long grey hair ruffled in the breeze. His silver beard ended in a point, and his glasses balanced on the edge of his nose. He was wearing a long patterned robe that seemed important to this ceremony. He held a thick leather worn book in his hand, reading its forgotten language before shutting it and, turning to them along with everyone else, he bowed.

Angel stood uneasy, frozen, and plastering a fake smile on her face before the crowd turned their attention back to the child.

"Why did we call her Isis?" Angel whispered, not taking her eyes away from her daughter. "Isis? It means 'supreme' in the old language. A name like hers would be given to one of the seven sisters of the goddesses. It is a very powerful name that you chose. In the old land there was a queen that had a child named Isis, and that queen became a strong and powerful ruler," he replied, squeezing her arms with approval. "What's her last name? I just realised I never asked. How will I know when we meet, that it's really you?" Angel said, watching her daughter curl up into a tiny ball. Ready.

Isis took a deep breath, filling her lungs. Her ringlets fell around her like a waterfall, covering her face, as her white flowery dress touched the stone table – she looked like a tiny fairy kneeling on a mushroom.

"Black, Isis Black. And you are Angel-May Black, my Queen," he replied, watching Isis – a light glowed small and round, covering her mid section. Angel watched as it grew, getting brighter and brighter. Her stomach started to flutter and her palms became hot and clammy. Angel knew something was wrong; she could sense it somehow. She wanted to move, but forced herself to stay, shifting from one foot to the other. *What if something happens to her? What if it hurts her? I can't bear anything to happen to her.* Thoughts ran through Angel's head, faster and faster.

Isis screamed. The high-pitched noise shredded the silence, stinging the onlookers' ears, and causing everyone to gasp; they were helpless, forced to look on in fear. Isis was in pain. *Go to her. She's not strong enough!* The voice of a man whispered to her. Angel reacted before he had finished. Reaching out to Isis, Angel felt her put her tiny hot wet hand in Angel's. Angel pulled at her. She wanted to protect her, to give her own life if that would save the child from this pain. Angel pulled Isis to her lap, joining them together. She saw the shadow of wings around her. Wrapping her arms around the small body, cradling Isis in a mother's embrace, Angel rocked her back and forth. "Shh baby, everything is going to be alright," Angel whispered, stroking Isis's golden hair as she clung tightly to Angel's waist; Angel still rocking as her daughter sobbed with pain.

Angel felt power. An energy so strong and pure, and which came from deep inside Angel, telling her she needed to give this to Isis, to help her in the change; her daughter was not strong enough to go through it without her, she didn't have that power or energy to heal from it. Angel closed her eyes. She could feel it building, thrashing inside of her, begging to be set free. She focussed on Isis, pushing it towards her, letting it flow through their bodies, keeping her safe, helping her to change. But her power wasn't enough. She needed more to take more from somewhere. She needed to give her more.

Pull it from around you. Use the land, the sky. It's all there for you to take to help her! The same voice spoke, feeling him in her head, warm as the sun, with strength of steel. He was familiar, her soul lit up. She could feel it glow through her skin, pulling him to her as he guided her. Angel did as he said, pulling light to her, letting it entwine with her own energy before forcing it to Isis. Thunder rumbled above them, rumbling loudly, making the earth around them shake. Then sparks of lightning hit the ground next to them, over and over, creating a circle, making a barrier untouchable to others as Angel pulled it in. Then on the last strike, it hit them, crackling the air.

People ducked on reflex. Creatures cowered in the shadows. Its energy lit them up so brightly that it was blinding. Suddenly, it exploded, causing mother and daughter to collapse onto the table, motionless. "Angel, Angel!" His voice was a panic, but she heard another in her head.

Angel, wake up. You did well, she's changed, but you have to wake up now. It was this voice that woke her. The sound of his worried voice terrified her; she could feel his fear examining her, wondering if she was damaged from all that power. She could feel him wanting to come nearer, but he had to remain distant, forced to stay away from her. *Angel please.* It was this sad whisper echoing under Zared's begging voice that plagued her ears. She blinked, seeing flashes of afterlight.

"How is Isis? Is she OK? Where is she?" Angel felt her body panic. She knew she was OK, he told her that, but she still needed to see her. "She's fine, Angel, she's fine. She's with Madoc, she's safe. What the hell were you thinking? You could have died!" he said annoyed. "You're not your future self yet. You could have killed yourself, or Isis!" He sounded more angry that she had risked her *own* life. "She needed me. I had to give her my energy." Angel didn't understand it and she couldn't explain it to anyone, but she had had to do what she'd felt, and that was to do whatever it took to keep Isis safe. "I know, but still, you could have damaged yourself. You're our Queen! We need you. And as your warrior, your protector, I ask you not to do that again. Not until the time comes when you know how to use it. You have to remember that you are not the Angel of now. You don't know how much power you possess, or how to control it," he said, pulling her into his arms.

Angel saw the worry on his face, making his scar noticeable again. "I don't care. I would do it over and over again for her. She is my daughter and I'm not going to see her in pain!" She felt angry that he had made her feel that this was wrong. "I know, I'm sorry. But you scared the hell out of me. You never told me this is what you did. You just said you would do something that you couldn't tell me, just in case I stopped you." He held her tightly. His lips brushed her cheek, causing her to blush. She could hear him taking a deep breath, almost tasting her, but something else was there, hidden at the edge. Suddenly, he released her, stepping away. He let her take his hand, entwining her fingers into his, squeezing lightly.

"Who is Madoc?" Angel suddenly asked, aware she had never met him before. "I'm forbidden to tell you," Zared replied, "but you will meet him soon."

"Why?" Angel watched as he looked away. He wasn't going to answer. She could sense that this was forbidden territory, and no one was to break this rule.

"Mummy, look!" Isis said, her voice filled with joy, Angel pulled away from Zared; his secrets irritated her. She moved through the crowd searching for Isis. She followed her voice and found her standing on burnt grass, looking remarkably tall and proud – as if she had grown a few feet. She was a vision. Her five-year-old daughter radiated gold and silver light. She had wings that spread to an amazing width – pure white with a band of black. "Do you like them?" she asked, jumping as she spun around to show them off. "Oh honey they're perfect. You're perfect." Angel smiled, bending down so that she could hold her in her arms one last time before she had to leave.

It's time for you to wake now my Queen. His voice was soothing velvet, touching her soul. She closed her eyes and sighed with contentment. "I have to go now," Angel said, knowing this was the last time. Her nose started to tingle as tears fell from her eyes, and her throat began to swell. "Isis Black, you are the most amazing thing I've ever seen. Don't let anyone tell you differently, OK?" Angel said, kissing her cheek – *Will I hear you again?* Angel asked him in her silent voice – "I won't," Isis said, tears forming, rubbing her hands in her eyes to stop them. "I'll be watching over you, and I can't wait till I met you again." Angel smiled, wiping tears off Isis's face, knowing that in a few years when she is older she would meet her again.

You will. Was all he replied, filling her with love.

"Come on honey, it's time to let mummy return," Zared said, picking Isis up, kissing her forehead softly, as her tears fell and her lips shook with the effort not to make a sound. "I love you always," Angel said, kissing her wet cheeks again. Running a hand over her hair, feeling its softness. "Watch over her. Keep her safe for me," she told Zared, brushing her lips against his briefly. Seeing his lips go crooked, Angel touched his face. It was soft, smooth, but she saw him pull away. Pain showed in his eyes again, before he looked away. Angel knew then that something had been different, and as quickly as they had come, they were … Gone.

Chapter Four

Six days had passed. She was on her way to healing: her cuts had scabbed and her bruises were coming out. She kept thinking of Isis and life with them.

Angel had felt something change within her; something more real than anything she'd ever felt before. Angel dared to believe more in this dream than in her own bleak reality. Over the past six days she'd begun to see the world and its possibilities with new eyes, and had spent every moment searching for the latent power within her. Every chance she had, she practised feeling for her father with her energy, knowing where he was in the house. She practised leaving her body, finding it easier each time, but she continued to find it difficult to throw her energy out and pull more in. She wanted to master this power that she had called to help Isis. It made her even more determined to see them again, to find him out there in this world and bring him to her.

Angel sat crossed-legged, resting her hands on her knees, closing her eyes and breathing in and out, slowly and deeply; she allowed the air to fill her lungs. Her skin tingled. With every breath she could feel tension releasing; her soul was finding peace, becoming still. Images formed in her head: images of bright light flowing through her. She could see it swirling around her, forming a ball of white light, protecting her. Angel saw pale green light coming up from the ground, travelling from her base to her head, making her feel warm and strong, and tainting the air around her with calming smells that made her heart ache. She could see pale red light descending from above her, flowing down through the top of her head. She was filled with peace and love. Her skin felt electric as the light travelled down her spine. She felt the two lights meet in her centre, swirling around, sending streaks of energy through her arms and legs, making them heavy as gold.

Angel's whole being was at peace. She felt herself drifting, swaying, and then she was falling with complete trust and surrender. She felt herself split: body falling to the floor as her spirit remained seated.

As she rose to her feet, everything around her seemed to slow down; air flowed through her, guiding her to leave her prison, to walk through the walls like a ghost in haunting. She passed through her bedroom door, walking down a narrow hall embraced by darkness. Stairs lay at the end of the hall, illuminated with a light that called her forward. Her father was on a chair staring at a box that showed moving pictures – she wondered if he had seen her.

Angel continued on, passing through another door before stepping out into the open air; its light so bright it filled her with joy, causing her to smile as her eyes adjusted. She could feel energy; it was so strong she could touch it. It was everywhere, everything that lived had an aura of light: there were different colours of light, even things that had never had life had traces of energy around them. "Wow," she spoke out loud, having forgotten how amazing this view was since the tree had grown and obscured the outside world.

Angel walked across overgrown weeds towards a thicket of heavy trees. She continued on, passing wide trunks with crinkled bark – this was freedom: no bars, no walls, no fear. She came to a round patch of grass that seemed to be waiting there just for her. Sitting down, she could see small purple flowers growing in the shadows of trees. When she looked closer, the deep purple flowers were shaped like small bells, as though they were ringing out to insects in the gentle breeze.

She saw white light hovering, flowing around them, and fading away the closer it got to the ground. Reaching her right hand out to touch it, she focussed on pulling; she needed to master this power, to help herself, to start fighting. She needed to escape her father's chains and start her life, to find Zared – the time had now come when she had the means.

Angel knew her life was on a countdown. She knew her father was planning something. He was going to kill her, she was as sure of that as the grass was green. He had started dating now, so how long would it be before she was in the way? How long did she have to save herself?

Suddenly she felt it. At first it was like she had lost focus: her ears whistled before the buzzing came, then she became light-headed, almost falling again. Angel concentrated, keeping herself calm; trying not to break the absorption. She watched her own light pulse, expanding – strange beyond this world. She watched with surprise as her energy entwined with that around the flowers; she could feel it pulling, drinking it down deep into her soul, filling her. It was buzzing inside of her. A primal hunger came over her, demanding more, to take every last drop, and giving her strength – a sense of immortality.

"No!" she commanded to herself, pulling her hand back, watching as the flower wilted ready to give itself back to the earth, its energy fading. She had taken its life source, only stopping before death and leaving only a faint last bit of light. *I can take it. Now can I give it?* Thinking of her dream, of Isis, and of how Angel had felt as she poured energy into her, Angel pushed her energy, feeling it buzz in her mind, spinning inside of her, ready to be let loose; focussing on the flower in front of her, she tried to give it life, but all she accomplished was a quiver of energy. *Your future self is stronger, you have to keep practising!* She remembered what he had said about her.

Angel realised time had run away; she had to return before her father did his checks, before he could find her body lying there without its soul. Focussing again, this time on her body, she pictured herself returning to it, entering it, becoming whole, merging her soul and body together. She felt a rush of air around her that picked up her ghostly presence, overpowering her with its strength, as it slammed her back inside her sleeping shell. Angel needed to rest; her experience had weakened her. She wasn't use to it yet. She found that her bed was very appealing to her as she climbed in, yawning, and fighting to keep her eyes open.

Chapter Five

Her dream began with her leaving her body, wandering around aimlessly, and passing trees covered in the same light she had seen earlier; but this was a different place, one she had been to before, only it looked younger. She looked around: something was missing, something that had been here before. There was a blanket of mist hovering above the ground, hugging the trees' trunks.

This place felt powerful, protective; this place that was meant to be her home. She watched as people approached her, bowing with respectful smiles. She looked around, there were other people. They were standing near her, strong, fearless, holding weapons, watching the trees, and scanning the crowd. She remembered the stone table; the one Isis had curled up on. She knew this place.

Then she saw a man – whose features were indistin-
guishable, but with jet-black wings half spread with red
tips – walking towards her, dressed in navy and gold
clothes. He took her hands in his, looking into her eyes
smiling. She saw nothing but sparkling bright light looking deep into her soul. Angel felt her face burning and
turning red.

"Do you take Angel as your queen, your wife, your
lover? Will you protect her with your heart and soul?
Will you die for her?" the old man said, his glasses still
balancing on his nose. "I do," the younger man replied,
kissing Angel's hands, making her skin tingle. Their
connection was so intense, stronger than anything she
had felt before.

Suddenly, her dream shifted to a large hall with people wearing strange clothing and masks – everyone was
wearing a mask. Then he came to her, walking past the
dancing bodies. She had never seen anything like him.
He was tall, at least six-foot. He looked dangerous: a picture of death. Yet, when she laid eyes on him, some part
of her stirred. She could feel that there was a connection
between them: her body kept saying to her mind that he
was hers.

His jet-black hair lay straight and messy around his
face, cut to different layers with strands touching his
shoulders. His perfectly sculptured face was half hidden

by a fringe that fell over his left eye. She could see, on his pale skin, a scar that ran from beneath his fringe, across the bridge of his nose, and over to his right cheek. *Zared?* she thought, watching him, forgetting everything else around her. "Angel," he said, looking into her emerald eyes. She saw a faint smile come to his lips as he walked past more bodies, no one seeing him.

He was wearing a velvet black coat with Gaelic patterning on its high collar, down the edges that fastened it, and around the edges where it stopped just above the black buckled boots that could do some damage. He wore a black tight top underneath that also had a high collar, and what looked like combat trousers, only they had chains and knifes connected to them, hooked in the belt loops. A thick strap circled his broad chest, holding a weapon she couldn't see. He looked like a warrior fallen from the gods, with wings that were as black as night with blood-red tips. They reminded her of her daughter's. She had never asked if he was Isis's father. She must be a part of him.

Angel smiled, her heart pounding the closer he got to her; her insides twisted with nerves, afraid to speak just in case her voice would break. He was a vision that took her breath away, and Isis was a blend of them both. "Zared," Angel whispered, hearing only the pounding in her ears. "What age are you now?" he asked, brushing a finger across her forehead, making her melt; her legs began to wobble. "Seventeen still, but I'm seeing you more now than ever before," Angel said puzzled. "I'm not complaining, it's just I'd rather see you in another way." She heated up. "That's good," he laughed, "because you're close," he said, smiling. "Close to what?" Angel asked. "Your eighteenth birthday and your freedom," he replied, stepping closer. His scent filled her, she breathed in deeply, filling her lungs, trying to hold on to him. "You are the one that brought me here. Your powers are waking, growing stronger by the day." He stepped closer again. She could almost feel him now. "And because I am the person that comes to you. I am the one that's waiting not far from your living world." He smiled, holding out his hand. "And because I am the one that belongs to you; just as you belong to me."

Angel put her hand in his, wrapping her fingers around his, as though it was the most natural thing in the world. "I wish I could believe you, to know you are real, that you are coming for me," she said, her voice filled with sadness. "But I am my Queen, and soon, you shall see. Before your eighteenth I will come. Keep your faith, it is time." Bending down, his face only inches away: "You must promise me something …" Angel nodded. "Be careful. There are many enemies that wish us dead; some will control you by trying to cause my death first.

If this happens, fight them, don't give in. You have more power than any person born of any kind." He spoke softly, placing a hand around her neck. Her heart pounded louder, racing in her chest. She nodded in response, unable to speak, forcing her lungs to keep working. "How soon will I see you?" Angel asked. "Soon." He smiled as she leaned towards him, his lips brushing hers briefly. "Soon. I'm just a few blocks away. When you wake, find me." His words were barely a whisper on his lips before hers met his; his kiss filled her with passion, starting with the lightest of brushes turning deeper, pulling her to him, his warm lips crushing against hers. It was a kiss she had long waited for; a kiss time had taken from him. There was a longing, almost forbidden, coming from him: a desire – a desire for more.

Angel felt it too, holding him tighter, wanting more. His fingers tugged at her hair. Her breath mixed with his, as his scent covered her, marking her body so all would know that she was his; she could feel their connection getting stronger, buzzing around them as an unseen force. Angel could feel her chest pounding. Pressing her body against his, her blood heating up, having parts ache for him to touch, she felt the smoothness of his fangs brush her lips; she touched them with her tongue, feeling their sharpness, teasing him, feeling him through their bond. She was breathing heavily into his mouth, trembling to keep control. He released her hair and wrapped his hands around her, holding her so tightly, as if, should he let go, she would disappear. Angel felt his chest move as he inhaled her in; he was keeping her as a memory.

"I don't want you to leave," he whispered, pushing her away reluctantly. "Then I won't," she replied breathlessly, pulling him back. Their kisses were filled with emotion. Her body aching for her to take him; that this was right, that he wasn't forbidden, that nothing mattered except being with him. She was meant to be at his side for eternity. "You have to. This is wrong." He pulled out of her arms. He was shaking just as much as Angel. She could feel the coldness where he had once been. She looked into his eyes and saw they were ablaze behind his hair. They were red, rich ruby-red. He turned from her, hiding his hunger, his desire and tears. "No! If I go, I'll lose you and you might not return. I lost Isis. I don't want to lose you … I don't think I can survive it." Tears filled her eyes as she clung to his coat. He was her long-time friend. She couldn't bear the thought of him never returning, of being alone with her father forever.

Zared turned to face her. His eyes had returned to their golden colour, leaving only the track marks of his fallen tears. He placed her face in his hands. She felt his lips just inches away from hers. "You will never lose me. I promise you that. I am bound to you by soul. What you feel, I feel. Our thoughts speak to each other while around us is silent. I have your blood within me, and you have mine. Angel-May, I gave my life for you because I am yours. I love you. Remember I will *always* love you." His lips met hers. Her skin sparked with joy, but there was a sadness in his words. "You must return. Find me! That's when our journey begins," he said, pulling away from her and stepping back. She watched as he faded away. "It's time, my love. Remember I will always love you." His voice whispered around her, fading away as he did.

Angel woke in her bed. Coldness surrounded her. The dream was gone and she was alone. She felt confused. She wanted to cry, to sob uncontrollably into her pillow. Her chest hurt now more than it had ever hurt; she felt loss. A part of her was broken in two. He was gone. She knew she wouldn't see him again.

"Soon," she said out loud, wishing, hoping he was right, that he was real, that he would come to her. *I have to find him.* She remembered what he had said.

Chapter Six

At nightfall her father came to her again, waking her from her dream state, standing over her, his eyes unseeing. She was no longer his daughter, just a punch bag to release his stress-filled day or his rage-filled mind.

Angel felt the large lump in her throat again trying to make her gag. Anxious at his unwarranted presence, she felt sweat begin to lace her skin. Her flesh rose in tiny bumps, turning her cold. Her stomach twisted with its sickly churn. Her pulse raced as her body froze, unwilling to obey the commands her mind was shouting. Her chest tightened as her lungs lost their smooth rhythm and began shaking violently. Her trembling reverberated through her mattress, making the old rusty springs squeal out. Her breath quickened suddenly as he raised his arm

– the silhouette in the dark swung down fast and hard. Angel felt the thick wide strap of his leather belt gripped in his tanned hands. His shining dark hair tossed around like someone had run their fingers through it all night. Angel's bright-green emerald eyes turned bloodshot as tears threatened to spill. She was shocked that he didn't let her skin heal, didn't give her time to recover.

He grabbed the sheets that covered her, whipping them away before they hit the ground behind him in a pile. He raised his hand again, swinging the leather strap down onto her bare skin. The force impaled her body with the buckle, which burned into her skin, ripping it apart and stopping her from breathing as immense pain shot into her and, vice-like, gripped every cell that had life.

Angel gasped, coughing forcefully, coaxing her lungs to work; she instinctively curled into a foetal position, holding her furious stomach. She lay there unprotected by her bedding, feeling her skin burning under her night-shirt. Another raging hit. She screamed out as the cold hard metal of his buckle ripped into her again, with more savagery than before, almost hitting her skin in the same spot through the thin cloth. Hot wetness spread across her nightshirt as her blood wept out, making her raw edges cry out. Her throat swelled up with the echoes of screams that surrounded her ears. Tears of pure terror stained her face, dissolving into her pillow. Blood started to form in pools around her, staining more of her worn mattress.

Another hit – it wrapped around her right arm and across her back, the buckle hitting the base of the neck. She cried out in another agonising scream, feeling the cold metal bounce off her bones and stopping her breath once again. Her hands flew up to protect this area as well as her face, just in case she had another painful hit there. Exposed, his next hit had a clear shot across her right side, shredding her waist and causing her to turn onto her stomach, screaming into the damp pillow that had muffled many of her beatings. He laced into her back over and over with rapid lashes. The buckle landed, crashing against her fragile ribcage, cracking bone. She could hear his ghostly breath, remorseless as his last strike caught her lower back, hitting her spine. Her body had been ripped apart.

Covered in blood, she began to go numb: her lungs continued gasping for air. His savagery was over. His breathing was fast and heavy; his body still hovered over her. She wished he would leave. She wished for death – his death.

Her father had only paused; now he had his next wave of energy. The beating felt as though it lasted for hours. Her strained voice lost its sound. Her mind lost focus, and now Angel lay there unable to move. Her body screamed out; she was left a broken shell, scarred beyond recognition. Unconsciousness claimed her as she allowed herself to fall into darkness.

Angel saw gold strands pulsing towards her, guiding her to follow. Her instincts told her that this was the journey she had to begin; this was what he had spoken of. Then she felt him only a block away. It was a fever that always burned, like hunger, that always craved to touch him. His bond had always instilled in her hope, golden warmth – the same colour as his eyes. She knew he was near. The connection strengthened the closer she was to him, humming to her in a silent melody imprinted only on her – a way their souls would recognise each other.

Turning the corner, Angel's heart almost stopped at the sight of him. She had waited for so long to be with him, to touch him with her own hands, to speak to him with her own voice. He was now in her present: no dream, no vision; he was real. Or, at least she hoped he was.

Zared was wearing a black T-shirt under a green–blue open shirt, and blue jeans. He was with another man who reminded her of the one she has seen at the house: same hair – short-cut, smoothed down and with spikes across his forehead. Its colour was almost black with a hint of blue. His eyebrows were the same odd shape, pointed, with the same richness of colour as his hair. His eyes looked menacing, evil. She wanted to cower under his gaze which projected from behind thick black lashes. He was dressed in a white shirt with blue jeans. Angel stood just a few feet away from them, watching, afraid to get closer in case he wasn't real – that this was just another dream. And if he wasn't, what would she say?

All of a sudden she was afraid to speak to him. They didn't notice her at first. They were deep in conversation about something.

Angel took a deep breath, she couldn't stand it any more. The urge to touch him was too great. Walking towards him, she felt the air around her: its cool pressure gliding over her skin, making it feel painless after the burning. She came to a stop inches away from him, fascinated with how different he looked to the last time she had seen him. Her eyes connected with his. There was no tint of green in them. There was no scar, no wings resting on his back. But she knew it was him; she was certain of it. His eyes had told her this much. Their bond sang out to her; she felt his hunger, his desire, heat burning inside of her. It called out to be tamed; begged to be satisfied.

Still hidden from view, she could feel her heart pounding with their connection, which buzzed, silently throbbing. He had felt it too.

He studied her and began moving towards her. In him awakened a protectiveness that had been sleeping for a long time. Feeling her presence seeping into his pores, he controlled the urge to rush over and embrace her.

Zared and his companion both watched Angel as she looked Zared over silently. She looked like a bloody ghost: her green eyes bright as emeralds in the sunlight. He felt his protective urge roar, to hunt down the person who had done this. He wanted to find her, to guard her until death claimed one of them. To hold her and tell her he was here, and that she didn't have to be afraid any more.

He gazed upon her pale creamy-pink skin, tinted with purples and murky yellows, some of which was fresh bruising. Her form was almost translucent. Her golden hair reflected the colour of his eyes, but in the light of the streetlamp he could see strands of golds, coppers and a tint of browns – all glistening as they curled softly around her. She was a vision; one he had been waiting to find for a long time. And at that moment, Zared knew if he had had breath she would have taken it away. Even underneath her mask of violence, she was perfect. Zared noticed again an electric connection growing stronger, almost opening her up to him, making him aware of her pain, and her feeling of liberation, of freedom, when she floated in this form. And trust, he could feel complete trust in him, which made him uncomfortable.

Confused he tried to shake the feeling off; he brought down his inner defences and tried to shut himself off to her – and to any implications of this unfamiliar charge between them.

Zared spoke to the man by his side, not taking his eyes from her: "Barret, what is going on?" he asked tensely, trying to push the presence of her away. "I think she's a ghost … she's got to be dead, there's no way someone in that state can still be alive," Barret replied looking down at Angel's battered body, blood seeping through cloth, skin sliced, as she left bloody footprints on the cold concrete beneath her feet. "Then what the hell is she doing here?" Zared asked, stepping back from her ghostly figure, reeling with shock. It hadn't occurred to him this was a ghost. Why could he feel this pull to her? Would he ever see her again? Ice ran through him.

"Zared, I have no idea." But Barret was fascinated with how focussed she was on Zared; she was oblivious to everything else. It was as though she couldn't even hear Barret's voice. The only voice she could hear was Zared's.

"Ask her, she seems to have taken to you intensely." Barret could smell Zared's annoyance, and there was another scent, something new – lust. Hormones secreted from the skin, faint, almost impossible to detect with human senses. It was an unusual response for a vampire to feel anything along those lines: emotions like this were a human condition, and vampires had lost that the minute they turned. It radiated from him in small waves. Enjoying watching the effect she had on him, Barret played with the idea of taunting Zared. Vampires saw every creature as food. When they mated it was for fun, nothing more involved. They never became attached, other than to the wound they drank from – it was impossible.

"I'm not a ghost," she suddenly spoke out, noticing that there was another person speaking to her – not really interested in what he had to say but realising she ought to acknowledge him nonetheless. "I'm just taking time away from my body. I will return when I'm ready," she continued, returning her focus to Zared, her head tilted, mesmerised by his appearance. "Then you need to return *now*," Zared told her firmly, feeling uncomfortable again, feeling her touching parts of him that had been dead for far too long.

Zared could see Barret out of the corner of his eye: a small grin contorted his lips; he watched, amused, as Zared squirmed with uneasiness. Vampires feared ghosts – he guessed it was because they envied them: death had claimed them, allowed their spirit to wander, proving that there was another place for them. For their kind, natural death was an untouchable dream: their souls would never meet the other world, never return to another body, they would just turn to ash, dust that would blow away with the wind.

"I will soon. I was told to do something first, and now I've done it. I just need a bit of time before I go back. I just want to know if you're real," she smiled, her voice fading to a whisper. "What did you have to do first?" Barret asked, curious, watching her move closer to Zared, feeling invisible again. As a man that was five foot nine, well-built, with jet-black hair, he was extremely difficult to miss.

"Answer the question!" Zared snapped, stepping back again. He had never felt the urge to step away from anything or anyone before. This was new to him: she made him different. Unnerved, there was a distant part of him that tried to speak up, to control his body, trying to tell him to pull her into his embrace.

"I was told to find him for my life to begin," she stated, not looking at Barret, only watching Zared, moving forward into his vacated steps, still not believing that he existed. "Who by?" Zared asked, stepping back again, anxious that this was a trap, a spell of some sort. "You," she replied, stepping closer to him, making sure that she was the only thing that filled his vision. Angel couldn't help herself, she had to touch him. She didn't want to miss her chance. Reaching out, she put her left hand on his face: it was smooth and warm. Her touch sent sparks throughout his system, letting them both know that this was real. She could feel the shock from him vibrating in their bond. He pulled his lips back showing fangs, but he didn't move, he couldn't; Zared wanted to run but his body was frozen to the spot, as if held by her presence.

Suddenly, he started to hiss in threat, showing that he was dangerous – proving to himself that he was still a killer, and that he should be feared. Angel didn't move, instead she shocked him again: standing on her tiptoes, she placed her lips on his. His fangs disappeared instantly, drawing back as if ordered by her. He could feel her touch, eerily warm. Her presence made his empty body yearn. Her energy poured into his hollow hunger, taming it, cooling the fire that was constant, giving him a sense that he had returned: that he was home.

Her gentle kiss turned into something more as he kissed her back. His arms wrapped around her warm body; she was solid against him.

No! he thought as she pulled back; smiling at him she knew how he felt. She felt his shock, his fight to remain himself: a killer, a monster that had taken time to earn the reputation he had – to put fear into those that crossed his path. Then she felt his joy as he surrendered. "Who are you?" It was barely a whisper on his lips, but his voice echoed in her mind. "Angel-May," she smiled. Speaking to him in silence, just as he too had done many times before: *You will come to me soon.*

"Why do you say that?" he asked, knowing that she

was a stranger to him. She had spoken to him silently – something that was rare. Barret watched on in silence while Zared still held Angel in his arms. "Because you're the one I've been waiting for," she replied, stroking her thumb across his lower lip. Zared felt her touch tickling his skin. He felt enjoyment, a gentle peace cast over him. He didn't want her to stop, but another part of him was telling him to move away, that this would only lead to danger – this would make him weak; this could kill him!

"I've never seen you before," he stated – this was true. "No, but I've seen you many times." She wasn't making sense to him. "Follow your instinct. You'll find me." A broad smile appeared on her lips, her eyes sparkled as she gazed at him. Zared felt her hand brushing over his face again. *How are you so sure I will find you?* he questioned her in silence. *Because you need to. You can feel it, I know you can because I do.* Her hand moved over his chest, feeling the stillness of his heartbeat. Zared stopped himself from reacting, he realised this was becoming too dangerous. Barret was now a witness, and this could be held against him if they found her.

"You're nuts! Leave *now*," Zared ordered, forcing himself to step away, removing all touch, all trace of her presence. He reminded himself that he was a vampire: condemned to walk the shadows alone, taking life when he desired. His kind was at the top of the food chain where they belonged. Then an image came to mind: he was sinking his fangs into her delicate skin, draining her rich-tasting blood – nectar filled with life – hearing her last heartbeat, her last inhale before death claimed her. Then he felt despair. If he killed her, nothing would make sense. His existence would be meaningless. He would be plagued with her death. The thought filled him with despair, he quickly shook it off.

Soon you will come to me. My future is with you. Angel was happy that she had found him, that he would find her, that her freedom from her father was now only a breath away.

"You're crazy woman." Zared started to growl under his breath. "You're a witch … You must be to know who I am. You and your coven have put a spell on me, and if we do meet, I will kill you myself…" He felt anger at his body's betrayal. After all this time it chose now to want, to desire – and it happened to be for a ghost.

You would never harm me. Angel smiled gently, her voice spoke to him alone. *What makes you so sure?* He gave her one of his cruellest grins; a smirk that reaped fear in many – even his own kind. Angel reached out to him once again: without fear, she moved with such speed that he couldn't move fast enough even if he tried. She put her bruised lips against his, moving them slowly.

Zared followed the motion, then, something new happened: a bright spark. His hands looped around her waist again. He was kissing her back, more fiercely. Her eerie warm air covered his mouth, providing him with his own breath. As the warmth from her hands ran through his hair, she felt even more real to him as the world around them disappeared. Her solid body beating in his embrace called to his lust. Another spark of pure bright light and he was being pulled to become one with her. His ears throbbed to her racing heart; his blood heated with passion. He had to claim her, he needed to claim her. "You are my protector, my sweet warrior and I will see you soon," she whispered breathlessly as she pulled away.

Then, as quickly as she had come to them, she was gone, leaving behind only the cold night air caressing his fevered skin.

"I can still smell her," Barret spoke, his voice strange in both their ears. "Can you follow it?" Zared asked, wondering what he was doing and why he felt compelled to do it. "Yes," Barret replied, still feeling flushed after witnessing the intimate act. Zared nodded as to say "let's go."

Barret crouched down, letting his body convulse – ready for the change. He heard his own bones snap and pop as they left their joints. He could smell animal from himself, growing stronger as he changed. He watched as fur pushed out from his skin before settling into a steady growth that covered his whole body. Seeing Barret's nails grow longer, curling, getting thicker, scratching on concrete, Zared watched as Barret's face flattened: changing into the skull of a larger animal, with teeth long and sharp, and canines extending from his upper and lower jaw – designed to tear flesh from bone. His whiskers were long and thick against his black fur, which was tinted with royal blue. His tail swayed frantically left to right. Purring rumbled from his mid chest as he sniffed the air picking up her scent. Racing off, he followed it, with his vampire companion close behind.

Chapter Seven

Angel was back in her body. Pain flooded her senses. She didn't want to move. She didn't want to breathe. Every cell burned with white-hot fire. Her body told her that this time she wouldn't be able to get up and move. This beating was a bad one. So, she kept her eyes shut, and slept a little more.

"Angel?"

He sounded oddly tense: a hint of fear hidden deep in his voice. It was a feeling that was abnormal to him having abandoned it along with his human life. But still, it was there within him; he could hear it in his own voice, and she knew the sound well, as she fought the drifting blackness.

"Angel, open your eyes." He shook her gently; she did as he asked, briefly feeling hot liquid pour into her mouth:

it tasted rich, thick, hot as it glided down her throat making her dizzy. "Drink," he commanded, as the smell of death lingered in the air around her. Angel followed his directions for a short time; she trusted him completely. "I told you you would come," she gasped, moving her head away from the exotic liquid.

She was still unable to open her eyes, they were too heavy and she felt too weak. "I kept my faith," she whispered before drifting off again.

"Yes Callie we have her," he said, then paused. "Yes, last night." He paused again, pacing the room. "Not yet. She needs to heal before we can move her. She was beaten badly this time." He paused again. "That's not a good idea. As we discussed earlier tonight, it's already there. If she does, then it will be too strong and killing it will be hard." He paused, tapping a hard surface. "OK, but she has to trust us first before we plan that." He paused again, briefly this time, sighing out loud. "Fine. I must go now, I hear him." He waited for a reply. "Yes. Soon." Then, she heard a click as he sighed again. The door opened to her left.

"Has she woken up yet?" he asked; his voice was familiar – their bond flickered with his closeness. Her heart pounded at its response. Her soul recognised his presence: it was a golden light that filled her, travelled through her every cell, their connection growing stronger the longer he was by her side. "No," Barret replied.

"You came," Angel suddenly whispered, forcing her eyes to open, knowing it was him. "I thought you weren't real."

"We both came, and yes, I'm real – very real." Zared pointed towards Barret, letting her know it was a joint effort. "Thank you ... both of you." Angel smiled, moving from her prone position, feeling stiff. "Where are we?" She gasped as a wave of pain hit her like a wall. Zared growled suddenly: it was involuntary as it bubbled up, feeling her pain too. Angel grinned – it hadn't been the first time he had done that. She remembered as a little girl she had been hit too hard by one of the guards. The pain that she had felt then had made him react in the same way.

Angel looked around seeing a room with old paper that had turned yellow over the years. The room had two narrow beds dressed in thin sheets tucked all the way round, and a dresser that sat in the middle parting the room in two. There was also a lamp that had started off cream, and an old TV box that rested on a small wooden table which leaned to one side.

"In a rented room. We'll leave as soon as you're strong enough," Zared said, walking over to an old ripped patterned chair that had some of its stuffing missing. "But, until then, you need to shower." His face twisted. His body was rigid. He spoke with emotion in his voice, but he tried to stay cool towards her, as he passed, staying well clear of her as dried blood scented their room with its sweet aroma. Zared sat down and placed his left ankle on his right leg. He covered his mouth with his right hand and stared at the wall behind her. His coldness made her feel uneasy, unwanted.

"OK," she said, staggering to her feet, putting a hand on the wall for balance as another hand grabbed her arm, making her jump and stumble slightly. She turned to see Barret. His eyes looked sympathetic, but evil was still there as well. *Was this one of my enemies that he warned me about?* she wondered, still reeling from the touch of another person. A part of her was waiting for something to happen. "Thank you," she said with a shaky voice as they moved to the bathroom slowly. Trembling under his hands, she watched them carefully, waiting to see if they would be raised in threat. "Would you like me to put the water on ready for you?" Barret asked. Angel nodded. Her voice wouldn't work. She watched him turn one of the big taps that was in the middle of the bath – a wide metal pipe led up to the shower head – before leaving.

Angel fumbled to undo the only remaining buttons she had left on her worn, ripped night shirt, letting it drop off her and land in a blood-soaked pile on the floor. Her back faced the door, forgetting that it was still open, that she had people other than herself there – that they still existed. She stood there alone, naked. Angel spotted a large mirror above a clean white sink and wondered how bad she looked. She walked in front of it. Her trembling hands gripped the rim of its white bowl to keep herself steady.

The mirror had started to steam up from the shower that was heating up quickly; but Angel could still see her reflection. She still didn't look like herself. She looked like she should be in a cage, displayed at a secret carnival for freaks like her. Her face was covered in blood where the strap of his belt had sprayed blood after each strike. She could see scabs from her cuts, dark brown. She touched them; they felt hard and bumpy. Her face looked multicoloured from bruises, old and new combined, but the thing that caught her attention the most was her eyes: they looked sad and empty, there was no strength there, no peace, no self worth. Looking down, she saw her arm: skin, raw, curled at the edges where it had turned yellowish – a sign of it dying. Underneath, she could see reds, pinks and white of new skin. It looked smooth with thousands of lines.

Painfully, Angel lifted her arm, poking one of her fingers into one of her skin's jagged cuts. Sharp stinging forcing her to take a quick inhale of air, blood welled up with a layer of clear liquid above it. She looked at the rest of her arm. She wanted to cry, to be held like a child in their mother's arms. He had damaged her, and every day she would have to see the reminder. Her skin wasn't whole any more. She turned, stretching to look at her back: she could see the imprint from his buckle burned into her flesh from its metal design. Parts of her body were just red-raw, with chunks of flesh gone, ripped away in his torturous rampage. She realised then that the only place that hurt mildly was her stomach, which had turned almost black as blood bubbled up from under her skin, trapping itself there for all to see.

Angel heard an animalistic growling from behind her. She felt the anger building in Zared, then a deep-throated rumbling hiss that sounded even more deadly, almost primal. "I should have killed him while I had the chance!" Zared was livid. His voice projected his feelings to everyone's ears. Fear rippled down her spine. He sounded every inch the cold-blooded killer. Angel turned to see both Zared and Barret staring at her naked body, which was unrecognisable even to her. She saw Zared's eyes. They were red just like in her dream. Only this was caused by a different reaction than before. His hands gripped the doorframe hard, fingers digging in, pulling at the frame and splitting the wood from the wall – releasing his tension, his urge to kill, to hunt down the perpetrator and dismember his body.

Barret didn't look at her; his eyes were focussed on the bloodstained pile of clothing. He breathed heavily, deep in thought, then, after what felt like forever, he turned slowly and walked over to Zared, whispering something in his ear in a low voice – something Angel couldn't hear. She saw Zared struggling to control himself; turning to look at Barret, his eyes closed, he dropped his head and slowly nodded. Barret left, pushing past Zared as he loomed in the doorway, staring down at the tiled flooring.

Angel could feel her eyes glazing, threatening to spill over. Her body throbbed hard, but Angel refused to cry in front of Zared, so she turned her back on him, pulling back the white plastic sheet and stepping into the steaming hot water. She felt it sting her wounds. It caused her to quickly reach out: flattening her hands on the damp, cool tiled wall, scraping her nails on its smooth surface, and biting hard on her lower lip to keep from screaming out. She took sharp short breaths. Then they came; she couldn't stop them. She put her shaking hand to her mouth and sobbed. She tried to stifle the sound. She pushed the palm of her hand to her lips to muffle her strained gasps. She didn't want him to hear her over the water. Her legs suddenly felt too weak; she couldn't hold her own weight any more. She slid down into the tub, curling into a shaking ball, feeling the water spray over her. She cried like she had never cried before. Her hands covered her face. Her body shook violently. It was the release, finally, that had been long awaited.

Her eyes were bloodshot from crying. Her skin was wrinkled and tender, feeling almost soft. After a couple of hours, wrapped in a large bathrobe that had been hung on the back of the closed door, she re-entered the room to join the boys. She could feel her skin beginning to get sticky as it caught on the robe's fabric. Her jagged wounds throbbed. Her hair was dripping with water.

She slowly made her way to the bed, trying not to rub the fabric on her wounds too much. "Where's Barret?" she asked, noticing Zared was on edge, shifting in his seat. His body looked tense. He was trying to keep his eyes off her. His left leg moved restlessly. His hands were resting firmly on his jeans.

Angel felt a sudden nervousness about his presence. She knew he wouldn't hurt her, but she still had a cold fear clenching at her stomach. "He's gone to get you fresh clothes," he replied through clenched teeth. "I need to heal you." It sounded like a demand as he quickly rose. Zared felt the darkness of rage fill him. He wanted to taste her, but at the same time he wanted to rip everyone's head off because she was in pain. He wanted to spill blood for each tear, for every drop of blood she had shed.

"How?" She moved to the bed, sitting on its edge and holding on to her robe, nervously staring at him, her palms sweating. "Well, I'm a vampire, and with vampires they heal quickly, so to help you I'm going to give you some of my blood." He said it with force; it, again, sounded like an order. He looked briefly at her face.

"I know what you are, but in all the time I've known you, we never did this, and you never told me about this … Will you turn me?" she asked, as he rubbed his palms up and down his legs. "No, you'll just heal," he said, confused by her statement. When the time came, he would have to ask her about it.

"You have given me some already?" Angel asked, remembering having swallowed sweet hot liquid. "Yes, I had to. You were dying. So I gave you enough to heal the wounds on the inside. I would have given you more but you passed out," he replied, now making eye contact with her.

Angel realised that she was safe now, that no one could hurt her. *He is your warrior. He is bonded to you. He won't let you die … and I won't allow it!* It was that voice again; the one that had spoken to her before. She didn't know who this person was, but she felt him constantly inside of her. He had spoken to her again on Isis's fifth birthday. He would always fill her with the feeling of pure love, no matter what.

After a brief moment, Zared forced himself to walk over to her, sitting next to her. "You ready?" he asked. She nodded in reply. Her heart was pounding at his closeness. "Good. When you see blood, drink it. I'll let you know when you have taken enough." She took a deep breath. Now she was nervous, and he was getting a scent of her blood, arousing hunger.

"Will it hurt?" She was half smiling – not wanting to show him that she was as weak as she felt and looked. "No, it will make you feel better … stronger. As it runs through your veins, it will make you feel warmer. You should feel your skin tingle as it heals," he replied, shifting, trying to hold himself in check. His insides were twisting, burning. Tension called to him, telling him to feed on her. "Will it taste the same as the first time?" she asked, as their bond burned, heating her up. She couldn't tell any more if it came from him or her. "Yes, only better," he said simply. He was getting more impatient. With every question, the urge to taste her was greater.

"OK, I'm ready" she said, turning her body towards him. Zared brought his wrist to his mouth, making a quick movement, ripping at his skin; blood welled up, spilling over in a waterfall of red. He pushed his wrist to her ready for drinking, but Angel didn't move. She was staring at him, fascinated by his face: his eyes were ruby-red; blood stained his pale lips. She had forgotten how stunning he was, how she felt for him. Seeing him in this state filled her with a need. Their bond burned together, drawing her to him. He had tried to block it, but only failed. She watched as his fangs fully extended, making his skin even paler against the redness of his blood.

Zarcd had an unseen power that surrounded him, making him dangerous, unpredictable, seductive. His features looked carved from ice: smooth, flawless – nature's most lethal weapon. Zared looked up to see her staring at him. It wasn't fear or shock, and she didn't want to scream like a mad person. What he saw at that moment was curiosity, recognition, trust and … then, she shocked him for the second time: her hand came up slowly as his bloody wrist disappeared out of sight. She was looking intently at his fangs. She was smiling, shyly, itching to move as she chewed on her lower lip. *Stop her!* a strange voice shouted silently, breaking his paralysed state. He grabbed her wrist, just as she touched his lips. Her fingertips brushed his skin, reminding him of their first encounter. He let her come closer. He wanted her closer. He wanted to feel her skin on his. Everything around them seemed to disappear. He could feel the air around them thick with anticipation. She was calling to his dead heart, pulling at him, making him surrender his will to hers. *What's wrong with me?* he thought, confused; he had never had this reaction to anyone. Her soft delicate finger brushed his fang with the lightest of touches. An explosion of wanting twisted at him.

The tip of her finger traced its smoothness, sending forgotten pleasure throbbing through his body. He couldn't move. He didn't want to. Things were stirring in his soul: a primitive reaction; an overwhelming need to claim her had returned, awakening lost emotions. Zared's eyes closed. She was torturing him. He could hear her heart pounding like a trip hammer against her chest. Her skin called to him with its scent of sweet honey, growing stronger with every beat, making the smell of the autumn rain fade the more excited she became. He wanted to call to her mind; to invite her to swim in his hypnotic words, which he had used on so many others before her. But he wanted her to want him of her own free will. He wanted it so much it burned intensely, making him fight the monster that wanted to grab her and have her, willing or not. Her touch aroused him strongly, teased him. Then, there was a pressure that exploded making him gasp out. She was forcing her finger under his left fang, right on its tip, climaxing his throbbing, begging her for more as the scent of her blood filled his lungs.

Yes. One thought escaped his throat as a deep rumbling moan. Grabbing the bedding between his fingers, he squeezed it tightly. He felt a pop, breaking her skin for the first time. She gasped as it split, but she didn't pull away.

Their bond began to open them up to each other. She felt him overpower all of her senses. She felt his longing, his intensity, as their bond crashed over her in waves. Blood bubbled up, bursting into his mouth, filling him with its sweet life. Her breath shuddered. Her chest heaved as he closed his lips around her wound, suckling on it gently, running his rough tongue over it, caressing it, causing it to bleed just a bit heavier. He moaned again, this time he heard her reply in the same way; breathing in a wanting way, as her skin heated under his touch. Zared tightened his grip on her wrist, pulling her closer, moving her hand to a position so that the joint of her wrist was exposed to him, ready to be tapped at any moment.

His desperation for her overwhelmed him. His lips released her finger, allowing it to glide softly down, her hand brushing her skin. He found it: the perfect spot just above the joint where all her veins met, turning her skin almost blue against its whiteness. He could smell it pumping just under the surface; its rich nectar summoning him to sip. Zared wanted her so much, but not in this way; it had to be more intimate; it had to be her neck. He couldn't take her like any other. He didn't want to. She wasn't food. She was something else … something more.

Moving slowly, savouring her scent as it intoxicated him, his hand wrapped around her neck. His fingers glided through her damp hair, tugging at the strands. She made sounds which thrilled him; they were sounds of pleasure. Zared pulled her closer to him. Their lips met, brushing over and over again, rapidly. He could feel her hands sweeping over his body: one resting on his arm that held her, while the other rested on his back, pulling him closer to her. He could feel her fingers tightening, gathering his shirt in her hand, both groaning into each other's mouths; eager to take their passion further – their kiss moving to a gentle rhythm. She could taste her blood on his mouth. Her tongue gently brushed his lower lip, parting them wider, feeling his sharp fangs brush her own lip when his mouth moved with hers. The tingle of her skin exciting her more.

Angel could taste her own blood but she didn't mind it – it made him want to taste her more. Zared slipped his tongue into her mouth, finding hers: rubbing, brushing, caressing it over and over. Feeling their kiss deepen, he felt like they were almost one, complete, their connection changing again, opening her up to him, he could feel her burning desire, her aching flesh that had stopped scream-ing out in pain. Angel felt like nothing she could ever have imagined: excitement, longing, desire, and a want-ing to become one with him. His hand tightened around her neck. Her hair was entwined in his fingers. She felt him pull her head back, gently tilting it to one side as his lips left hers and slowly traced the curves of her neck, kissing her skin softly, over and over. Her heart skipped with every touch. Feeling his tongue licking, flickering from between his lips, tasting her softly, she felt giddy waves shivering down her spine. Zared parted his lips. She felt his fangs brush her skin, scraping lightly. Her breath quickened in anticipation.

Stop, the voice shouted in his head. *Stop!* it hollered again. Only Zared didn't want to. He wanted more, not just of her blood, but of her body too, to satisfy her hunger, her desire, to take her, and make her his. Her grip tightened, pulling at his clothing. "Yes," she whispered, unaware she had spoken out loud.

Zared pulled back slightly. There was no fear in her voice, no pain that held her still. The only thing he heard was the invitation she gave him. The only thing he felt was the suffocating craving she had for his touch, causing pressure to build up underneath her skin, to the point where she wanted to explode.

"I trust you," she whispered, closing the empty space. Her acceptance was all he needed.

His fangs touched her skin, again scraping lightly at the place of her beating pulse. She held her breath, waiting, gripping him tightly. He penetrated. His fingers gripped her hair, pulling on it lightly as he crushed her body against his. Angel felt them pierce the crease between her neck and shoulder. She could feel them sinking deep through skin and the fat that lay just beneath. Then she felt the sting as they penetrated again, felt the burn, just like the first break, before it disappeared and turned into an unnatural pleasure.

Hot liquid poured into his mouth. She could feel him drinking, suckling gently at her skin, his lips hot on her heated body. She felt his tongue touching her wound over and over, lightly caressing it in a smooth motion. He pulled her closer, letting her fit into his hard curves, making her shudder under his embrace. She wanted to move him, to push him down, to obey what her body cried out for, to experience this raw passion that was devouring her senses, to position herself differently upon his willing body; she had a powerful desire to straddle him. Angel knew these urges even though she felt they were unknown to her. She had no idea where they came from, or why this feeling to be united with him was so strong. Her fingers grabbed at his clothes. She wanted to remove them, to rip them off his firm sculptured body. Zared knew what she wanted to do, and everything in him said to go with it, to allow her to rule him. He couldn't explain why he wanted this so much, but his claim on her was too intense.

She is destined to be with you, but not this way, the voice spoke to him as he drank her rich sweet-tasting blood. *You are here to be her warrior. You were sent to protect her!* Zared suddenly felt the truth of its words; the future this connection held. It scared him back to reality, and to what he was doing. "No," he whispered, pulling away, scrambling to his feet, fighting his body.

"What's wrong?" Angel asked, shocked at his sudden reaction, that he had broken their intimacy so quickly it had left her reeling. "Nothing. I just need a minute," he replied, forcing himself to walk to the bathroom, closing the door behind him.

Zared stood looking into the mirror, which was still damp from Angel's shower.

"What just happened in there?" he asked his reflection, hearing his hoarse voice, still feeling the uncontrollable urges trying to take him over.

He gripped the white porcelain sink tightly, closing his eyes and focussing on calming the beast inside of him. *Go with the plan. Give her your blood then get out of there,* he commanded silently to himself, before looking at his reflection again. He wiped his lips, removing the evidence of her blood that still lingered. Zared took a mouthful of water, spitting it into the sink, and watching the last of her wash away. *Control yourself; she'll trap you otherwise.*

Re-entering the room, he saw she hadn't moved. She waited for him, her face solemn. "You have to drink," he ordered, holding his feelings back now. He forced his voice to sound cold, detached, making it as menacing as he could before returning to the bed. His eyes lingered on her neck, seeing trails of blood run down her soft flesh. "When we finish, wash your neck before Barret sees it," he said, averting his gaze from the fresh red streaks that tainted the air and filled his lungs with the promise of life that had cooled his hunger with skin that tasted of sweet honey. He licked his lower lip, remembering that taste. He shook his head quickly, trying to remove all thoughts, looking only at her bright emerald eyes, and hearing her pulse returning to a steady pace, as her breathing slowed to normal. "OK," she said, nodding, trying to not let his numbness upset her.

"Don't tell anyone what happened," his voice sounded odd – a strained plea was hidden within his tone. Angel nodded again, knowing from his reaction and the feeling of their bond that if she did say something, it could be bad for both of them. A sadness ached in her chest, making her realise that this person in front of her was too different. Maybe he wasn't her best friend, but only the image of the teacher she knew so well and loved dearly? The Zared she wanted the most was not of this time, and this thought made her throat tighten and her eyes become glassy. Angel had finally got the man she loved in front of her, at arm's length, and still she had to wait … waiting and not knowing if he would ever come to her, if they would ever be together.

Zared ripped his skin again. This time he needed it to be quick, before Barret returned asking questions: questions he couldn't answer and didn't want to. Angel cleared her throat, taking a deep breath and exhaling in a sigh before she looked into his eyes again. His face was strained with hidden emotion, as he fought against himself. Zared's eyes tried to hide a longing that was forbidden to him. He was aching as much as she was. He reminded her of his last visit; how sad he had been then – how much he had wanted to stay with her. Angel said nothing; she just did as he asked.

Closing his eyes, Zared focussed on nothing, trying to keep her out of his mind as he felt her sucking deeply at his wound, giving him more pleasure than it should. He fought from wrapping his fingers in her damp hair again. He could picture picking her up, having her sitting on his lap facing him, licking her honey-scented skin slowly, before tapping into her once again, bringing her into a lovers' embrace. He was seeing their golden thread filling a loneliness he had become accustomed to, letting it pulse with its own heartbeat drumming away to its own musical rhythm.

He could feel her presence vibrating loudly through their connection, and he was finding it even harder to fight his desire. She was shifting uncomfortably as she drank. He wanted her to feel comfortable, to not feel her robe scratching at her skin as it started to heal. He pulled her up to her feet. Keeping hold of her, he spun her as she drank, and pulled her back against his aroused body, wrapping his arm around her neck, so that his wrist was still over her mouth. Her lips still touched his skin. His arm rested on her delicate shoulder, as his other hand lay on her hip, resting in the small curve with her heated back against his chest.

Angel could feel how close he was as she drank. Her body relaxed, leaning against him as his head lowered towards her ear. She felt his husky groans vibrate through her, his soft lips brushing her naked neck slowly, kissing it with the lightest of touches, and stopping her in her tracks. Lust gripped her. It had changed. Something deeper was taking over. She lifted her head; her breath was heavy, raw – she had been untouched and her instincts were primitive. Her free hand glided behind her, feeling bulging cloth, teasing it to break free. She could feel his hand leave her hip, his strong fingers pulling at the belt of her robe. She rested his hand on her chest letting it glide up around her throat; she felt him squeeze gently, smothering her air, exciting the fire that burned inside her. Her hand rested on top of his, squeezing it, inviting him to do as he wished, tipping her head back and resting it on his shoulder, allowing it to roll to one side – their bodies swaying to a soundless rhythm. She felt his lips on her neck again, kissing her with just the right amount of pressure, making her giddy. She turned slowly in his arms, sliding her hands under his top, feeling his carved muscled toned skin hard against her body. She was pulsing like a beacon, begging him to satisfy her throbbing core. His lips touched hers again. Passion, lust, filled their colliding bodies. Only instinct guided her, as her thick fingers began undoing his buttons – knowing in her heart that she couldn't undo them fast enough. Zared's hands worked like hers, only quicker, as they found her belt, undoing it in seconds.

Angel opened her eyes to see what she had seen before: his eyes were red as rubies. He wanted her as much as she wanted him. Then, she felt his strong arms around her body, picking her up without effort, and laying her down on the bed. His body followed, hovering just above her. Her legs wrapped around his waist as his hands held onto hers. She felt his kisses on her neck making her flesh ache in pleasured pain, arching her body, crushing her into him. She could feel him licking her skin; his hot tongue glided down her collarbone and over the peaks of flesh of her naked breasts. She moaned for more as he circled her hard nipple, sucking at it softly. Her nails scraped across his back making him shudder in pleasure as he flicked her alluring cherry, feeling her legs pulling at his body, bringing his throbbing erection closer. His kisses became pressured on her flesh as he ventured slowly down, her legs falling away freely as he moved teasingly. She felt his hands gliding down over her curved waist, continuing down to the heated wetness that touched her inner thigh. Zared's fingers found her burning core stroking at it gently. She felt her body gasp at his touch, rocking her senses, as it travelled through their connection, exciting him more and bringing his fevered body to a standstill as his pulsing fullness bobbed, waiting to enter her forbidden cave, summoned by its inviting prize. Angel's hip moved back and forth against his playful hand. Her breath shaking with excitement, skin buzzing with energy. She was almost there, almost ready to climax.

Enough! the voice shouted, shattering everything, shooting pain through his mind, stopping him completely in his tracks. *Leave now!* It demanded him to obey. "Enough," he said defensively, he was losing his control around her. He wondered how this could happen. Suddenly the pain blinded him, he found it hard to think, he suddenly felt vulnerable – a vulnerability he had never felt before. There was something more powerful out their warning him, watching his every move, making him nervous. He had to get away from her fast. She must be a witch, it's a spell that she's casting over me!

Angel stopped. She felt breathless, frustrated. Meeting his ruby eyes, he turned away from her in rejection. Quickly standing to his feet and rearranging his clothes, he headed for the door, his head easing. He left Angel lying there, hurt. She saw the cold bitterness in his eyes. He made her feel ashamed as he sent anger thundering at her through their unbreakable chain. Angel wrapped her robe close to her wanting body, forbidding herself to cry.

"Go clean up." His voice was like ice, just as cold as their bond had become. His back remained facing her. She could feel his loathing pounding at her. Zared made his feelings disappear just as quickly as they arose, allowing his head to clear. The voice that warned him had now gone. He turned to see something inside her shattering. He felt her happiness crumbling, causing her more pain. She disappeared quickly to the bathroom, to wash her neck, erasing any sign of him, and removing the victory he would feel to see tears spill.

Zared really didn't want to hurt her, but he had no choice. This power that came to him was more powerful than either of them. It threatened his being. It was clear that his job was to protect her and nothing more.

Chapter Eight

Barret entered just as Zared grabbed for the door handle. He looked at the lust-filled vampire, seeing all the signs of sexual intent. He could smell its sweet scent lacing their room. Barret averted his gaze, focussing on the wall next to him.

"I've done my job. I'll leave now," Zared said, hoping never to see them again. She was someone he couldn't be around, not if he wanted to remain his evil disturbing self, or keep the unnerving feeling of death that came with her away. "No, Zared! I'm afraid your plans have just changed." Barret's mouth curled up at one corner, his dark eyes flashed. "You're coming with us. Callie has also summoned you." He turned his eyes to Zared's, staring into his liquid gold eyes with utter disgust, seeing Zared's resentment at him for forcing him to remain in their company. "You will come, or I will tell her about what's just happened." He half grinned. His eyes went wide briefly, giving him a menacing look, a smugness of knowing he had won. "Nothing happened, and I don't appreciate being blackmailed," Zared snarled back, wondering how much he really knew and how much he really saw. "I didn't say it would be all true." Barret gave a low chuckle, his body filling the doorway, arms crossing his chest. "Who do you think she would believe, a vamp, or a long-time friend?" he continued after a short pause.

"I'll meet you on the plane," Zared said, knowing that he had a point, and if he didn't come along, then Barret would send his henchmen. Zared didn't fancy looking over his shoulder every two seconds.

"When do we take off?" Zared asked, his jaw clenched, eyes narrowed. "Three a.m. Be there, or I'll make sure Callie will have you cooking before the week's out." He gave him a dazzling sinister smile. Zared wondered if he was planning something else, and if that was why he had been ordered to Callie's. Zared said nothing. Callie worked for some powerful people, people no one had met socially, as far as he knew – and those that had met them never returned.

Zared pushed past Barret, forcing him to step aside. He needed to escape now more than ever. He felt the darkness inside him mixing with her golden light, tempting him again. Anger began to rise. He felt she had trapped him somehow. He wanted to rip someone's head off, go hunting, just to feel the pure joy of it flowing through his system, flushing her out. He was going to be stuck with Angel for awhile now and the tension in his muscles had to rest before setting off on a plane and being trapped in a confined space, suffocating with the fevered knowing that she was near and untouchable. This didn't settle well with him, especially when she made him feel so much.

Barret walked over to Angel as she returned from the bathroom. He was holding a handful of bags and tipped them onto the bed next to her, along with a jacket for when they were ready to leave. "These are for you," Barret said, looking her over. "Your old ones are no good, and I don't think it's right for you to meet your grandmother in a bloodstained shirt and panties," he announced. "Please pick what you like and we can get rid of the rest later." He smiled, trying to make his voice sound gentle and light, careful so as not to scare her.

"I didn't know I had a grandmother. Why did it take until now to find me?" Angel asked. "She didn't know you were still alive, but then when a traveller spotted a picture of your mother, he said he had seen you standing in a window. He thought you were the woman in the frame, an easy mistake to make after all you look so much like her," Barret said, sitting down. "What's my grandmother like?" Angel asked, holding up tops, liking him a little bit more even though she still didn't fully trust him. Something in her told her only to trust Zared, but at this moment she didn't trust herself. She had felt Zared's anger and annoyance towards her returning, his emptiness. She tried to block out his hatred as much as she could.

"She's a sweet old lady. I've known her all my life. When I was a small boy she took me in after my parents died; then, when your mother passed and your father took off, she searched for you, even though she thought you were gone too, and when I was old enough, I joined her team." His voice brought her back to him. She noticed how his words sounded, detached, empty, as he recalled his memories. "Callie would help any one. She has her own island, where many of her friends and the people she's helped live. She created a sanctuary for people like us to go to, where there's no fear, hate, only protection and peace." Suddenly, Angel felt something in her saying this was definitely a falsehood. "Do you live on this island?" she asked, trying to figure out if her intuition was correct.

Angel picked out a navy-blue T-shirt, and jeans that covered her feet, trying not to let him see her face, just in case he could read her. "No, I left there a year ago so I could find a bigger territory," he said warmly. That was true, her senses told her that much. Barret's eyes were on her, watching her, scanning her quickly. Angel walked away, returning to the bathroom to dress, closing the door as she changed.

"What do you mean by that?" Angel shouted through the closed door. She didn't know what that word meant. She had never heard it before. She looked into the mirror and saw that all of her wounds had healed and all sign of them nearly gone, but some remained, looking like they would stay with her for the remainder of her life – maybe because they were too deep to disappear like the rest. She saw that even those on her neck had gone: no sign of Zared's bite and their exchange of blood. Her skin glowed, looking healthy: pale pink with no blemishes. She blushed when she thought of Zared – before remembering that he wanted nothing more to do with her. Angel felt used. He had gotten what he wanted, and now threw her away, leaving her with these strangers.

"I mean, I had to go out to the main land and find my own land so I could hunt more," Barret replied loud enough for her to hear. "Hunt? What do you mean hunt?" she asked, sounding shocked as she finished dressing. "Animals. Rabbit. Deer. Anything I can catch really," he replied, as she entered the room again. "Why?" She was looking at him puzzled. Why would a man like him hunt animals and what did he do with them? "Because I need to. It's something we all do when we change," he replied simply, seeing her face questioning silently. "*Change*? Change what?" She was really confused now. "We change into animal forms: mine is a panther, it's a really large cat, but if we lived on the island, then we can only hunt in certain areas."

"Oh," was all she could think of saying. "Will I see your animal form?" Angel asked, after a short pause. "Maybe," he replied, looking at his watch. He suddenly asked her if she was ready. "Yes, let me just brush my hair first," she said, finding a comb on the side chest. Barret could smell her scent bursting towards him with every brush, filling the air, covering Zared's scent of faint death, as well as his own wild odour.

"I never asked: how do you feel?" Barret asked, clearing his throat as he spoke, looking at her confused face as she tried to figure out what to do with shoes and socks. "I feel great! My skin no longer hurts; it has a few scars but that's all, and I feel strong and awake … and I know it sounds funny, but I don't feel afraid any more. I feel like I'm safe, that this is where I'm meant to be." She smiled, handing over the sock when Barret held out his hand. "Did he bite you?" he enquired, showing her how to put the sock on, watching her face carefully, but Angel kept it blank, trying not to picture their earlier activity, concentrating only on Barret's hands as he scrunched the sock up and put it over her toes, pulling it up her foot and over her ankle. He left her to do the other one; copying his method, she scrunched her sock up. "No, but he did bite himself," she replied after a small hesitation, which was true, only there were other things that had happened as well, things he didn't need to know.

Barret then showed her what to do with her shoes; he had gotten her caramel trainers that fastened with Velcro. "That's fine, that's all I wanted to know," he said, feeling suspicion about her response – either she was lying to protect him, hypnotised by Zared's voice or she was too involved. Either way it niggled at him. Barret took her shoe pushing it onto her right foot and pulling the Velcro across. Angel smiled, copying, not saying any more. She knew she had to remain quiet about the rest of it. Something inside her compelled her to do so in spite of Zared's anger towards her. He was drawn to her, and right now she didn't want to enrage him any more.

"Let's go, I've got a car waiting outside," Barret said, looking at his watch and realising that time was moving quickly. "You know, this feels odd," Angel said, following him, feeling the shoes restricting her feet. "They feel huge." She walked, feeling like a clown, watching the floor and being careful not to trip until she was confident enough to walk without stepping on herself. "What?" he asked, not understanding what she meant as he closed the room door behind her. "These on my feet. I've never had them covered before. It just feels so strange, and kind of painful around my toes …" She stopped a few steps behind him, rocking back and forth on her heels as she explained. "You'll get use to it over time, then it will be normal," he replied, walking her to the waiting car.

Chapter Nine

Their plane landed on a private island outside of Boston: she could see the city lights illuminated in the distance, sparkling and flashing in the night sky.

"Where's Zared?" Angel asked, looking around, opening herself up, feeling that he was near. Their bond had been pulsing throughout their journey, revealing only things that scared her, that made his presence feel prickly and untouchable with its iced fury. He had sat as far from them as he could during the flight, his body tense from the moment he had stepped onto the plane. He had instantly felt her, smelling only her scent all around him, as her presence burned in his thoughts, churning away at him, summoning him to leave his seat and return to her side.

"He's on his way," Barret replied, sounding tense. He knew that there was something between Angel and Zared and it was strong – but how did it start, this is what had him so puzzled. "Good, then we wait till he's here," she said, standing at arm's length to Barret on the dark tarmac, and feeling warm air around her – it must be summer still, she thought, not really knowing what season it was, or why she had insisted on waiting.

"Can I ask you a question?" Barret said, looking directly at her, his dark eyes flashing like a cat's in the darkness. "Yes?" she replied, studying his face, fascinated by his reflecting eyes, which kept her at a distance. She watched the way he stood, almost sealing himself off to her and everyone else around him. It was a lazy expression for him, but one which screamed danger to those that got too close. "Why are you so attached to the vampire?" He cringed at the thought of Callie's grandchild having chosen a leech to place her trust in. "Because he belongs to me," she said simply, knowing the statement to be true, and that he meant so much more than even that. "How? You've never met him before? How can you say that?" Barret was shocked to hear Angel state this fact out loud. "But I have. He's called me to him and I've called him to me." She smiled at the memory of her dreams, then she felt him approaching, flattening all of her happy memories of their future, wondering how they

95

would get to that place when she could sense his begging for their chain to fracture, to break cleanly, allowing him to be released from her suffocating hold.

"He's close." She sounded irritated by Zared's presence, and turned her body away from his direction.

"When?" Barret asked, before Zared arrived. He watched as her expression turned to misery with Zared's approach. Barret began to wonder if this connection to him, or whatever it was, had been forced upon her, that a powerful spell might be able to remove it and make her forget Zared had ever existed. "Why does it matter so much?" she questioned him, feeling irritated by his tone. "I just wondered. He said he had never met you before; he doesn't remember your face that's all." She felt he was lying. There was something he was after and it felt bad, very bad. "He may not remember my face, but there is something deeper inside of him that knows me; unfortunately, it's something he can't remove, no matter how much I repulse him," she snapped, giving Barret a sarcastic smile, tilting her head to one side as her eyes narrowed in Zared's direction. She folded her arms across her chest as if to keep her heart from leaving, and pulled her back up straight. "He feels it too alright. Don't you Zared?" Anger filled her voice with venom, her back remained facing him so she didn't have to see the disgust in his eyes.

She stared into the distance, rocking herself on the spot like none of this bothered her. Zared walked up behind her, standing so close that they were almost touching. Angel's heart betrayed her by skipping a beat.

"How did you know he was there?" Barret asked with a wide grin. His eyes shifted from hers to his, feeling relief: seeing there was a hatred there, a mutual loathing that was plain and clear, something that he could use to his advantage – and if that hate for the leech grew stronger, then she wouldn't mind if he exterminated him.

"She feels me the same way I feel her! I don't know how this happened or how to get rid of it, but it gets stronger the closer we are." His voice was as cold as ice as he stood by her side; his dark energy encasing her. Angel couldn't help but step away, her insides flipped making her feel sick. She never thought that this would happen. She had put all of her trust into this man standing near her: she had given him her heart, her faith. He had watched her grow up. He had come to her when she most needed to see someone, to take away the pain. He was there to keep her sane, and feel what life was meant to be. He had kept her going for all of these years.

Her eyes began to sting. She turned away from both of them, blinking her tears back, focussing on the darkness before her, and trying to block out their voices from her pounding ears.

"What else do you feel when you're together?" Barret asked, watching Angel cringing beside him. "Protective," Zared said coldly, looking at Angel's back, seeing her shoulders tense, knowing that this was only a part of what he felt for her; but this was not going to be something he would admit to. This was something he was going to ignore completely, making their connection as hollow as he could, sending her feelings of contempt, making her feel as if she were nothing to him, just a blood bag ready to drain at any time.

Angel backed away. He had to admit that it was working to plan, but he felt guilty that he was making her feel pain, when only hours ago he had wanted to kill the person who had harmed her. "And the rest!" Angel felt repelled, sealing herself off to him as best she could. She knew how he truly felt now: it made her skin crawl. She wondered that if it weren't for the ache in her chest, if she would even be able to tell if she were standing here alive and breathing. "Like what?" Barret asked, feeling even more curious, eager to widen their rift. "Oh! What … about the anger … loathing … how I repulse him … seeing me standing here make's him feel physically sick? He wants to be as far away from here, from me, as possible. If, … if he could kill me right now, he would. I disgust him. I'm nothing to him, and at this moment in time I really wished you'd left me there. I knew how my father felt about me, but at least I didn't have to feel him every damn second. I didn't have to deal with *this* ..." she was shouting by the time she'd finished, tears rolling down her face. Her hands flapped around in the air, unable to find the words to finish.

Both of the men were watching her: Zared's eyes filled with hostility. Barret was amazed at how much she sensed from Zared. "Is that how you feel?" Barret asked, watching Zared carefully, making sure it wasn't an act put on for his benefit. "Yes!" he hissed out.

There was no sign that she was feeling him wrong. But, hearing him say it out loud made something twist inside of Angel. She couldn't breathe, she felt a pain so powerful that it made her legs buckle. She wanted to throw up, to run away somewhere and curl up into a ball; to close her eyes and never open them again.

"I may feel protective of her, but I don't intend on doing anything about it. I'm pissed with this. I want it gone. And why the hell are you giving me the third degree?" His teeth were clenched, trying to keep his anger in check again. Glimpsing at Angel out the corner of his eye, he could see her shaking, silent tears were tearing her in half. He had caused this. Her hands were wrapped around her waist, as she bit down hard on her lower lip. "Because Callie is going to ask and I need to know what the truth is before I explain it to her!" Barret snapped back, bringing Zared's attention back to him, just as a long black limo pulled up. Angel did what she did best: she pulled herself together, gave out a cough, held her breath to stop her misery, and made herself go numb for awhile. She dried her face on her sleeves, hearing a faint sniffle as she composed herself.

Angel walked behind Barret, and as far in front of Zared as she could get. "They're real," she whispered, spotting the long shiny black car with blacked-out windows. Zared heard her. It wasn't the first time she had said something like that, and he really wanted to know why; but at this moment she was in pain, because of him, and he doubted she would talk to him again.

Their ride didn't take long. They soon pulled up to Angel's grandmother's house. Stepping out of the car, she didn't notice how big the house was, not until she was stood in front of it.

"This is her house?" Angel asked, in awe. It was a large old white building with a white porch that went all around the front, with columns evenly spaced out, holding up the porch's extended shelter. From the large gravel driveway steps led to the front door. The lawn was stunning green, trimmed short, with striped patterns on its surface, and covered the grounds around the house. Colourful flowers sat in borders. Beyond the grass was woodland, with tall thick strong trees of different types. She could hear animals moving around, and birds flying above her. The soft breeze stroked her skin, reminding her that there were no more bars, no walls, just wide open space.

"Come on she's waiting for you." Barret started to head for the door, his hands were stuffed in his pockets.

"This feels wrong," she whispered to herself – something felt off to her. Angel's instincts were telling her not to go in there. She stared at the door. Zared had stopped beside her. She felt the urge, now stronger than anything she had felt before: she could feel her body wanting to panic. She took a few slow deep breaths to mask her fear. "Just keep your guard up," Zared whispered in her ear before walking ahead of her, fighting his own urge to take her hand in his; to give her his strength to help her face whatever was waiting for them. He could feel a darkness inside of her growing. It was telling her she was in danger. It took all of his strength not to turn around, sweep her up in his arms and run – run to a safe place where no one would find them.

Zared shook his head pushing the desire away. *How can she do this? It must be some kind of spell.* Zared's mind was racing. *If it is a spell then Callie will sense it; if it is, she will find a way to break it, and if it's not, then she will try to kill me.* That thought didn't appeal to him, but if he could escape this, then he would. If he couldn't, and the time came to them taking his life, then he would go down fighting, taking as many of them with him as he could.

They entered a grand entrance hall covered in pale-pink and white marble tiles, with a dark cream staircase that matched the walls and split at the top to go to either side of the house. Thick red velvet curtains covered glazed windows, each of which would cover an entire wall of a normal house. Pale-pink marble pillars held white vases, centred at each window, and filled with bright flowers: sweet pea, carnations, larkspur, and chrysanthemum.

"Callie," Barret said, bowing with respect. Barret stood a foot away from her. Angel went to stand by him, while Zared remained just behind Angel on her left-hand side.

"Hi Callie," Angel said copying Barret and bowing as though she were stood in front of a queen.

Callie looked at Angel with soft strong eyes, which were a darker green than her mother's bright green eyes. Angel noticed her gaze seemed slightly off, distracted, then her gaze fell on Zared. Her gentle face changed. Angel could see wrinkles form on her skin, giving Angel an eerie feeling. Angel couldn't help herself, she stepped back cowering, going to a place she felt safest, even with all of her anger: she stood next to Zared, getting as close as she could to him.

"Callie." His tone was cold, distant. Angel realised that they really didn't like each other; he had no respect for Callie and she had none for him.

"I hear that my granddaughter *appeared* to you." Her voice was shaking with its raspy sound. "That she sought you out."

"Yes, she did," Zared replied numbly, keeping his face motionless, giving her nothing. He felt Angel's arm against his; she still came to him for safety, to feel comfort, to feel his strength.

"Why did she find *you*?" Callie stepped closer to Zared. Angel felt a shift in energy; she could see Callie's energy surrounding her aging body. Angel could feel Zared's anger building, transferred through their bond; she felt it building to boiling point, ready for them both to snap.

"What is so special about you, vampire?" Callie was making him feel worthless, as she tried to drag an answer from him. Her energy was wrapping around him, sparking, causing him pain.

"He is special to me because he is mine!" Angel felt a darkness with a power that was making her light-headed as it grew in strength. Callie's energy was lashing out at him, binding him. Something in Angel wanted to destroy the old lady. She was hurting him, using something against him that he couldn't fight.

"What did you do to her, vampire? She has been alone for years, and now she appears to you? I see her need to be at your side, which tells me that you must be controlling her, because in a matter of hours she has bonded to you, and to you only. So I will ask you one more time, vampire: what did you do to her?" she snarled, stepping closer to him.

Angel felt his energy darken. She could feel his strength seeping into Callie; she could see Callie's energy sparking around him, almost pulling at his own black energy, making him weaker – trying to make them both weaker. Angel began to feel like she had in the woods, with the flower: hunger to take life.

"Stop," Angel snarled, stepping in front of Callie and looking her in the eyes. "Stop using your power on us," Angel ordered, as if she and Zared had merged into one person. "Out of my way child, this is not your business," Callie said, anger blazed in her eyes, power flowed from her, hitting Angel with pressurised waves. Callie didn't like people to interfere, no matter who they were. "Barret take her!" she commanded. Barret moved towards Angel, ready to grab her.

"Touch us and you will die!" Angel felt darkness flooding between them. She wanted to use the energy that was inside her. She had used it once to help Isis, now it was to help them. She could hear Zared hissing beside her, crouching, warning Callie and Barret. Barret froze. He felt the power flooding from Angel and Zared. It shielded them as it grew. Barret realised that it would be Angel that would have to kill Zared. Even when she hated being with him, no one could touch them. Angel felt energy trap her. She could see its chains around her body, holding her still. It felt strong, and it was coming from Callie.

"Callie! Stop. There's something I need to tell you first!" Barret shouted. "Guards!" Callie yelled over and over, until they appeared holding swords and daggers made of silver. "Take Angel-May to her room and lock her in there until I'm ready to see her. And as for this vampire, kill him," she said, not listening to Barret's pleas.

Angel felt something building inside of her. Callie's power that held her was also fuelling her. Angel drank it like soup, seeing Callie's face straining as she tried to strengthen her hold over Angel. Angel focussed on her breathing as she had practised before. She had mastered it now, with it only taking minutes for her to leave her body, and with a shield in place as protection – a gift from her future self giving her the possibility of what she could do, even though she'd seen it only a couple of times as a child. Angel saw light surrounding her and called it to her, drawing it in, allowing it to fill her soul and wrap her body in its blanket. She closed her eyes, blocking out the noise of everything around her – the sounds of the guards attacking Zared; Barret's swearing as he tried to grab her; his protestations to Callie that there was a force field around Angel's body shocking him.

Then, she felt it: dizziness, then, falling. She relaxed, telling her body to go with it. She felt her soul come away, as her body fell to the ground – still protected, for now. She saw Zared hissing, crouching, one hand crab-like on the ground, his clothes ripped, ready to fight, his fangs extended and dripping in blood.

"You will not harm him. He is mine." Angel felt pure deadly hunger. She moved to one of the guards that was on the attack. He had something in his hand. She didn't know what it was, except that it was short thin and lethally sharp: a dagger. She knew this would cause his death, and that made her stronger, more focussed – no one would take his life.

Zared was under attack from another guard. He blocked the guard's strike, knocking his hand away before ducking to miss the blade as it swiped back. Then, another guard grabbed him from behind, wrapping his arms around Zared's chest. Zared grabbed his arm tightly, and threw his weight forward, causing the guard to follow his quick motion, tumbling over Zared's back and landing on the hard floor.

Just then, the first guard brought his long sharp blade down. The blade was made from silver; it reflected light that caught Angel's eye. It sliced Zared's skin, starting from his right cheek, over the bridge of his nose, and across his golden eye, ending below his fringe. She felt him clench at the pain, keeping himself from shouting out, trying not to show that he was hurting, but letting out an angered grunt.

Angel could see his blood, his wound open, as it began pouring down his pale face. Zared became unrecognisable, half of his features hidden under the red veil. He wiped at his wound, removing thick liquid from his vision. He couldn't see; he was completely blind. Without saying a word, Angel could feel the pain throbbing. She knew he was wondering if he had lost his eye. He pulled his hand back, his palm covered in blood. He smiled at the men grimly; his teeth flashed briefly. "Lucky shot, it won't happen again," he snarled, standing up straight, licking the blood from his lips, and seeing the fear in some of their eyes.

Angel quickly glided to him, and stood like a ghost between them as the guard went on the attack. She reached out, placing a hand on both of them, she pulled the energy that surrounded the guard; she felt it tear out of him up, uproot with force, causing him to shout out in agony. She pushed her own energy at him, forcing it to entwine with his. It seeped in as she drew it back: now, it was flowing freely. It gave her pleasure as she drank it up – it was his life source, and it was making her stronger than she realised.

Her eyes found Zared again, she pushed the energy towards him, making it flow through their bond, growing so that it filled his body, taking over his darkness, and soothing his hurt. She watched as his own energy gulped hers down with enjoyment – his black light turning liquid gold, the same colour as his eyes. She watched as his face healed, leaving the scar that she recognised instantly. "There you are," she whispered with a smile, releasing the guard that was almost drained of his life source. "There's my warrior," she whispered, moving nearer until she was almost touching his radiant body. "My lover." She smiled, brushed her lips over his, and felt his warmth and his shock as he returned her affection with control.

Another three guards attacked together. Angel kept her hand on Zared's chest, throwing out her free hand, she pushed her energy out again. It snaked around the guards, connecting with each of them, one by one. She could hear them scream. She thought of Zared. She wanted him safe by her side. She could feel their energy pouring into him as it travelled through their bond, igniting them like a supernova. She felt herself drink and drink

… feeling the guards' lives slipping away. She could feel Zared taking in their lifeforce through her, enjoying it, as though it were blood feeding his thirst. It was then that he realised she too was a vampire, just like him, only she drained energy, while his kind drained blood. The thought comforted him. He relaxed with the realisation that she wasn't human, she was something else – she was a new kind of vampire.

"Stop!" Angel heard the raspy voice in the distance, commanding her to obey. Anger swelled up inside of Angel; she pulled away from Zared, releasing the guards, hearing them fall to the floor in a heap – none would die but all would take weeks to gain their full strength. Angel turned her attention to Callie.

"You tried to kill us," Angel said, speaking for them both – his anger still boiling deep inside of her. "I had no idea that you were connected; bonded as soul mates," Callie tried to reason. Angel realised for the first time that the energy Callie had used to keep a hold on her had gone. She could still see it, but she could feel that her own power had overridden Callie's. The old woman seemed frightened. "If I had known that, I would not have commanded the guards to kill him," she said, making her hoarse voice sound softer. "Please return to your body, and I will arrange a room for him." Her energy changed, changed colour too, but there was a feeling that she was trying to work something out; something that told Angel that this wasn't over.

"You will kill him if I return," Angel hissed, moving towards her. "I will not touch him. You have my word," Callie replied quickly. "I will not harm him. It is too dangerous for you and for us." Angel looked at Zared, who stood by her side. He nodded in agreement, but she could feel his concerns hidden deeply. Angel allowed herself to calm down. She focussed on her body; she felt a drifting, a pull slamming her back.

"Barret, I will talk to you alone," Callie announced, as Angel came around, blinking hard, clearing her vision of the dancing spots, as coldness from the marble floor touched her back. Barret bowed in agreement. His black hair shone in the light.

"Zared, you may stay in the north wing while you are here. I will need you to help Angel control that anger of hers, and that power she possesses before she burns out, or kills one of my people," Callie said bitterly, before shouting for someone called Avery, ordering her to take them to their rooms. "Barret come with me please," she rasped at him, walking away, slightly hunched. Barret flanked her side, taking a shaky arm to provide her with extra balance.

Chapter Ten

"How do you feel?" Zared asked Angel, taking her hands and helping her to her feet. He hated feeling as close to her as he did – with their connection still burning through him – but the fight against it was getting harder.

"Fine. Soulmates! Is that what we are?" she said, brushing her new clothes down, hoping they weren't torn or stained. "I guess," he replied, not really knowing what this meant – the soul mate or bonded mate was a fairy tale for his kind. They had heard stories about such things, told to them by the first walkers, but no one had heard of any vampire finding it. Just like the stories of their kind that had once walked in the light, and had had children, all were just dreams, the invention of some traveller.

"How are you? You took half of what I took from the guards. I could feel it go through our bond," she said, holding on to his hands as he lifted her without effort. "Different. Almost … alive, if that doesn't sound crazy," he said, suddenly putting a hand to his face, remembering that he had been wounded by the blade. In normal circumstances it would have taken a few hours to heal, leaving only a red mark before disappearing the following day. "It won't go you know," she pointed to it as she watched him follow its line. "You look like you're supposed to now," she said, still not forgiving him. "This is how you came to me." She remembered he was so handsome: a warrior from god, she had thought.

"You called me 'your warrior', 'your lover', why?" he asked, looking at her, as they started to follow Avery at a distance. Zared made sure he didn't touch her; she had a way of making him lose all control. He didn't want her to be his soulmate, he became cold again, distant, a screen of ice. "Because that's what you are. You've always been that to me," she replied, anger filling her voice. She could feel him rejecting her again. She cut herself off from their connection as much as she could; she felt the ache that tightened her chest.

"When did you see me? The first time I mean?" Zared hissed, puzzled. Angel didn't answer. Zared grabbed her upper arm, squeezing it tight. Angel bit her lip, stopping herself from making a noise as he pulled her to a stop and made her look at him before repeating his question. "When I was about four, maybe five," she snapped, trying hard to keep her voice low. "Only then, you were a lot nicer than you are now!"

"How could I? We've never met, remember? So who the hell gave you my name? Someone told you about me, and you're going to tell me who it was!" He refused to believe her. His hand was still clasped around her arm in an iron grip, pulling her towards him as he spoke. She sounded stupid to him, and he made it very clear through their web that he thought she was lying to him. He would get it out of her at some point. "Your future self told me." He still didn't believe her. "Zared, *you* told me. You were the one that helped me talk, read and write. It was you that told me what you were, and it was you who introduced me to Isis …" She smiled faintly at the name. Zared could see love in her eyes for this person. Suddenly he felt envious of Isis, and of what she meant to Angel. Jealous that she thought of this person with affection. He shook the feeling off quickly. "Who is Isis?" he whispered harshly, not knowing if the question was a wise one. "My daughter. Maybe your daughter too, I don't know," she hissed back under her breath, stinging her throat, trying not to look at him as they began to walk behind Avery again, continuing their arguing.

Zared started to laugh making Angel jump; it was a rich laughter like the time of the ceremony. "Now I know you're mad, because vampires can't have children," he hissed, his lips still curved slightly. "We have a witch who's a grandmother to Isis. Her name is Jurisa Sand. She met me a long time ago, with you, of all people! She said that our journey would start together, but mine would start in two ways: that I would go backwards before I could go forward, and that my vision would help me find you." Angel could feel her anger boiling over as her voice began to rise. "She also said on this journey we have to be careful. Death will touch us. So if we want more help, we have to find her; she is the one that starts this whole thing off, and if you want to get rid of me, then you're going to have to help me find her too!"

"Calm down and try to keep your voice low," he said sharply. Angel took deep breaths, calming herself; he was irritating her so much right now that she couldn't look at him, or speak for a few minutes. "Jurisa Sand? I know that name." He was speaking to himself, trying to figure out how and from where he knew this name. "How many times have you and I visited each other?" he asked. "I don't know … maybe once or twice a week, but in the past year it became more frequent: about three, maybe four, times in just a few days." She couldn't really remember how many times he had come to her over the past month; she only knew she had seen him more and more often.

"What did I do on my last visit?"

"We were here; we were in the entrance hall. There was a ball, with people wearing masks and dancing. Then, you came to me from nowhere and told me that we were destined to be together … that I was yours and you were mine, and that I had to promise to be careful … that there are many enemies that wish us dead, or will try to control me through you, and you said if this happens, then I had to fight them, not give in … that I have more power than any person born of any kind," she said, keeping her voice emotionless, trying to recall their last conversation.

"If I hadn't come to you, would you be so attached to me?" Zared asked, wondering if this bond would still exist if she had never known him. "Of course! This thing between us … it isn't something that we could have avoided. It would have happened … unless you had never showed of course …" She glanced at him briefly. "And, besides, it's not just that, it's everything else you showed me. Think about it Zared, do you really think I would be the way I am now if you hadn't come to me? Do you really think daddy dearest took the time to help me, to stop for a few hours a day to teach me anything? *No!* You did, and others within the house … you were there for everything. Jurisa explained a lot to me as I grew older, and when I was in danger, you were sworn to protect me as well as Isis. I know this because *you* told me!"

She saw the look he gave her. "Would you have saved me, if I hadn't told you what was coming?" he asked, wondering how he could even start to think that all of this was real. "Yes and no. I would have tried in my human form because of our bond … and failed. If you hadn't come to me, told me about my future self having so much power, and that I just wasn't able to control it at that time, I wouldn't have known that I have this gift, so therefore, I would never have known to practise letting myself fall … finding out that I could travel without my body. I wouldn't have been able to find you that night … like you told me to. It was your warning that pre-pared me. My power or gift had to be controlled, ready to protect you *and* me, because you told me not to trust them. And I don't," she whispered, as they walked slow-ing down to get more distance. "If you hadn't have come that night, we would both be dead. I know it. And if not, then I would certainly have been by now," she said final-ly, turning to look him in the eyes; showing him that she was telling the truth.

"If you knew you had all this power then why didn't you save yourself?" Zared asked. "I tried, so many times

I tried. But, it just didn't work, it never showed up!" Tears stung her eyes. She blinked them away rapidly.

"Angel, you will be staying in the west wing. We have a room prepared for you." Angel jumped at the sound of Avery's voice, bringing them both out of their conversation. Angel looked at Avery, but Avery didn't turn around to face them; she gave the impression that it was beneath her to look in their direction, making Angel irritated. "Zared we don't have a room for you yet, but they are preparing it as we speak over in the north wing. It won't be too far from your woman," she said with distaste, her black high heels clicking on the marble floor. Avery was dressed business-like, wearing a tight knee-length black skirt that had a small split at the back, and a white blouse which ruffled at the wrists and collar. Her hair was sandy-brown, with streaks of silver, and flowed down her back to her hips.

"What do you call energy around people?" Angel asked Zared, suddenly, keeping her voice low, so that Avery couldn't hear her. "Aura. Why?" he replied, wondering why the sudden change of subject. "Because hers is different. It pulses. I can feel it moving," she said, her tone still low.

"So, Avery, what are you?" Zared said out loud. He wanted to vent his frustration at someone, and he had found a perfect target. "Shifter, wolf, witch, fairy, pixie, demon, dragon … or other?" He didn't really care, but if he knew what was watching him, it could be useful if he needed to escape this prison. It was always helpful to know how to kill a creature. If she were a vampire like him, it would be sun, fire, or beheading – wooden stakes were a myth; shifters: silver daggers to the heart and fire; same with wolves of every breed; fairies and pixies you had to catch first and remove their wings; and copper for changelings and goblins … if you could see them coming. Demons were very common; they're like a virus, just harder to get rid of, but anything holy. To detect one, you had to have an amulet from a witch. Even then, the body they possess has to consume the holy item – not a pretty sight if you have a weak stomach. Dragons were the hardest to kill, and at this point they were still trapped by the coven's spell. They were almost impossible and could only be destroyed by a sword made by the gods and given to warriors, another form of angel. Then there were other supernatural beings that ranked lower in their world. Some were not important enough to worry about, but if you needed to kill them, a simple spell or cleansing, or even any of the creatures from the list above would do – they loved to feed on lower creatures.

"*Other*," Avery replied, this time looking back at them over her right shoulder, smiling. "I'm a silver-blade," she said proudly, her head held high with honour. "Aren't there only ten of you left in the world?" Zared enquired, grinning at her. "Sadly, yes." Angel watched her; her voice sounded musical, singing in their ears. "I was wondering if the rumours are true? That the only way to kill your kind is by beheading – oh, and … how can I forget … *vampires*? Apparently your kind taste quite delicious on toast!"

Everyone stopped suddenly. The sound of Zared licking his lips was audible as he chuckled away under his breath. Avery whipped around so quickly, Angel could feel the air glide across her skin. "Do you want to test that rumour?" she snarled, pushing her face into his. Zared laughed, louder this time. He had pissed her off which meant what he heard was true. "Be careful vamp, the sun's coming up soon, and I have no problems in turning your ass to *dust*!" Sarcasm filled her voice with venom. "Damn! So touchy. Must be irritating keeping your feet firmly on the ground? After all, a bird is not a bird when their wings are clipped." He winked, watching her face heat with rage. He smirked, feeling like his old self again.

"Look, Avery. I'm not staying in the west wing," Angel spoke out, breaking their challenging stare. "I'll stay near Zared, thanks," she said. Both Zared and Avery looked at her in shock. "I'm sorry, but I have my orders. You are to stay in the west wing," Avery said, turning around and setting off again. "Fine. Then Zared can stay in the room with me." Angel was angry with him, but something told her to keep him close. She still trusted what she had felt … even if he didn't. "No. He will have a room to himself." Avery looked flustered. "Then you find a room next to mine, or with me, or I'm leaving," Angel demanded, stopping Avery in her stride. Angel wasn't going to let Zared out of her sight, especially after his warnings, and certainly not with how she felt at this moment. Panic had begun to grip her again. She held on to it, keeping her face blank as Avery scrutinised her.

"You can't leave," Avery said sternly.

"Watch us," Zared replied. He didn't want a room next to Angel – the further away the better – but he could feel her panic, which was enough to concern him and keep his mouth shut. Something was very wrong; she knew something. She was there to keep them alive within this house filled with enemies. "Hold on. I need to clear it with Callie," Avery flustered, racing off, heading in the same direction they had come from.

"It's not important Angel. You can still feel me no matter where we are in this damn place," Zared stated coldly.

His bitterness sliced through her. He was looking past her, only seeing cream walls and closed doors. His eyes followed Avery as she disappeared from sight. "I know, but I have a really bad feeling about this." Angel stopped. He watched her face getting paler, her right hand clenched the fabric over her wrist twisting it between her fingers. "Look something's wrong. Something bad is going to happen."

"Nothing's going to happen, you know that. Callie gave you her word," he said, looking at her face. Her eyes were filled with worry, making him anxious. "I don't care! I lost you and Isis once before. I won't go through that again. You *will* stay close!" she commanded him, "And you can hate me all you like, because I really don't care." Angel looked Zared straight in the eyes. He realised she was not budging on this one. "*Fine*," he hissed, stepping away from her. "You do know you never actually lost me in the first place? It was all some nutty dream." He turned to look at her again, hating the fact that she felt so strongly about this. "I don't care! I gave you a promise, and so help me I will not watch you die!" She sounded strong, her voice like steel. "Fine! We get a room next to each other." He gave in to her demands, but Zared needed the last word on this situation that he found himself in: "But you stay in your own room. You don't step foot in mine," Zared said, grabbing the tops of her arms when she didn't answer. "OK?" his voice was demanding as he looked at her sternly. "Why would I go near yours? You made it very clear how you feel about me," she snapped her reply at him, trying to yank her arm away. "Good! Because I don't want them getting the wrong idea about us," he hissed, letting her go quickly, pushing her arm away brutally. "And what idea would that be?" Angel snapped back. "The idea that we are involved in anything. We may be bound together, but unlike you, I don't want the world knowing that information," he responded, hoping Avery would turn up soon.

"What do you mean by that?" Darkness burned inside of her. She found that when she was around him, she felt strong, fearless, able to speak her mind. She had felt healed since she had had his blood, and she felt that in her was a part of him.

"I mean, I want you to stop calling me 'your warrior', and don't use the word *love* to me again," he hissed, glancing around to see if anyone was in earshot. "I'm not your friend, Angel. I never was. I never will be. So, other than my job, I want you to stay the hell away from me." His voice sounded menacing, sinister. His golden eyes narrowed making his appearance change in her eyes. He saw the pain in her face; he could feel it stabbing at him through their bond. Her eyes started to glaze at his words; her gaze went blank and distant.

Zared put his hand on the back of her head. His fingers wrapped around her curls, forcing her to come closer. He watched as she looked at his chest, fear showing in her eyes. Her breathing was unsteady. He got close enough to smell her skin, to hear her heart racing.

"I think Callie is right. You're still a child: naïve, stupid. Your powers are too strong for you to control, so now I have to baby sit. But soon you will have control and I can leave. And when I do, I don't want to see your ugly mug again," he snarled, jaw clenched. His voice sent chills through her body. Zared released his hold, stepping away and beginning to pace uneasily in front of her.

"I'm nothing to you, am I? You don't want me. You never have." Her voice broke, sounding weak. She backed away from him, stunned. Every word was echoing around her. Zared came at her quickly making her jump. His face filled her vision. "I want you to listen to me very carefully." His hand moved as he spoke to her, giving her the full impact of his words. "Callie is the only person that will want you to stay. She is the only person that will love you, that will tolerate your snivelling. And when my job is done, and it will be soon, I never want to see you again. Do you understand? *Never* again. Because if I do, then I'll kill you."

"But Callie called us soulmates … we're connected," Angel whispered, her eyes still distant, her voice low. "We're only bonded, and it's easy enough to break," he hissed. Angel finally looked up; she saw his eyes, they were blazing. She felt the humiliation of years waiting for this person cut through her. She felt so stupid. She felt like she was dying. He had shattered her heart again. Its pain wanted to claim her for the second time tonight.

"I have to go. I have to leave now." She held on to her tears long enough so as to be out of his sight. She needed to run somewhere. She needed to think. She needed to be away from him: the one she thought of as her soulmate; the one she had put all of her hopes into; the one that had been coming to her all her life. Maybe it was just a dream? *He came to me, telling me lies, so I would go to him.*

She raced down the stairs, tears rolled down her cheek. *If he thinks I'm nothing then what about our bond? Is what I'm feeling real, or did he trick me?* She was questioning herself. Running out the door, she sprinted for the woods. *He's just like father, hurting me. Only this hurts more.* She wiped the fierce tears away. *Why am I so stupid! I'll always be stupid, father was right! I'm nothing. I'll never be pretty, or strong and fast. I'll never be wanted. I'll never be ... loved.* Her voice spun round and round in her head, bringing her to a stop.

Angel stood in a thick woodland, breathless. She felt hollow; a black emptiness that made her sick; a kind of sickness that twisted her stomach painfully. She wrapped her hands around her waist, letting her legs give way. Her chest ached. Her lungs fought to work: she was suffocating. Her throat stung as if she had swallowed a dozen razors. She could feel herself being ripped apart, the pain stealing her warmth.

"Leave me!" Angel raged out, sensing that there was someone behind her, watching her from the shadows. "I'm sorry miss, but I'm to keep an eye on you," a male voice replied apologetically. "Like hell you do!" Angel snapped, looking in the direction the voice had come from, hearing only silence. "Stay out of my sight," she commanded, feeling her anger rising, its power encasing her.

I'm stupid. I let him in. I believed his lies ... all these years, why? Just to get a little bit of hope? I'm nothing to him! And I'm nothing to them. I never will be. They're going to kill me sooner or later, just like father would have if I'd stayed there any longer. I'm nothing but damaged goods. Her mind's voice shouted at her. "Shut up!" Angel said out loud. *Look at yourself, pathetic! All those years he beat me, and I could have stopped him. I had all this power. The only reason why they saved me now, is because I showed myself to him. And where did that get me?* It continued, spinning faster and faster in her head. "Stop it!" she shouted out to the breeze that was growing in speed around her, just like her silent voice. Holding her head in her hands, she rocked back and forth on her knees. *Go on you cry baby. Cry! That's all you're good for ... that, and being beaten. No one would want you. You're nothing. Even he hates you!*

The conversation in her head had changed. She felt split in two as she rocked faster; darkness thick and sticky seeped from her skin, like wet tar, as a film of black energy engulfed her – helping the darkness to grow inside of her. Angel's skin was on fire: blue and green, as it leapt from her pores, buzzing, crackling, getting louder and louder, deafening her ears. *No one wants you. No one would care. You'd be better off dead. Just end it all right now. It would be so much better ...*

Angel screamed as loudly as she could, everything around her crackled and sparked. Her skin was alive, turning her fire to oranges and reds. She screamed as loud as she could, releasing energy. She felt it explode out of her, driving into the earth, hitting it so hard that a wall of dirt filled the air, throwing a blanket of dust over her, concealing her from the world. Her dark rage still burned, growing in strength; she was pushing it out around her, wanting to cause extreme damage. The air around her started to spin, entwining with the blanket of dirt howling around her ears as it circled. Her heart started to beat faster, helping the whirlwind speed up around her, feeling her own body linked to it, as it began to pick her up off her knees, helping her to her feet, lifting her up, hovering her inches above the ground – along with loose foliage, spinning around, joining her tunnel of raging air, as she rose higher and higher. She looked up to the night sky to see no stars; to see only the storm that was forming. Her anger was growing to boiling point. Clouds above her sparked with grumbles, a sign of what was to come.

Angel screamed again, feeling it slice through every noise around her, commanding all to silence. The sky lit up: lightning flashed streaks across the vast open sky before it darted into her tunnel of howling air, striking, travelling down, blue light hitting the ground beside her, throwing up mud and grass, and the smell of burnt earth.

She stretched her arms out wide. Her skin felt raw with every cell awakened. Her dark mass of anger had burst out into a ball of rage, pulling her flames of hatred into one mass. Angel watched it hover at chest level; it burned brightly. Veins of red flames poured into it, helping it to grow. It was everything that she was holding in her heart. She had let it build up for all these years, waiting for a time to be released. It kept spinning, gathering in speed, pulsing, growing, waiting for her to aim it.

"*Angel* stop!" It was Zared's voice shouting from behind her. He watched as she turned, still hovering with hostile air and sparks of lightning protecting her. Her emerald eyes had turned to pure white. Her skin was as pale as a ghost's against the dusty background. Zared could feel her power through the tornado that was deafening the silence that hugged the woods. He watched as her golden curls lifted, swaying with their own life.

"You lied to me!" Lightning hit her as if it were nothing. He watched her energy engulf it, giving her unknown strength, her voice striking out. Her energy quickly licked at him causing him to step back in fear. He felt guilty. This was his fault, but he didn't want her to love him – he couldn't return her affection, it was unknown of. She had all this faith in him, which he would shatter in the end.

"I'm sorry. I just think you have the wrong person. I can't be your mate," he said. That's when it happened: blazing heat coming at him, only giving him enough time to duck as it hit a tree's bark, exploding above his head and showering him in hot embers. "Angel, listen to me. I'm a *vampire*! We don't have soulmates. We don't feel love, or so many other things. Angel everything you want, are things I can't give you. These are what humans and shifters and other kinds can give, not *my* kind! My kind can only bring you death …" He was trying to reason with her, to calm her down quickly, and he didn't want her to turn him into dust.

"I hate you," she snarled, as he stepped closer, his hands out as a sign of peace. "Good. Because one day I will leave you. So you hating me now is the best thing for both of us." Zared stepped towards her again. He had to be careful; in this state she was far too dangerous to him. "Like now? You could've told me from the beginning, but instead you stringed me along. Why?" she replied, not making sense to him.

Angel threw her hands up, lashing her energy out, pinning him back to the tree that had protected him earlier. Her eyes, an eerie white, held no sign of her returning to a calm state.

"I've told you! You're becoming too close Angel. It's not good for us. It will only lead you to more pain," he said, trying to push away from the trunk, feeling her pushing him back, as if she had a dozen hands on him.

"I trusted you. I trusted everything you said!"

He watched as tears fell from her white eyes. "That's because there was no one else to trust. All you saw was a dream and you put all your hopes into that." He watched as everything around her started to slow down. "How can you love someone you've never met?" he asked her. It was the truth, how could she? "You've been with me all my life. Why do you fight it now?" Angel felt her anger burning out as cool rain started to fall. "Because, I don't understand it? It has to be a spell. To make you believe it was me, so that when I was sent to collect you, you would trust me without question. Think about it! If you are so important to them, then they will have used what they could to get you here," he replied, with truth in his words.

"No, that can't be true. You're here because we have a bond ..." she replied, shaking her head. "That's because I had to heal you. If you were injured it was my job to heal you, and the bond is an illusion to keep you from running. The witches have put it on you, so you wouldn't leave my side," he lied, but he needed her to believe him. Zared pushed himself away from the tree, again stepping closer. "Look at me. Does it look like I'm lying?"

Angel said nothing, but he saw her eyes returning to their bright green, tears still falling from them. He looked away. He didn't want to see himself in her eyes. He had seen it in many eyes before. He had seen it from eyes like those disappointed in him. He had thrown away many lovers before he got attached. It was the same look when they realised he was a monster – a heartless vessel. She was trying to understand it, but it was hard. Her anguish was all over her face as she shook her head. She couldn't believe it – was all this really a spell? Zared forced himself to lock eyes with her, putting on his best mask.

"You were in on this. You did this to get me here." Her eyes were distant. He couldn't feel her in their bond any more. She was gone. "No. They did. I was just the guy that was told to rescue you," Zared said, keeping his voice calm, neutral, not wanting her to get upset again. He watched as the sky cleared and the wind settled, as she returned to the ground – the walls of dust collapsing at her feet.

"No, I won't believe that, I know you … you're linked to me …" Angel stepped towards him, feeling his confusion going through her.

He leaned against the tree, looking everywhere but at her. He was mad, she saw straight through him. "Do you still feel it really? Because I don't. What linked us is gone," he bluffed, making himself feel nothing, just hollow and empty, the way he once was, before Angel. "Like I said, it's a spell, one that was very powerful. They need you, and will do anything, even make you believe in a dream," he continued.

She was so close he wanted to hold her, to feel her against his cold skin, her gold light that chained him to her, tempting him with her every breath.

"There's one way to find out," she whispered, placing her body as close to him as she could, "If the bond is still there, then it will appear again even if you block it … that's when I'll know for sure if you're telling me the truth." She pulled her hair to one side. His blazing eyes fixed on her neck, seeing her pale skin throbbing from the beat of her heart. "No." He started to turn away, forcing himself to ignore the urge that she was challenging him with. "Do it! Show me that there's truth in what you're saying." She pulled cloth away from her skin, revealing more. "No!" he snarled, grabbing her arms, spinning her around, throwing her hard against the tree. "There's no bond between us, and there never will be so drop it! I'm here for one reason: to control you and get paid. I tried to be nice about it, but after this I'm gone … as far away from you as I can possibly get. You're nothing to me, just another blood bag. One word from them and I'll be happy to end your life, but for now, you're important. You're a part of some big plan, and they're going to use you in it. After that, you'll be someone's blood bank or baby machine. After all, they can't let all that power go to waste. There are families that will pay highly for off-spring with your gifts …"

His voice was cruel, menacing, as he whispered to her, his hands were flat on the bark either side of her, her back pressed against it, knowing she was listening to his every word, as he leaned closer to her ears to make this more personal. He felt guilt brush his dead soul as he watched it sink in slowly; her thoughts telling her that what he had said was all true. Her eyes went glassy, empty.

"You're just another slave now. They will watch your every move, and when they lose interest in you, you'll be locked up in a small room with just four walls … and if you're lucky, they'll send in a playmate, something you'll enjoy … it'll remind you of home …," he continued, his finger brushed her wet cheek. She cringed at his touch, turning her head away, closing her eyes, squeezing them shut, hoping that this was another nightmare. She heard Zared laugh, sending cold chills down her spin. "I should have killed you while I had the chance. And in a few days you'll be begging me to," his voice hissed in her ear. His lips brushed her skin. Angel stopped breathing.

Then she heard him curse, hitting the bark; she felt it vibrate through her body. He turned, leaving her.

Her eyes flew open. Her held breath choked out. She watched as he walked away, disappearing through the shadows, leaving her alone, trembling violently as her legs went weak, thankful she had something solid behind her. "I waited over sixteen years for you," it was barely a whisper as it left her mouth. It was the only thing she could think of. Suddenly everything in her world was gone. Her body was numb; his words drowning her. Everything was false. She had gone through life being beaten, forgotten, unloved, and now used for someone's sick joke – to be sacrificed at their choosing.

Angel's mind went still, every thought had gone. She noticed a stick, thick and sharp, and broken into a point. Her eyes were drawn to it, focussing only on that one thing; she felt it call to her. Calmness claimed her. A peace. A knowing of what to do.

She pushed herself away from the tree and walked over to the stick. She felt a desperate urge to disappear, to end her misery, to wash away her memories.

What was the point of being alive? Her voice spun around in her mind: ice cold. She picked up the stick. It was rough in her palm, but solid in her grip. She felt like she had no control over what was happening to her, that life hated her for reasons she couldn't explain. Watching herself from the outside, she sat where she had stopped, her hand raised high.

Chapter Eleven

ngel's name was called from a distance, but she
didn't really notice. With the stick firmly in
her right hand, she drew in a quick breath,
then slammed it into her left wrist: red hot burning pain
erupted. She gasped out in pain, convulsing, refusing to
throw up, pulling her arm to her chest protectively.

She looked at the stick half buried in her flesh; her fingers unable to move without causing agony. Biting her
lip hard to stop herself from screaming out, she grabbed
it again, getting a solid grip on its wooden handle. Blood
bubbled from under her teeth; she felt them sinking
in sharply, before the tingling of numbness took over.
Blood started to pour from her wrist. Angel held her
breath and dragged it towards her, opening her wound
up more. Tears flooded her eyes as she gave out a silent

scream. Blood gushed out fast and thick. She yanked the stick out, pulling at it with all her strength.

This time she did scream. *It's over now,* she thought, as she watched the ground below her turning deep red. In a matter of seconds her blood had soaked the earth, seeped down her legs, and travelled through her jeans, expanding its warm wetness. She quickly transferred the stick over to the other side. She did the same thing; knowing what to expect this time.

Angel finally felt her body going light, as she began to tilt to one side, rolling off her legs that were tucked under her weight, landing on her buttocks, as a giddy smile came to her lips. Her hands rested on the grass; her choice of weapon rolled away.

Relaxation washed over her; the pressure of her hands on the earth causing her wrists to bleed faster. Her tears had stopped. For the first time in a long time, she felt truly happy. No one could take this from her. This was her choice. No one could hurt her any more.

Tiredness called to her as she fell back with a thump, knocking the breath out of her lungs. She lay there look-ing up at the night sky above her, thinking of nothing, blood pouring out, adding itself to the puddle that had already formed. She felt coldness come over her as she gazed at stars flickering, watching her, waiting for her to fall into a never-ending sleep.

Faces came into her vision, calling her name; only she heard no sounds, only seeing their lips moving, a giggle surfaced uncontrollably, as she lay on her back, arms resting on the ground beside her. Then she recognised them: Zared and Barret. They started shaking her, telling her to stay awake, calling her name over and over, while they grabbed her opened wrists holding them tightly, trying to slow the bleeding.

"Give her blood, she'll die otherwise!" Barret panicked as he held her arms above her head. His palm trying to seal her wounds, blood squeezing through the small gaps and running down her arms, tickling her numbed skin.

Zared had already opened his wrist and was pouring blood into her mouth. Angel coughed it out, turning her head away, clamping her lips shut. Angel didn't want to be saved.

"Hold her head she keeps moving it," Zared ordered. "She's slipping away. If she doesn't drink, then she won't live." Zared felt a knot grasp his stomach. The thought of her dead scared the hell out of him. Her emerald eyes grew distant, heavy, the life in them was fading. She closed them, letting darkness take her.

"*Angel!* Wake up!" Barret shouted at her. "Come on Angel, wake up!" He was shaking her now, shouting at her, but it was all for nothing, she was slipping away. She had past the point of no return.

"Barret, it's too late; she's gone," Zared said placing her arm on her still stomach.

"You did this." Barret backed away, dropping her arm, wiping her blood from his trousers. "You killed her!"

Zared said nothing. Barret was right, he had. Everything that had happened in the last few minutes was his fault. He killed her to keep her away, to make himself feel better. Barret turned round and ran into the shadows. Zared knew where he was going: he was off to inform Callie that her granddaughter was dead, that she had bled at the hands of Zared – her so-called soulmate.

Zared knelt over Angel's still body, looking down at her drained face. Hair had fallen across her forehead. Pain began to ache at his body, growing, throbbing, screaming out at him. In six hundred years, he had never felt this ache before: it burned deep inside him, hollowness quickly filling with grief.

Hell was now calling his name. His torture was just getting started. Anger began to rise. He remembered their conversation: he had told her he wished he had ended her life, that he would never love her, that she was just another blood bag, a baby machine for the supernaturals of this world. *This is my doing. I was meant to protect her! Instead I killed her. I'll pay for this! Every single day.* His voice raged at him. Tears came to his eyes. Zared felt the shock and amazement as they fell. Touching one on his cheek, he felt its cool wetness covering his finger-tip. Zared touched more of the wetness running down his skin. She had made him cry. She had given him tears. *This is what happens when you love someone and lose them. You'll live with a broken heart – it's your punishment. It's the price you'll pay every day. These tears will rip you apart.* A male voice taunted him.

Zared looked down at her still body, touching her skin, which was losing its warmth. He brushed loose hair from her face. Another tear dropped, and another. The ache he felt was growing stronger; daggers were ripping though his chest. It was worse than the hunger. At least with hunger he could make it go away, but this was here to stay.

Zared pulled her up, pulling her into his arms, cradling her gently, tears flowed more easily now, dropping freely from his eyes. He bent his head forward, resting his lips on her hair, smelling the last trace of her autumn rain-scented skin. His lips touched her lifeless forehead, before the scent of death became too overpowering. Squeezing his eyes shut, something snapped inside of him. He was broken. Zared started to rock, something was shattering, as his tears fell on her soft curls, holding her tighter, bringing her closer, not wanting to release her. *I'm sorry, I'm sorry!* he repeated over and over, as he rocked with her back and forth; his fingers gripping her golden hair. *Please forgive me,* he begged, as his quivering lips crushed against her skin.

Chapter Twelve

Angel found herself surrounded by darkness. No light. No heaven or hell. Just the emptiness of a black hole.

"It's not your time." A male voice spoke to her from out of the darkness. "Who are you?" she asked, trying to see who the voice belonged to. "Madoc," he replied. "How do you know it's not my time?" she questioned, still unable to see. "Because you had to do this to begin your path." His voice was strong and calming, even with his cryptic answer. "I don't care. I don't want …" She didn't finish. "It doesn't matter. I will come to you when the time is right," he said, as a warm breeze brushed her skin with the lightest of touches. "Great! Another one. Why do you all want me?" she snapped, backing away from his presence, which enveloped her. "Isn't it enough that they take my mother, then make my father hate me. And now Zared …" She couldn't say it.

"It wasn't planned that way. You were hidden from me. Here you're not," Madoc said. She felt him closer to her again. His breath ruffled her hair, making her jump. "Why me? Why am I so important to you?" She felt tired all of a sudden. "You are my Queen. I am your equal, your protector, and Zared is your warrior," he replied. "He and I will always be at your side. He has been marked now. He will look after you, keep you safe," he continued. "I don't think so. He hates me," she huffed, in reply to his last statement. "No, my Queen. He was scared. He wants to keep you at a distance because he loves you, and it is that emotion that he hates," he replied, making her more confused. "I doubt that. He made it clear to me he wants me dead … that I'm nothing to him!" Angel folded her arms across her chest.

"My Queen, you have to remember he is a vampire. It's in his nature to kill, to feel nothing, to hunt for enjoyment. They don't feel like humans. Emotions die when they leave their human life. So you have to give him time. He has lived as a vampire for nearly six hundred years without feeling anything towards any human. He has felt the calling to come to you since you were born. But he had no understanding of this calling; it was unknown, a niggling torment. He fears being with you. He fears he will harm you … it's something he can't allow himself to do. He is fighting his protective urge to keep you safe, because he can't *remember* who you are; who *he* is. He has fought to keep you safe for so long. He doesn't understand it. He doesn't trust those that want you. And he doesn't trust the way you make him *feel*. He has lost you many times before … and now you have returned."

"Still I don't want him near me," she rapped back. "I'm afraid you have no choice in the matter. He will be your shadow from now on. His need to give his life for you is getting stronger. He will never leave you now. His mark will link him to you again," Madoc stated, brushing her skin again. "Why me? Why am I the target? I'm sick of it!" Angel felt nothing but anger. "That won't change. They are scared of you … You will come to rule them," he said softly.

"I've heard that already, Madoc … Let me see you!" Angel asked into the blackness that surrounded her. "I'm sorry my Queen, but I cannot show myself … it's forbidden," he said, his voice soft to her ears. "I don't care. Show yourself to me now!" she demanded, wondering why it was forbidden.

"My Queen," he submitted, as light grew around him. Angel could see his shape, with outlines of wings. He was extremely bright to her eyes. He had no features. She couldn't see his face in the bright shining light, but she saw his eyes … they were recognisable. They were the colour of pure silver: a colour she would never forget. She could see the silhouette of his body, with golden light that filled it. She still didn't know what he looked like, but she had known from the moment she had seen him, from the moment she had seen his eyes, that she would know him again.

"What are you?" she whispered. "Let's just say I'm a warrior … your warrior," he said, placing a glowing hand on her arm, bringing her close to him. Angel could feel his warm skin on hers, sending sparks throughout her body, making her feel faint. His arms wrapped around her, until she felt steady again.

"How do we know each other? Why do I feel like I'm not meant to be without you?" Angel felt like she knew the answer, but she couldn't find it in her thoughts. "It's because you belong to me. My soul is joined with yours … it has been since your first birth. This is the strongest bond created. For every life you have, I must return to the earth to be at your side until your death," he said, holding her close. "I don't understand. What do you mean by first birth? I've only been born once," Angel said, letting her body relax against his, feeling his solid chest against her exterior. "You are what they call … an old soul. It means you are born over and over. Humans call this reincarnation," he replied. "How many times have I been born?" she asked. "Many," he replied simply, running a golden hand through her hair. "Why don't I remember them?" She felt her face tingling from his touch as he tugged the strands of her hair. Her heart started to pound; her stomach knotted. She was nervous. "Because it's too much for the human mind to handle," he said softly. His voice seemed to float through her.

"So what will happen to me in this life?" she asked. "This life shall be different for you. There is a war you must fight with powers given to you by the gods," he stroked her right cheek. "When your mark appears, so will I." His face glowed as if he was smiling with child-like excitement. "What mark?" Angel stepped back from his arms, looking into his silver eyes. She still felt his touch on her skin. "This one." He touched her left arm bringing it into view. Angel looked down to see a mark on the inside of her left arm below her elbow: there were three deep red makings crossing each other with sky-blue around them – they were the same as the one on his neck. "This mark means that your powers have summoned death to give back life."

"This is a dream isn't it? I'm imagining you? I'm going to wake up any minute aren't I?" She couldn't believe she had survived, or this strange conversation she was having. Madoc laughed. She knew that laugh, she had heard it before, but where?

"It's not a dream ... and soon you will wake up!"

"He saved me didn't he?" Angel swore, cursing under her breath. "Yes he did ... with a little help." He glowed; she pictured him smiling at her. "As I have told you before, it is not your time."

Angel suddenly felt lost, confused – why did Zared save her? why did Madoc hide himself from her? why were so many things forbidden, and what war was she meant to fight? – all questions unanswered, and questions she knew Madoc wouldn't answer even if she asked them.

Madoc bent his head forward, his face inches away, his silver eyes locked with hers. She couldn't look away; she didn't want to. Angel felt her skin heating up. She knew that her face had turned red.

"It's time for you to return." He stroked her face again. "When your mark comes, I will be with you, I promise you that ... but, until then, you have to return to Zared. He will do as you ask ... he will stay by your side. But you both have to find a way to leave. You're in too much danger there, and I can't protect you yet. Zared won't be able to do it on his own. You must find a way to help him." His voice was low.

She could feel his breath brush her lips; his skin smelled sweet. She fought the impulse to take a deep breath, to imprint him in her memory. Her heart skipped a beat as his lips met hers. They were warm, full, kissing her with a teasing pressure, begging for her to return his kiss in the same loving way. Madoc pulled her closer, golden light surrounded them, filling her up. She heard a sound of air moving quickly. Pulling back, she opened her eyes and saw wings with golden light beaming from them. Angel couldn't help but smile as she looked back at his silver eyes.

"Keep your focus. Practise using your power. Control it. Use it to your advantage ... that will help you both. You're strong now, and don't let anyone make you feel any different." Angel nodded, she couldn't help it. He made her feel safe and strong. "When you are both free, find Jurisa Sand. Go to her. She will keep you both safe ... and don't trust anyone else." Madoc pulled her close, his golden face inches from hers. She could see his eyes: there was a loss in them. Madoc wrapped her in his strong arms, pulling her close, breathing in her scent. She closed her eyes, relaxing into his hold, her soft hands covering his chest.

Madoc wished at that moment that she would never leave him – but he knew it was impossible. Her time with him was over. His lips met hers for the last time.

Chapter Thirteen

Angel woke up on soft white sheets, which smelled clean and fresh. Looking around her room, she saw it was large and bright. She lay in a four-poster bed, which was wrapped in white veils. A large double wardrobe was to her left; a fireplace to her right. In front of the fireplace was a cream sofa, a small table that had a flower-patterned lamp, and a bookcase filled with books. Angel couldn't help but smile. She had never been in a room like this, with so many different books at her disposal – none of them looked like those at her father's house. Sheets soft and clean, new under her skin.

To her right was a large machine with numbers and lights flashing, and wires that led towards her, disappearing under her bedding. To Angel's left was a long pole with a hook at the top holding a bag with clear liquid that also had wires leading towards her. At the end of the pole were wheels, making it easy to move around.

Angel then remembered what she had done. Pulling her arms out from underneath the covers, she saw her wrists wrapped in thick white bandages. In the back of her hand was a needle embedded in her skin, stuck down with white tape, and connected to a thin tube made of plastic that came from the clear liquid. Underneath her vest top were more wires connected to white pads that stuck themselves to her chest.

Angel pulled them off, feeling the tape and pads pinching her skin, not wanting to release her. She then started to slowly unravel the white bandage from her left wrist, wondering how deep her wound was – did she have a large scar? was there bruising to her skin? Angel stared in shock at her skin: nothing. No marks, no sign of what she had done. There was nothing.

She dropped the bandage, grabbing for the second one, unwrapping it faster: nothing. Her wounds were gone.

Angel felt the urge to scream so intensely that she couldn't stop: "*Zared!*" – followed by kicking her arms and legs around frantically in frustration, looking like a mad woman, throwing the sheets off of her, her hair falling in front of her face. "I'll kill him! How dare he!" she screamed. *If he thinks I'm going back to that life,* she snarled, silently. *I'll die first.*

Suddenly, the door flew open. Angel reacted like it was her father storming in with a belt in hand: fear shot through her, terror made her roll off the bed and duck behind one of the machines that had started beeping at her. Her back was right up against the wall. She gave out a mental scream. *What are you doing?* She was ashamed of herself, cowering like an animal. Angel got to her feet, standing straight, forcing herself to be strong.

Zared followed moments later: hair messy from sleep, dressed only in navy pants, his toned sculptured chest bare. His naked feet pressed into the soft, springy, carpet.

"I heard you screaming, then banging," the guard said, still looking fierce as he walked over to her, turning off all the sounds that surrounded her ears.

"*You!* You did this!" Angel snarled at Zared, showing him her healed wrists. Zared looked at her wrists expecting to see scarring, but there was nothing, only a faint red patch that was slowly disappearing. He felt their connection pulse, vibrating at his dying numbness. He was feeling her emotions. He tried to block them, but no matter how hard he would try, it wouldn't work, not any more.

"I hate you!" she snapped, picking up one of her pillows and throwing it at him. The pillow hit him in the chest, before sliding to the floor with a thump. Zared smiled, his golden eyes revealed happiness, relief that she had woken, that she was alive. Even if she never forgave him, she was still here, and he could still feel her. "I think we should leave so she can dress," Zared stated, waving for the guard to leave. "Yes, of course. I'll be outside miss. Good to see you well again." He bowed and followed Zared out.

Angel looked down at herself; she was wearing a blue vest top with shorts. She wondered how she had got into these clothes. Her hair was a tangled mess. Once she was washed and dressed, she put on the pair of stone-washed blue jeans that had been placed over the back of her chair along with a black top, which looked ripped in places – a fashion that was in style – and the cream trainers that had been placed under the chair.

Angel left her room and collided with Zared as he exited his. Her breath caught in her throat. He looked good in his blue jeans and the tight black top that showed off his defined body.

"You saved me. Why?" she asked, feeling calmer. "I didn't … I tried giving you blood but you rejected it. Barret and I did everything we could, but it was too late you were gone … our bond was broken … the light that links us just disappeared, and the smell of death surrounded you," he replied, trying not to look at her. "So why am I here?" She grabbed his arm pulling him to a stop, forcing him to focus on what she had asked him.

"I don't know. I was losing you … I could feel you go and I wasn't fast enough to save you. Everything I did … that I caused … I'm sorry," Zared said looking past her, remembering their last conversation before she had taken her own life. "Then something hit me. It was like an electric current passing through me and into you … it used our bond to pound at your body, hitting you with everything it had until you started to breathe again … your heart suddenly started to beat and your wrists sealed," he said, his eyes going distant.

Then, he felt her shock. She backed up, pulling up her sleeves, looking at her arms. "What's wrong?" He sounded worried, almost caring. "When did you get that?" She pointing to his neck. "After you returned, why?" he asked, watching her move away from him. "No reason … it's nothing. Just a dream I had." She was making no sense to Zared. "What was the dream?" he asked, watching her. "Nothing. Forget it. Let's go, I'm hungry." She forced a smile. "Did you enjoy your meal?" she asked, knowing that his hunger was satisfied. "Angel?" Zared said waiting, but then he realised she wasn't going to tell him. "Yes, I did, thank you!" He returned the forced smile, watching her carefully as she sneaked glances at his neck.

"I have to start helping you, starting from today."

"Fine, so what's first on the list of things to do?" Angel asked numbly, as they made their way downstairs. "First job is to get your strength up, so you need to start going to the gym and start training to build up your muscles," Zared said. He knew she was weak. All those years of being locked up and not having enough food had made her muscles useless – a deliberate plan on her father's part so that she couldn't escape. Now Zared had to build her strength up, ready for Callie's first orders.

"Then what?" Angel asked. "You have to attend counselling sessions, and also learn how to use your power with some control," he said, remembering their woodland experience. "OK, but I don't want to do it inside for everyone to see, so when we practise we'll use the woods," Angel said, thinking about how much danger she had been warned she was in – first by Zared and then by Madoc. *Could this all be real?* she wondered as they walked across the marble floor.

"Are you sure you're OK? You've been acting strange since you saw my neck," he whispered as they approached the dining hall. "What do you care? I'm nothing, *remember?*" Her words were venomous and made him cringe. "Angel." He grabbed her arm pulling her to a stop. "Let me go! Do what you're told. The sooner you do, the quicker you get to go," she snarled, pulling her arm from his grip. "Angel, please. I'm sorry for what happened. It was stupid of me to say those things. I said them to keep you from getting too close. I'm sorry … I thought it was for your own good." Angel watched him through narrowed eyes, trying to figure out if he was lying or telling the truth. "Please forgive me," he continued, waiting for her answer.

Forgive him. It was Madoc's voice in her head. *Things are different now. He has felt the loss of losing you. He will stay by your side until the time comes when he is no longer needed,* Madoc's voice continued, soothing her anger, *He loves you.*

"You hurt me," Angel said, feeling her tears bubbling up. "I know, I'm sorry. It won't happen again," Zared told her. It was true; he couldn't risk losing her again. "OK, you're forgiven … for now, but the next time I won't use the stick on me, I'll use it on you," she said. Her eyes narrowed again. "You won't have to. If there's a next time I'll do it myself." Zared smiled; it was a genuine smile. The air had been cleared; she had forgiven him and that's all he needed.

Chapter Fourteen

As she entering the dining room, Angel saw a long narrow table with chairs pushed under; all were made from a rose-coloured wood and intricately carved by hand. They looked expensive and fragile.

The room was filled with bright light, which reflected off the mirrored walls, giving the illusion that the room was larger than it really was. As they approached the table, Angel could see that a cloth covered only where they were to sit. Plates of fruit were laid out, and a cooked breakfast of bacon, eggs, beans and toast was waiting for them. Angel could barely eat. All her stomach would allow her was some toast, bacon and a bit of egg. Sat opposite Zared, she wondered what he was thinking. She remembered Madoc's words.

"Come on," Zared said, standing up and walking away, leaving her to catch up. "Where are we going?" she asked, moving quickly to his side. "We're going to look around so you can digest that food before swimming." Zared grinned, taking her hand in his. "I can't swim," Angel replied. Zared's hand felt so right in hers – as if it belonged there, after everything that had happened, all this time passing, all leading to this, to him being hers at last. "You're going to learn," he smiled as they headed out towards the front door.

True to his word, an hour later they both made their way to the pool, her hand still entwined in his. They had talked about everything. Zared had needed to explain his actions, to prove to her that he had meant every word he had said.

"Now it's time to swim," he smiled as they walked across tiles before stopping in front of a lounger. "Swim?" She was unsure of how to react. She saw a long pool with plants along its glass walls, and overlooking a garden filled with moonlight. "Go to that small room. There's a costume in there for you to put on. Then come back here," he commanded, pointing in the direction of where she should go. "Leave your clothes in there. You can change again after." He grinned at her as she walked away.

Five minutes later, Angel was wearing an all-in-one blue swimsuit that left half of her back bare – showing off the scars from the years of beatings. She wrapped her hands around her elbows, feeling naked, hearing her bare feet padding along the dry tiles which made her skin cold.

Zared was waiting for her near to the pool's edge. She re-entered the room, seeing him pacing, wearing only swimming shorts and a chain of golden metal. Her eyes glanced over him. His eyes were fixed to the floor; his soft lips strained. "Now what?" she asked, trying not to look at his muscular defined body. She could feel heat rising to her face. He made her pulse quicken. Her stomach was somersaulting, making her glad that her food was now digested. She wanted to be closer to him. Her anger had finally gone, and he was different now. She felt as though she belonged, was protected, loved, and that he was now what Madoc had said he was: her warrior. She suddenly wished his lips were on hers again, his skin brushing against her, heating her up. Her breathing started to become unsteady at the memory of their time alone in the rented room. She shook herself, trying to push her feelings away – this wasn't the time or the place, and he still wasn't completely forgiven.

"Come on, we're getting in." Zared grinned, taking her hand and leading her to the shallow end. Zared dropped into the water, his body submerging quickly. "Come on!" He signalled holding out his hands. Angel's nerves fluttered madly as she sat down on the cold tiled floor, getting as close as she could to the edge. She slipped her feet into the water. Coldness hit first, as small waves rippled up her legs, giving her warm skin a shock. Her hands gripped the edge. She lifted her body up as Zared grabbed her waist, his muscles flexed, giving her support and guiding her trembling body, subsiding her fear, letting her know she was in safe hands. "Oh! It's cold," she said, breathing sharply.

"It'll warm up when we get going," he said, guiding her body slowly down, water rising higher, getting deeper as she went in. She transferred her grip from the pool's edge to around his neck. Zared could feel her fingers gripping his shoulders. They were warm, making his skin feel hot. He could hear her heart beating, speeding up at every touch. Their bond had strengthened. It had changed. He could feel a part of him waking up, but another part was still lost. Yet, when he was close to Angel, it was the closest he could get to feeling whole. The faint gold light that linked them had grown brighter, more powerful, and was pulling him closer to her. It was getting harder to fight. He had been able to deny to himself that he could be her soulmate – as Callie had called them. But now, he was starting to believe the myth.

The water stopped around her chest. Her feet touched the bottom. She shivered. Her breath quivered. He pulled her close, feeling wet fabric against his cool skin. Looking into her green eyes, he forgot everything around them. He could see the vision of himself her eyes: he was no longer a monster; he wasn't someone that just caused her pain. There was a new look that was just for him; one that no one had ever given him before, even in his human life. It was a look he would see in others around him. A secret they shared with each other; a secret he wasn't invited to know. Yet, he had watched as strangers held hands, or enjoyed stolen kisses in the park.

"If you get fully wet, it won't be as bad," he said after clearing his throat, looking away briefly. Zared released her, but stayed close enough so he could grab her if she got into trouble. He went under, coming back up quickly, removing water from his face, as he wiped a strong hand over it. "Now hold your breath, and bend your knees so your head goes under."

Angel's insides knotted as she grabbed for his hands, holding them tightly. "We'll both do it after three. Remember, hold your breath," he said, showing Angel what he meant by take a deep breath, bopping up and down, getting ready. "One! Two! *Three!*" Down they went, then back up. Angel pushed her hair back, wiping her eyes, breathing quickly, and coughing as water went up her nose. Zared grinned, putting an arm around her waist, keeping hold of her while she relaxed. She grabbed hold of him for safety. Her vision was blurred. It had shocked her system.

Angel grabbed his shoulder and blinked repeatedly, wiping water off her face until she could see clearly. She saw his grin turn into a smile that she had seen before, a rarity for him. Her weightless body floated towards him, guided by his arm. She was so close her hand rested on his chest. Heat burned her face. Their eyes locked again; his liquid gold and blazing with temptation. She felt his free hand slowly glide up over fabric that felt invisible. Shivers erupted down her spine as his fingers touched her neck causing her body to react in a way she had never experienced. She wanted him again – now more than ever before. He watched her emerald eyes sparkle and then close as pleasure erupted through her. He felt her heart stop for just a second. Her head was tilted and her lips, slightly curved up at the corners, parted.

He couldn't fight this any more. He wanted her. He couldn't let anyone else have her. He had to claim her for himself, and soon. Angel glided closer, her head still tilted; their lips touched again. It was the final proof he needed. She had finally come back to him. He was home. She was his home no matter where they were. Their kiss turned from slow gentle brushes that barely touched, to something much deeper. He felt her grip tighten; her nails indenting his skin. She was pulling him closer. Her breath was warm, shuddering in his mouth. Passion and hunger burned inside him, wanting her, wanting to yield to her, to become as close to her as he could get. Something bright flashed between them. His mind filled with her presence, pools of greens and golds mixed behind his closed eyelids.

I can't fight you any more. It was his thought directed to her, Angel heard it in her mind. There was a sound of hunger, a desperation to fulfil his desire, as they moved to a secret dance, their bodies entwined, flesh moving against flesh. Submitting to his control, he guided her back until they came to the wall.

Then, don't. It was her voice and not his that replied, giving him a shock, bringing him to a stop. He pulled away and stared at her in wonder. Angel clung to him, pulling him back. His lips moved with a trace of a smile down to her neck, brushing her skin lightly, causing it to prickle with goose bumps. Breathing heavily, she fought with herself to stay quiet and in control of her heightened senses. *I want to taste you. I want more than that,* he said, silently, returning to her lips as his hands moved smoothly to her thighs, lifting her up, allowing her legs to wrap around his waist. He heard the sounds of excitement rise in his voice. *I want you.*

Yes! he heard, her voice growing again, louder and clearer in his mind. Pulling away, Zared looked at her, studying her face. *Are you sure?* He had to ask. He still found it strange and unbelievable. Angel was just smiling. *Yes, I want this.* She was still grinning widely, nodding to confirm that he had heard correctly. She ran her fingers though his hair. Zared smiled back, beaming at her, at their new connection, at being able to do this with her, something that no other person could ever do with him. His eyes turned blood-red, hunger filled them, a hunger to claim her.

He leaned slowly in; Angel felt fangs brush her skin, finding just the right spot. He penetrated. There was burning as her skin broke, making her body arch, as she moved in a sexual way against his pelvis, which was already throbbing with desire. He was aching with the anticipation of making her his. He heard her suck in a quick breath as she bit down on her lower lip to stop herself from crying out. *Yes!* Her nails dug in to his back, scraping at his skin, fuelling his desire even more.

Angel was hot; he was burning her up. Her body was alive, following its own rhythm, calling to him. Her heart pounded with his touch. Every cell was telling her what to do, waking a part of her that had been sleeping until he had come into her life. It was a natural urge, one that was imprinted into every part of her DNA. Zared felt her legs tighten around his waist. She was pulling him closer. He could smell her skin; it was intoxicating, mouth-watering. Forcing her body to press hard into his, his already aroused bulge found her heated cave fitting in to her effortlessly. He wanted to remove the thin fabric that blocked the area that he wanted to invade. Her breathing was heavy against his ear. Her body trembling, rocking, teasing him to the point of no control. Pressure was building inside him. He could feel the intensity of her need. Her nipples hardened against his chest as her frantic pulse called to him. He wanted to feel his fullness inside her, to hear her moan for more.

Zared grabbed the pool's guttering, gripping it hard, his knuckles turning white as sounds of hissing escaped his clenched jaw. Angel could feel him, raw with lustful need. She could see the images in his mind of what he wanted to do to her. *Yes.* She was giving him permission to go ahead. He had stopped drinking, trembling against her. He was trying to keep control as his lust-filled body screamed at him to claim her completely, to mate with her, and make her his.

Angel pulled herself to him completely, slowly running her tongue up his neck, hearing him suck in air this time, his fingers twisting in her costume that sat low on her back. "I want you to taste me," Zared whispered heavily in her ear.

Angel pulled away slowly as Zared let go, slicing his skin with one of his fingernails in the same place that he had taken her blood. Angel's eyes focussed on the wound, blood welled up. *Please.* He spoke to her silently, begging her to do it. Guiding her with his hand on her back, he pulled her closer. Moving slowly, Angel put her lips over his wound. His blood was intoxicating: sweet, strong, as addictive as a drug as she drank. He could feel her sucking, taking his life source. She felt his chest heave. He was finding it erotic on so many levels that should be wrong. Her hands began moving slowly down his back. His skin crackled with the electricity travelling down his body as it followed her fingers. He moaned with pleasure in her ear. His desire intensified, it merged with hers as their blood intermingled. He gripped the guttering harder, something cracked under the pressure. He was ready to explode, to impale her. He was a bomb ticking, and this excited her more.

Then their bond did something new. He no longer just felt it pulse or vibrate, it now opened her up to him completely: every touch she felt, every breath she took, everything that burned inside her, he felt it too. Their souls had merged into one, and this union would change them for good.

Zared felt her heart beating inside him. Her blood hummed through his veins, heating his own body. Her breath filled his lungs; he felt his once still lungs moving in time with hers – the oxygen making him giddy. His body didn't know how to react, but one thing was clear, he didn't want it to stop, and he didn't want her to stop him claiming her. His soft lips were on hers, passionate, deep, excited. His hands moved over her aching flesh that was thrusting against him. His fingers grabbed at fabric pulling it from her shoulders, pulled it down her arms gently.

Her legs were clenched, half in fear and half in excitement. Begging him not to stop, her fingers found his waistband. Her nails gently scraped his skin. She heard him groan as she moved them around teasingly, until she found the small loose knot and pulled its strings free. Feeling it come undone, she slid her hand under, caressing, feeling it pulsing with excitement under her grip. Her heart pounded as he groaned into her mouth, gripping her costume tightly, and wrapping the fabric around his fingers.

I want you now, she whispered to his mind, unable to control herself as her body shook under his touch. *Yes!* he replied, letting her legs fall from his waist, feeling her fingers grip his swimming shorts, pulling them slowly down, feeling the top of his …

"I hope I'm not interrupting?" A male voice rang through their ears making them both jump. Angel froze. Zared lowered his head, his forehead touching her shoulder; his hair brushed her neck. He pulled her costume back up while she pulled his shorts back to his waist, both feeling starved of satisfaction, disappointed at the interruption. Shoes were heard on the tiles behind Angel: squeaking rubber soles approaching, making her nervous as she stayed close to Zared, her heart still pounding madly. Her face was hot; her body refusing to calm as her flesh continued to ache for Zared's touch. They had been caught.

Zared let out a low throaty growl. Angel had felt it rumble up, escaping from his throat. She felt Zared's anger. This was something they had both longed for, and it had been a long time coming for Angel. She had waited years for this. Every time he came to her, she would hope that this would be their time. Zared grabbed a bar that went around the pool just below the water line. Angel felt her body still throbbing, amplifying his presence. She straightened herself up, pulling herself together to turn and face the intruder.

"What do you want Barret?" Zared asked, teeth clenched. His breath was still heavy in her ear as he tried not to show Barret his hunger-filled eyes, or another part of his body, that were still filled with lust – a promise that had to wait. "Nothing. I was just passing, and thought I would come watch," he said, studying them suspiciously. *He can't see us like this,* Zared said silently to her. *If he see me like this, then they will make sure you never see me again.* The shock of that travelled through her. That couldn't happen. Angel turned slowly in his arms, moving her hair over her bite marks, which were healing quickly, helped along by Zared's blood. She stayed in front of Zared covering him carefully so Barret couldn't see any clue of what had just happened.

"As you can see, he's just teaching me how to swim." She smiled, still feeling Zared pulsing through their private link, trying not to let it heat her up again. She blocked images of them claiming each other. Angel kept her back against Zared. She could feel his hands on her waist loosen as he started to regain control.

Keep him busy I can't control myself just yet. His voice echoed in her mind. Their bond was still strong; their souls still merged. She could feel his desire alive in her.

"Why don't you join us? I could do with all the help I can get." Angel smiled, keeping eye contact with Barret. "I don't have any shorts, sorry. But I'll stay and watch," he said, smiling broadly.

Now what? she thought to Zared. *Tell him there's a spare pair in the changing room that I told you about earlier.* His knuckles were turning white around the bar as he moved closer. Angel felt him move, brushing against her. Her breath stopped, she tried to keep her face blank, her hammering heart quickening as seductive images prickled at her, giving her skin a touch of fever.

"There's a spare pair in the changing room, Zared said so earlier. Why don't you go put them on?" she said, still smiling, willing him to go.

Her pulse was still quickening as images entered her mind again. She couldn't determine if they were her own or his as she fought against them. More images came, having a powerful affect on her, causing her muscles to weaken. Feeling his grip on her strengthen, it allowed her to transfer some of her weight onto him. Images of them uninterrupted plagued her thoughts. Her breathing started to change as they raged at her in waves that she struggled to fight against.

Block them, I can't do this without you, his voice whispered to her, sounding sensual, captivating. His voice lured her, demanding her to forget Barret's presence. Zared's face was hidden behind her, his eyes, blazing red, hidden by her damp hair. His fangs extended, he sucked in air, filling his working lungs, exhaling heavily on her back, making her shiver with pleasure.

Zared couldn't stop seeing the images that filled her mind, or feeling her trembling body against him. Hardness slid up against her, parting her legs slightly, allowing it to bob within the small gap that formed against her buttocks. Angel fought against the urge to move, to let him guide her to where he wanted her. She forced her lungs to stay steady even though she was sure he could hear her shaking. Now Angel could feel Zared trembling. He was fighting his hunger to take her. Something inside her pulled at him. She felt it calling him to her. He couldn't fight her summoning for much longer. Something deep within her wanted him to surrender to it, and she was going to be obeyed. Her heart pounded. She had visions of his roaming hands touching parts of her body he wanted to sink his fangs into.

Zared cleared his throat, gripping Angel's waist tightly and forcing them to move apart. "Grab the bar and let your body float up." His voice was hoarse as he smiled at the clear images she was projecting to him. Zared's voice stayed low, with forced control, as he lowered himself further into the water, moving to her side, staying out of Barret's view.

"That's it. Let your legs float up." His voice broke slightly as he placed his hand on her hip. Sparks shot through their skin. She tried hard not to show any reaction, but to her surprise she heard a small moan escape from him.

The more your desire grows, the weaker I am to fight it. His silent voice spoke to her like silk wrapping around her soul, calling it to be commanded. "OK," Angel said, trying to hide her frustration from Barret. *Tell me how to fight it when you're so close. I want you more now than ever.*

"Keep hold I'm going to let go now." He sounded almost breathless, but he understood that the closer they were, the harder it was. The waves from his movements pushed at her body as he backed away. "It's OK. I'll still be here." He gave her a seductive smile, melting her heart, turning her insides to mush.

Zared quickly ducked under the water. Angel watched as water covered his head, bubbles floating up, before he emerged running his hands over his hair, pushing it back from his face, smoothing it out. The sight didn't help their situation when she wanted his chiselled body on hers.

"Now I want you to kick," he shouted, his back remained facing their watcher, his eyes still blazing red, which showed his pale scar more clearly. His placed his hands on her stomach, keeping her lifted. Her pulse jumped and a low sound escaped her lips now. She gripped the bar tighter, frustrated that he was now untouchable to her. *Sorry!* She smiled, biting the corner of her lower lip, trying to look anywhere but at him. Zared had to quickly look away too, he wanted to feel her lips on his, to feel her hands roam his skin.

Angel began to kick, splashing water around them. This distracted him for a moment. "OK I'll be right back," Barret announced suddenly, heading to the changing room. Zared dropped his hands as she returned to her feet. *Go!*

she said, turning to him. *Before he comes back.*

I'll meet you later. I'll be waiting in the woods, he replied, looking to see if Barret had actually gone, before closing the gap he had created between them. Angel smiled, her right hand gripped his neck, pulling him closer, leaning so that their lips were inches apart.

"One day I will have you to myself," his raspy voice whispered. She touched his lips, their kiss deepened again. She was fighting against her own body, keeping it from making him one with her. *Go! You have to leave. If you don't then I won't be able to stop,* she said, her fingers entwining in his hair. He wrapped her in his arms. *One day we'll be alone with no interruptions,* he smiled. His lips began moving slowly down her neck as her fingers drew down his back, circling his shorts. *Is that a promise?* she asked, giggling out loud and pulling lightly at his waistband, igniting his desire again, her fingers finding their way under. *You're a tease.* His fangs brushed her skin, making her shiver, letting her regain her hold on his bulge. *Only for you,* she smiled, her breathing deeper, her temperature turned up a degree.

Zared lifted her effortlessly as she wrapped herself around him. Angel felt his fingers move her hair showing him her pink puncture marks. Zared couldn't help but taste her; his fangs throbbed, burning through him. Fighting it was hard, stopping it was even harder, especially when what he wanted was right there in his arms. Angel could feel his fangs gliding over her wounds. Her legs gripped him, pulling him into her again. Her hips rocked against him as his tongue tasted her skin. She could feel his hands gripping her, pulling her closer to his body, crushing himself against her, his hardness between her legs inviting her to experience something exciting. Angel wanted to taste his sweet rich blood again, licking his hot damp skin slowly, nipping with her teeth gently.

Stop he'll catch us. It was a weak breathless voice that spoke in her head and it was coming from him. He was breathing hard in rhythm to her breath. A noise was heard from a distance bringing her back from where she couldn't go to yet. *No. You're right, not now, you have to go before he catches you.* She focussed on her muscles, forcing them to move, releasing him, pushing him away, her flesh screaming at her in protest. She reached for the bar; her knuckles whitened as she remained there, breathless.

I'll find you later. Her eyes remained fixed on the water as she slowed her breathing down. Zared came up close behind her, his breath hoarse in her ear. His warm fingers gripped her shoulders giving her violent tremors as she tried to pull away. *We can't get caught. I can't lose you.* Her voice was a begging whisper to him. Movement came from a door behind them. *I'll wait for you in the woods*. He kissed the back of her neck, his lips soft, sensual, sending cool shivers down her spine. She felt the water stir as he jumped out and disappeared through another door.

"Where's Zared?" Barret asked, walking towards her in red shorts, glancing around to see if Zared was close. "He had to go, so you're left teaching me. I hope you don't mind?" Angel said, smiling, still feeling Zared's presence in her mind and filled with lust and frustration. She was glad it didn't show on her the way it showed on him. "Of course not," he grinned, entering the pool. "It will give us the chance to talk." Angel didn't like how this sounded.

"How do you like being here so far?" He bobbed in the water next to her. Luckily he didn't have the same effect on her as Zared did. "It's alright so far, but I've not seen much." Her stomach twisted; he was fishing for something. "Well, why don't you go out with Avery, she knows the area well and that girl loves to shop," he smiled. "I'm sure you'll enjoy that. I can ask her if you want?"

His look didn't change even when he was wet. His black hair clung to his wet forehead making it look spiky, the hint of blue visible in the light. His oddly shaped eyebrows, pointed at the top, had the same richness of colour. His eyes, dark and confident, were surrounded by thick long lashes that any woman would die to have. His skin was the colour of mocha; his voice deep and lazy, with a hint of danger – as though he was talking to his next meal.

"No, it's OK. Me and Zared will go look around later." She wanted to edge away from him. He was making her uncomfortable and she wasn't sure where this conversation was heading. "Do you think it's wise to spend so much time with him? I mean you barely know him and yet you're at his side every minute." He grabbed the bar. "So?" she snapped. "So … I think it's time for you to meet others and spend time without Zared." He watched her reaction. "No." Angel started to turn, she wanted to leave now. "If you don't, then they will get rid of him." Angel froze. "I know he loves you and you love him, and I know he won't leave your side, not after you tried to kill yourself. But you have to do this, or Callie won't care if he is your mate … she'll have someone dispose of him."

"If I do this, will you say no more about us being together? Will you leave us alone?" Angel asked. "Yes," Barret replied. "Why are you telling me this?" Angel turned to face him. "I thought you hated him."

"Because I owe him one. He saved me from …" He shrugged it off, not finishing what he was going to say.

"Well, it doesn't really matter."

"What did he do?" Angel was curious as to the sudden change when all he had wanted was to get rid of Zared. "He brought you back from death. I don't know how. When I left you you were dead. You'd bled out. I returned to Callie to tell her … let's just say she didn't take the news too well, and then he turned up with you in his arms, still breathing … not strong, but you were alive," he said, remembering that day clearly.

"What happened after that?" Angel wanted to know everything. "Things were hectic for awhile, but they got you to your room, hooked you up to the machines, and then you had a nurse twenty-four hours making sure you were still doing well. Zared only left your side to sleep, but he brought in a guard from the outside to watch over you in the daytime, and then, when night came, he'd leave and Zared would take over. But Callie also had a guard outside your door … just to make sure nothing else happened to you," Barret continued, "so you see … I owe him." Angel was silent waiting for Barret to continue. "Callie has known me a long time but she doesn't really care. If you had died that day so would I have, and Zared."

"OK I'll do it. But nothing is to happen to him while I'm away," Angel demanded.

"You have my word." His smile was friendlier this time. "Just don't tell anyone I told you all this. It'll be my head rolling otherwise ... and believe me they're just dying to get rid of him."

"It's OK, I won't say anything." Angel smiled as they began her swimming lesson, aware that he wasn't as bad as she'd thought he was.

Chapter Fifteen

Angel got out the pool an hour later, wrinkly and very hungry. She found herself more relaxed with Barret. He went to the kitchen with her, hearing his own stomach growling, and offered to make sandwiches.

"Have you always wanted to be a panther?" Angel asked, as she watched him pull things from the fridge and drawers, carrying on their conversation from the pool. Angel began to feel every muscle ache after their session. She'd found it harder than she thought she would, sinking more times than she floated, with the chlorinated water trying to choke her as it filled her lungs and forced her to cough, gasping for air. "It's something that's in the blood, so there isn't much of a choice," he replied, as his made their sandwiches, smiling as he listened to their stomachs grumbling.

Angel sat opposite him, watching everything he did on the island in the centre of the kitchen. "If you had a choice, what would you be?" she asked, her head leaning on her hands as she rested her elbows on the counter. "A hawk!" His knife sliced the bread in half. She grabbed plates for him. "Like Avery?" Barret looked up at Angel, shocked that she knew what Avery was. He passed her a plate with the first lot of sandwiches. "Yes, kind of. She's a silver blade. They're the largest birds around, very rare. Her family still have arranged marriages so their blood carries on in the shifter world, but a hawk is just as beautiful."

Barret's look had changed over the last hour. He'd relaxed, becoming softer with her. He began talking to her as if she were a long-time friend he hadn't seen in awhile. "It's the feeling of freedom to glide through the air, to go anywhere you want without worrying, to feel the sun on your back, and the views must be incredible! Don't get me wrong, a panther is great, but it also restricts you. If a human saw me they would shoot, no questions asked, but if you're in the air, there's no one to hunt you."

He grabbed another plate for his sandwiches, and then headed around the counter to sit on a stool next to her.

"Are there a lot of shifters?" Angel asked, taking a bite of her ham and salad sandwich. "Oh yes, they're everywhere. I think there are more of us than vampires, and maybe witches," Barret replied, taking a bite of his too. "Are they the same as you, or are they different?" she asked, curious to know more. "Some are different. We can change into other animals," he swallowed, "It depends on what type of shifter you are. The main ones are the full-bloods; they're like the royalty of our kind. They can change into any animal by touch. Then, there's half-bloods, which I'm one of, so down the family line a full-blood shifter mated with a human producing half-bloods. The half-blood shifter changes into whatever animal the full-blood shifter had chosen to be before they mated."

Barret paused to let the information sink in. "For the half-blood to keep the shifter gene in the family, they would have to mate with another shifter, which is more likely to be another half-blood as full-blood shifters are rare outside their own kingdom. But, if the half-blood shifter mated with a human, the trait would slowly disappear, especially if their child mated with another human, and so on. In the end, it would just be another myth in our history books," he said, stopping to take another bite.

"So, is it your mum or dad that's the shifter?" Angel asked, trying to understand it all. "My dad and my grandmother were shifters, so it stayed strong in my bloodline," he said, jumping off the stool and going to the fridge again, grabbing two cans of coke and giving her one of them. "My mother? I haven't a clue about? I'm guessing so, but when she left she wasn't spoken of again."

"So what's after half-shifters?" Angel asked keeping the conversation moving after seeing how sad his eyes looked when he spoke of his mother. "Made shifters, which means they've been bitten by one of our kind in their animal form. For humans, it becomes an infection which turns them into the animal that bit them. So, on every full moon their bodies change like half-shifters and kind of like the werewolves of your human myths … except half-shifters can't ever change into wolves; they're a whole different different society in our world … It can be painful at first until the body builds up the cells to block the pain. It only takes a few minutes, and then they are changed, and the pain's gone," he said, opening his can, hearing gases escape, and taking a mouthful.

"Do they know what's happening to them?" she asked. "Yes, if a human is bitten then the shifter has to take responsibility for them by law; otherwise, they could tell the world about our kind and others. It would become a witch hunt, and we can't have that. If a shifter leaves without helping the victim, then, according to the laws of our world, the punishment is instant death for both the human and the maker, but it's rare that we change a human unless it's for war." Barret smiled to himself at a memory.

"So what about wolves? They're not shifters like you?" Angel asked, opening her can, still smelling the chlorine in her hair. "They're a whole different kind of breed. They're wolf full-bloods that turn into the actual wolves you see in the wild, or in books. They call themselves the Lycaons. Then there are Lycaon half-bloods, that's a human that's only partly changed, and a whole new breed: vicious, short-tempered, brainless – easy to control. They're a kind of deformed human with coarse hair covering their bodies, the head of a beast, large feet, and hands with sharp thick claws. Truthfully, I would say the horror movies of werewolves have it spot on with the look. And then, there are those that are made by half-bloods, which are humans infected by the half-bloods passing their curse on through a bite just like with other made shifters," Barret said, "but those that are made wolves have it worse than any other shifter. Their bodies can't cope with the shift back to human form, so every made wolf has to eat a heart, liver or a large amount of muscle to transform back to a human, otherwise they die. Their bodies just burn out."

"That's awful," Angel said, her stomach twisted at the image of eating a heart. "Is there any cure for them?"

"No, unfortunately it's permanent," Barret said, sadness touched his eyes briefly. "Are there any shifters like you living nearby?" Angel asked, changing the subject quickly, Barret nodded. "Could I see some? I've never met one before. Could you show them to me please?" she begged, putting a hand over his. "Sure, I'll take you to meet some tomorrow." He smiled and finishing his food and drink. "Well, I have to go. I need to run some errands," he said, getting ready to leave. "OK, see you later." Angel smiled, watching him leave.

Chapter Sixteen

*A*re you alone now? Zared's voice spoke to her silently, making her jump. Angel had been so caught up in her conversation with Barret that she'd forgotten to go and meet Zared straight after she'd finished swimming. *Yes, where are you?* she replied, standing up, turning, and jumping when she saw a guard behind her. *No, I have a guard!*

Come to the woods, I'm waiting in the clearing you know where.

What about my guard? Angel asked, as she slowly walked over to the sink with her plate and empty can. *Well, make him think you're practising to control your power. When you get here, we need to talk.* He knew she was already heading for the door. Angel's stomach had tightened at his last words.

"Zared!" she shouted, arriving at the spot in the woods. She could see him in her mind, feel the humming get closer, and followed it through trees and across long thick grass with flowers creeping out from the shadows.

"Over here," he called out, leaning against a thick old tree, his dark hair hanging in front of his face. "So, what am I doing first?" she asked, feeling her heart pounding as he looked up at her. His golden eyes glowed as he flashed her a devilish grin.

Angel sat down next to him. She noticed he'd changed from the clothes he'd had on earlier, and was now wearing a brown suede-looking coat that stopped half way down his thighs. It was fastened across his right side. Under his coat she could see the top of a black T-shirt. His dark blue jeans hung below the tops of his white trainers, making them stand out against the darkness of the ground.

"You need to practise the basics: control," he said out loud, intended for her shadow as she still had her guard following her. Zared knew he couldn't hypnotise him; Callie would spot the blank areas of his mind straight away, which would be very bad for all of them. *How is it that we're still communicating like this?* he asked silently. "OK," she replied out loud, looking around and seeing her shadow not far from the tree line. *I don't know,* she replied, giving a faint shrug that only he noticed.

"This leaf, it's light, so concentrate. See if you can make it rise." He placed the leaf in his outstretched hand. Angel went to grab it, but Zared was too quick, moving his hand, careful not to touch her skin just in case it set off the earlier reaction. *Look at it. Pretend you're focussed on it.* He was looking into her eyes. "OK," she replied, answering both requests.

The bond, it's changed hasn't it? her silent voice asked, studying his eyes for the answer. *Yes. But how? Is this going to be permanent? If it is then we're going to have to find a way to block each other's thoughts, or we're gonna go mad!* Meaning that he couldn't have her poking around in his thoughts; he was worried she would see the monster he was, to feel the effects of bloodlust hunger so strong that it hurt, the killer in him waking up for its daily feed – and that was something he didn't want Angel seeing, or feeling.

I agree. But you know now that you're meant to be with me. You can't deny it now, she said with a smug smile on her face knowing she was right. *That's true, and I'm sorry, I just find it hard to believe.* He was trying not to look at her. *Why?* was all she said. *Because you have so much trust in me, and I don't deserve it, not after everything I've done.* He paused, and then continued: *I've killed a lot of people, so how can you love me? I'm nothing but a murderer. I've taken so many lives.*

That doesn't matter to me. Soon I will have to take lives too. You *are what matters to me,* she told him, fighting the urge to talk out loud and use her voice. His hand rested on hers so that she could feel his reassurance. *Why did the gods make you bond with a vampire? One that has to fight his nature just to keep from killing you! To have to stand by watching you getting weak and sick, and what about the time when you do come to die, you can't prevent that, no one can. I can't watch you leave me again; it's too hard.* This time he looked at her. Her green eyes, bright as emeralds, saw the sadness as the memory of her death flashed through him. At that moment, he knew what he'd have to do when it came down to it.

You won't harm me, you never will, and as for me leaving you, that will never happen, she replied, looking back at her leaf. *How are you so sure?* He watched her; her flesh looked paler under the holes in her black top, which suited her more than most other colours. *Can you see into my mind, my memories?* Zared nodded. *Then look, and you will see why.* She closed her eyes and focussed on every memory she had of him and their lives.

Who is Madoc? he asked, seeing a flash of him. *He says he's my warrior.* Angel shrugged her shoulders, forgetting that they weren't speaking out loud. *But since I saw him that day, you have the same mark on your neck as he does, which appeared when you said I returned to my body. I don't know; it's confused me. He said he will come to my side when I call for him, but I don't know much more than that*, she continued.

Suddenly she wondered if she was doing the right thing by him. Was Zared happy with his life before she came along? Did she really force him to be with her? "That's good. Concentrate. Focus!" Zared said out loud, making her jump; his voice sounding strange in her ears, and caused them to throb briefly. *Don't think like that. I've chosen to be with you.* Zared wanted to reach out and touch her but it would look too suspicious. There was a new look on her face. He felt her mood change, pulling away from him, not physically but emotionally. *You could walk away still, before it's too late? I'll understand if you do. I feel a lot stronger now. I can cope with this on my own.*

No, you have me for life now! I won't leave you. He pushed his mind towards her, following her light as she pulled herself away from him. He wrapped his thoughts around her, feeling her warmth, making her return to him. *Good, but we have to leave as soon as possible,* she told him, knowing that this was critical. She felt time was running out for them.

What are you doing tomorrow with Barret? Zared asked with a stab of jealousy that she was going to be alone with him for half the night. Zared wanted time alone with her, to have her safe by his side, and discover everything about their future. *He's going to show me some shifters. Why?* she puzzled, scrunching her face. *That's great, it gives me a chance to leave the island and arrange for transport ... and a place to stay while the sun's up.* He stopped a smile, forcing his face to remain expressionless. He felt relief that they were leaving, especially with Barret looking at her with more than friendship in mind – even though Zared had smelled the scent of another female on Barret when he'd entered the pool room. *Will they let you? We haven't been here long, only a few days.*

We've been here over a week already ... only for some of it you were in a coma. He remembered the image of her lying in his arms, her heart coming to a stop before the lightning had hit him with such a force that he was amazed he was still in one piece.

I didn't realise it was for that long. Barret told me you stayed by my side. She looked up into his eyes again. *Yes well it was my fault. I was the one that put you in that bed.* Zared looked away. *Zared look at me. It wasn't your fault. It was me that did it, not you. I was the one that snapped. I was the one that wanted to end it all ... and it would have happened sooner or later ... it just happened to be while you were with me. I'd wanted to do it for a long time, only I couldn't, there was nothing I could use;*

he'd taken that choice away from me. Then when you came and got me, there were so many things that I could do, but I didn't know how or what was happening. It all became too much. I couldn't understand what was going on and that was the only way out that I could see. Angel looked into his eyes, showing him the truth of her words. *When I was sat with you, I was scared you would leave me again. I can't go through that, so promise me you will never do that again!* Zared forced his silent words to her, letting her know he was serious. *I promise I will never do it again.* She smiled. *Good, now let's go!* Relief flooded over him like a breath he had been holding for a long time.

"I think that's enough for now. Come on let's head back," Zared announced, standing to his feet and helping her up.

"If it's alright with you, I'd like to look at the box with pictures," she said, as they started to walk back towards the house, followed by their guard who kept only a few feet behind. Her voice sounded strange and squeaked. She cleared her throat. "It's called a television, or TV for short," he said, laughing at her description, while she played with a leaf between her fingers. "OK, TV. It's just, I saw one once and I've always wondered what it is," Angel said as they emerged from the wood. *You know there's so much I have no idea about, so you're going to have to show me as much as possible.* She gave him a side glance. *Don't worry I'll show you everything and more,* he replied seductively, wrapping an arm around her waist. *Now that worries me!* She grinned, letting him pull her closer.

Entering the house they both headed for the TV. Zared showed her how to turn it on, and how to use the remote control, pressing channels until she found one she liked. They sat on the sofa, sinking into the soft cream cushions.

Avery walked in, standing at the doorway, wearing a thin red top with black trousers and heels. Her sandy-brown hair was tied up, hiding her streaks of silver. "Angel, Callie would like to see you now," she announced, then turned and left. "You'd better follow. Callie is one of those people who doesn't like to wait." Zared glanced towards the door, moving his head slightly as if to say go run after her. Angel just nodded, heading off in Avery's direction. "Will I see you later?" She paused at the doorway, turning to look at him. "Of course, I'll be right here waiting." He smiled, turning back to the TV, changing the channel as she left.

Angel, be careful. I don't trust her. Say as little as possible. Zared silently warned her as their mind connection began to get fainter.

"This way," Avery said from down a long cream hallway that led to other rooms. "In here." Avery opened the door on her right, stepping to one side to allow Angel to pass.

"Angel. Please sit," Callie's raspy voice said to her just as Angel entered the room. Looking around the room, Angel could see it was like any other: light walls with a few paintings hanging of someone long forgotten for all Angel knew, and a sandy-brown carpet, which matched the sofa and chair well.

"I'd like you to meet Leeda; she's visiting from England." Callie pointed to a beautiful Indian-looking woman with long jet-black silky hair and smooth milky-coffee skin. Her large eyes were the colour of rich chocolate, and asked for your full attention. Leeda had full plump lips that wanted to be touched by men. She looked perfect, wearing a dress that had may patterns and suited her. Colourful beads hung from her ears and around her neck, with a strand of beads that had a white feather hanging from her hair. She looked like a goddess as she sat on her throne, watching as Angel approached.

"Please Angel, sit," Callie said, patting the space next to her. "Hi. Nice to meet you," Angel said, tearing her eyes from Leeda as she sat down next to Callie and opposite Leeda, who radiated confidence and power – a figure higher than Callie.

"It's so nice to meet you Angel," Leeda smiled, her voice seductive, hypnotising. "I've been waiting to see you for a long time now. Your powers must be getting stronger since you turned seventeen. Have you had much trouble with them?" Leeda asked, studying Angel very carefully with her deep rich chocolate eyes surrounded in long thick black lashes.

Angel couldn't tear her eyes away from Leeda's, whose eyes bored into Angel's thoughts, demanding she tell her everything. "No. There's not much I can do yet," Angel said nervously, feeling Leeda's eyes burn though her. "I'm practising as much as I can, but I'm not doing very well." Angel smiled, her palms were clammy.

"That's good to hear. I'm sure your powers will improve with all your practice." Leeda grinned satisfied with Angel's answer. "Tell me Angel, how does it feel to take people's life energy?" she continued, smiling in a smug way that only set off more warning bells in Angel's mind. "I don't know. It's not something I can do again," Angel replied, shocked, looking from Leeda to Callie and then back. Every cell in her body was telling her to run.

"Angel did it the first time she came to us," Callie said, her eyes narrowed as she looked at Angel. "Yes that's true, but it was only then, and that was because you attacked Zared. I've not done it since. I've tried but I can't," Angel added quickly so as Leeda wouldn't think it was something she could do at will.

"And what about what happened in the woods? The guard tells me that you called the elements," Leeda said using a tone of authority. "I don't know what elements are. I was just angry, everything was happening so fast. I just lost it for a moment." Angel wanted this meeting to be over as every fibre of her being told her to stop talking. "The elements are when you call earth, air, fire, water ... and some that are very powerful can also call on spirit," Callie explained. "Oh! But I don't know how I did it. I don't think I can do it again." Angel kept her face blank, giving away as little as possible. Angel knew she could call them again if she focussed and practised more.

"I heard that you and Zared were arguing when you called the elements," Leeda enquired, sitting up straight, her arms resting on the chair, waiting for Angel's explanation. "He came to me after I had called them." Angel stopped herself from shifting in her seat. "But your argument led to that, did it not?" Leeda asked, her voice smooth. "No, it was everything else that led to that, not the argument with Zared," Angel clarified.

"But it did lead to you trying to commit suicide?" Leeda looked tense. She was trying to figure out how Angel's new power worked but finding it difficult. "I had a weak moment where I wanted to end my life. Zared just turned up at the wrong time." Angel didn't like this line of questioning.

"I think your power is unpredictable and that you're too involved with this Zared," Leeda said, "If this continues then I think you should spend less time with him and more time with someone who can help you use these powers on demand," she continued. "Your emotions are too confusing at this time, and your strong attachment to Zared does not help the situation. So, for now, we need to remove him."

"That will be difficult Leeda. They are tied together in a soulmate bond. Zared has brought her back from the dead once already," Callie said, moving uneasily in her seat, ignoring Angel altogether. "This is interesting news. It happened a lot sooner than I anticipated," Leeda smiled, giving Angel the creeps. "Yes," Callie said, her raspy voice sounded worried; this frightened Angel more.

"Tell me child, how did you find him so quickly?" Leeda looked at Angel but it was Callie who answered. "She found him in her astral state, and that's when they followed her back and discovered it was the same child Barret was to bring to me anyway." Callie turned her head towards Angel, almost challenging her to speak; the look she flashed Angel let her know if she did dare to speak, she would feel Callie's wrath. "Well, I must say, I am shocked at this news. I didn't plan on this happening, but it has. We will talk about this problem later," Leeda said, looking at Callie. Angel knew instantly that trouble was just around the corner. "Tomorrow I want Avery to take Angel to the hall. We will practise spells and see which ones will help."

Something about the way in which Leeda had spoken made Angel acutely aware of the danger she was in; she heard the lie in Leeda's voice. "I can't. Tomorrow I'm out with Barret," Angel replied quickly, trying to prevent herself from being around this woman. "Really? Doing what?" Leeda asked. "I'm going to meet some of his kind," Angel said, shifting in her seat. "That sounds like a good idea, and what about Zared?" Leeda asked, watching Angel trying to stay calm. "He's staying here," Angel lied; there was something bad in Leeda's thoughts, she could sense it. "That sounds like an excellent plan. I'm sure it would do you some good to be away from Zared," she smiled.

"You can bring Barret to see me Callie. I've heard many things about him from Ashton who speaks very highly of him, and if he is well acquainted with people that Ashton has told me about, then I have a job for him," Leeda smiled, standing to her feet followed by Callie and Angel.

"The arrangements for the ball are in place I hope?" Leeda said looking at Callie. Evil sparkled underneath her beautiful exterior. "Of course," Callie replied, bowing her head slightly. "Good. We have many guests coming – very important ones. And if there are any problems then I will be very disappointed," she said, walking way. "Angel, I hope I will see you again soon? I would like to see some of this power you have." She disappeared out of sight.

"While Leeda is here keep Zared out of her sight!" Callie snapped. "And when you get back with Barret, you go straight to Avery, do you hear me?" Callie thundered at Angel, who nodded her head not speaking a word. Callie looked older today, overly stressed with having Leeda here. Angel knew one wrong word could make the old woman explode as she sculked off, heading in the same direction as Leeda.

Angel felt her heart plunge. She was in a lot of danger; she felt it stronger than ever. Angel felt the panic bubbling up inside her, ready to spill out. She needed to find Zared. She needed him to tell her there was nothing to worry about.

Where are you Zared? She sent the thought out, but all she felt was a humming coming from his side of their bond. She returned to where she had left him watching TV. "We need to talk right now! Upstairs. Away from ears." Angel's voice sounded frantic as she pointed in the direction of her shadow who was standing with his back against the far wall. "OK," he said, looking at her, feeling her anxiety.

When they entered Angel's room, she closed the door behind them, leaving her guard on the other side. Zared made himself comfortable, sitting on her sofa while she paced in front of him. "Angel, what's up?" he asked patiently, watching her as she moved back and forth. "Do you know a woman called Leeda?" she asked him. Zared swore and pulled himself upright, sitting on the edge of the sofa. He was immediately tense waiting for the reason that had prompted her to mention this name.

"Yes," he said, his teeth clenched. "Why?"

"Well, she's here. And something big is going on, I can feel it. It's just not right … " Angel said, watching Zared as he rose to his feet stopping her mid sentence. "Zared, I'm scared."

"Does she know about your powers?" Zared grabbed her upper arms, squeezing the muscles. "Yes, they've told her everything, even what happened in the wood before I …" She felt her panic increasing. Zared squeezed her arms again as he cursed under his breath, making Angel even more worried. She could feel Zared's own panic and knew he was on edge – a very bad sign. "Leeda also knows about our bond. Callie just told her … and how I protected you when we first arrived." Zared ran a hand over his mouth and swore out loud this time. "We have to leave now, tonight … before sunrise," he stressed as his fingers raked his hair back. "If we get off the island there's a safe house we can go to near here. I'll phone them when we reach land and they can pick us up." Zared started moving while talking through his plan, grabbing clothes from her wardrobe and putting them next to her bed, hiding them from view, ready for him to grab. "I need to get a bag from my room. We'll put a few clothes in to keep you warm at night, then we leave. I have money and we'll drop by mine before we go to the witch." Zared was moving silently trying not to let the guard know what they were doing.

"What's happening? Why now? Why does she scare you so much?" Angel asked. "Because when the sun rises, she will execute me to keep you here," he said, walking over to her, grabbing her arm. "I can't let you out of my sight not while Leeda's here." He raised her chin to look into her emerald eyes. He forced a smile that barely reached his lips – but Angel saw that there was something else in his liquid-gold eyes, and it was more than worry. "Act like we're just hanging out, don't let the guard suspect anything is wrong. We go to my room, grab the bag, and then come back and grab what you need," Zared said. "Everything will be fine. I promise." He kissed her on the forehead. "OK," Angel replied numbly, as Zared grabbed the door handle. "Ready?"

He smiled weakly at her. "Ready," she nodded, taking a deep breath as he pulled the door open.

Angel wished she could still read his thoughts as they headed across to his room, smiling as they passed the guard. "How are we to get past the guard? He's always there." She swallowed, forcing down the fear that threatened to overcome her. "We'll go to the woods. I scouted it out earlier while you were with Barret. At the far end of the woods there are some small boats with engines, just beyond a chained fence that we'll have to climb. Don't worry about the guard, I'll take care of him," he said, rushing around, grabbing the things he needed: his keys, wallet, and a few bags of blood to last him just long enough until they got to the safe house.

Back in Angel's room, she waited until the door was closed before speaking again: "Why would she execute you? You've done nothing wrong … and why does she want me so bad?" Zared was moving quicker that Angel could blink. "Leeda is the most powerful witch of all covens. There were others that were just as powerful, but if she couldn't control them, she got rid of them. Leeda needs to have complete control, and right now you're a big threat," he said, dumping her clothes into the bag.

"There were some like you before. They could summon the elements, but they weren't as powerful as you. Leeda saw them as a threat. She knew they could kill her, and kill those she works for. So, before their power grew stronger she had them executed. She has this book that talks of the chosen one that dies but is brought back by the one that is bonded to her. This child will rule. So any who have shown this sort of power, she's found them, tried to use them for her purposes, and then she would imprison them, keep them chained, starved, to ensure this prophecy wouldn't come true. For a long time Leeda has been planning something, and no one knows what exactly. But by the sounds of it, it's bad, and this person, the book speaks of, is to fight her … and the demons that are coming." Zared zipped up the large bag. "You have to understand this world is ruled by evil. If you live, then everything can change. I believe you're the one. I've never heard of anyone dying and returning, and as Callie said I'm your bonded mate … that is why it's too dangerous for us to stay. Now, put this on. We have to leave now!" he said, passing her a blue denim jacket that had been hanging in her closet. He waited for her to put it on before grabbing the door handle and letting her out first.

"We're off to the woods for more training, are you coming?" Angel asked the guard, as though this was an entirely normal thing to do. She smiled happily as she and Zared walked past him, pulling the remainder of her golden curls out from under her coat. "What's in the bag?" the guard asked, stepping closer. "Supplies. How else am I going to practise?" Angel gave him her most innocent look, keeping her body tense so she didn't start to shake.

All three reached the woods. It was quiet, dark. It felt eerie, different from how it had felt before. Zared grabbed Angel's wrist as they neared the clearing, slowing her down and allowing the guard to get closer to them.

"What's wrong?" the guard asked, stopping just behind them. "Nothing." Zared whipped around, grabbing the guard's head and twisting so quickly that bone cracked with the speed. Angel slammed her free hand over her mouth, stopping her scream from escaping. Her breath rushed in from under her palm, shaking like her legs.

"Something's wrong." Zared said, looking into the shadows. "It's too quiet." Something moved to their right, hiding behind a tree, covered by the darkness. Zared saw it. *"Run!"* he shouted at Angel, pushing her forward. "Keep running. Don't look back. Go straight ahead," he shouted at her as they ran.

Angel did as she was told. She ran, bearing straight ahead, moving round trees, ducking low branches, and jumping dark shapes that stuck out of the ground. Her chest was tight. It was getting harder to breathe. Pain was shooting through her lungs, making her want to throw up. She pushed through the pain, still running straight, when she saw from out of the corner of her eye something move quickly. Angel turned her head slightly.

Then she saw it. It was an animal running at her from her left-hand side. It was big enough to knock her down with one hit. She kept on staring at it as it came closer and closer, emerging from the shadows in pursuit. It was light brown with blocks of darker spots; ears flat against its long skull; its teeth dripping with saliva and ready to sink into one of her limbs.

Angel started to speed up. She could hear it laughing at her as it raced towards her. She ducked under branches, feeling twigs scratch her skin, stinging her, making her eyes water. The animal was so close now she could hear it breathing over her shoulder as its feet pounded the earth, breaking dried twigs.

Suddenly it leaped. Angel screamed, falling to the earth. She had tripped over the root of a tree, saving her from being mauled. She landed hard on her stomach, knocking the wind from out of her. Angel was gasping for air as the animal passed over her and landing to her right. She heard it skid to a stop, turning as it continued to move past bushes, kicking up dried leaves and damp soil as it grappled hard to find its grip.

Angel quickly scrambled to her feet, running for the direction of the fence, hoping she could get over it quickly, leaving the beast behind. But there was no hope of that. It was too fast. Looking back over her shoulder, she could see it gaining on her already.

Angel ran faster, dodging trees and jumping shrubs, trying to slow it down, but she could hear it thundering closer behind her. Her heart was pounding, her lungs hurt. Her mind went blank with panic. How was she going to get out of this? Where could she go?

Angel flew back. The force of the pull almost bent her in half as her feet left the ground. She heard the sound of her clothes ripping in the animal's jaw as it locked down on her. Angel landed on her back. What little air she had left burst out of her lungs from the impact. Her arms were spread out wide, feeling damp earth under her hands. Her head pounded as it made contact with something hard, that was sticking out of the ground.

The animal circled her as she grabbed for her head, rubbing the spot that hurt, feeling a lump beginning to rise, and the sticky wetness of blood soaking her hair. It laughed at her again, coming closer, stalking her. It began to snarl, baring its teeth; its pink tongue curled as it licked its peeled back lips. Slowly, Angel began edging away, pushing herself backwards with her arms. Her arms and legs where shaking violently, tears blinded her vision.

It lunged. Angel threw up her arms to block it from attacking her face. It grabbed one of her arms in its open jaw, sinking its teeth effortlessly into her thin flesh, shaking its head viciously as its grip tightened. Angel could feel muscle being torn from bone. She grabbed its ear, pulling it as hard as she could with her free hand as it pushed her down, flattening her to the ground, standing over her chest.

Angel was screaming in pain. It burned through her body, stopping her breath every time the beast moved. *It's going to kill me!* She suddenly thought. The realisation engulfed her as she kicked out with her legs and punched it over and over again in the head. The beast just snarled at her, growling, as she struggled to free her arm from its iron grip.

Call fire to help you ... Picture it burn! She heard the male voice but had no time to recognise it.

"Fire I call to me!" Angel yelled, grabbing the animal's neck, trying to stop it from ripping her arm apart. Angel imagined the beast getting hotter, flames bursting from her hand and igniting its coarse fur. Suddenly, there was a blood-curdling scream coming from the beast. It released her instantly as it dropped to the floor, rolling, dirt flying everywhere. Angel pushed away, spinning onto her front, getting to her hands and knees, and scrambling towards the trees for safety.

Heat filled the air around them. The sound of crackling filled her ears and the smell of burning caught in her throat. She turned her head to see flames covering the beast's body. She watched; her eyes wide with horror as its form changed into a human male. His body thrashed around, changing from one form to the other, screaming in two voices before collapsing to the ground and falling still. His body was black as coal, and thick dark red blood slowly oozed from the cracks of its expanding skin. Its eyes were still wide with terror, looking at her: lifeless. Its scorched mouth still holding its silent screams. Angel turned away quickly and threw up at the base of a tree. She could smell its burnt skin – a smell she would never forget. Another sound in the distance.

Angel used the trunk for balance as she pushed herself to her feet. She had to move. She had to forget what had just happened until she was safe. Even then she didn't want to remember. She cleared her mind and forced herself to start running again. Her body started to slow down, her legs were getting too heavy as her muscles burned and ached. *Where's the fence?* she thought frantically. Then she saw it. It was just ahead of her. She had reached it at last.

Angel turned to see Zared hitting a tall man, around five foot nine of medium build and with dusty blonde hair. He was hissing and growling like Zared. *Vampire!* she thought, as she watched the stranger hit the man she loved. Zared and the man began to circle each other. Zared threw a punch, hitting the stranger square on the jaw and splitting his lower lip. Blood bubbled up, then disappeared as it healed almost instantly.

The vampire seemed more powerful than Zared, older, as he leapt. His hands wrapped around Zared's throat, his mouth wide open, and his fangs ready to strike. The vampire lunged for him again. Angel watched as Zared's hand flew up, stopping the vampire from attacking his neck; its stained fangs sank into the thick flesh of Zared's palm. Zared used his elbow to hit him again and again in the side of the head until he was released. Zared threw a powerful kick into the vampire's side, wounding him and causing him to buckle. Zared quickly aimed another fist to his jaw before he regained his balance. But the stranger shifted quickly, causing Zared's hand to pass inches from his skin. Suddenly he punched Zared in the stomach, throwing him forward enough to get him off balance. The stranger picked him up and threw him hard towards the fence. Angel felt completely helpless as Zared flew past her and collided with the strong steel, bending some of the fence's links, and bouncing off it and onto the ground in a heap.

"Climb," he said weakly, looking into her worried eyes. "I can't," Angel replied, tears coming to her eyes. Her body was frozen as she watched him struggle to get up. "Yes you can. Grab the fence, put your feet in the holes, and climb. When you get over, jump and roll so you don't hurt yourself," he said, pushing himself up again, and staggering to his feet this time. "Take this. Get to the boat. If I'm not there soon, then leave without me." He took the bag from his shoulders and tossed it to her. "Now go! I'll hold them off."

"No! I won't leave without you." Tears were running down Angel's face. A hiss came from behind her. "Angel go! *Go!*" Zared shouted, waving for her to move before running at the snarling man that was running straight for Angel, working out the quickest way to kill her.

Angel lifted the bag, sliding her arms through its wide straps, and began to climb. Her muscles were shaking. Her heart pounded faster and faster as she climbed and reached the top. She blinked away tears that wouldn't stop falling. At the top, Angel swung her legs over, getting ready to jump, or just let go, whichever her body would allow her to do.

She glanced over to see Zared, praying it wasn't for the last time. He had the vampire on his knees in front of him, head between his hands. She watched as Zared made a quick movement, hearing the crack of bone going through her as Zared twisted the head into an impossible position. She heard Zared let out a war cry. It echoed through the night telling everyone that he was alive, and that he had made his kill. Then she heard flesh tearing, as bone broke free. An unimaginable sound that made her insides heave. Angel saw the vampire's blood spray the ground and trees around them. Angel watched in shock as Zared pulled the head free, blood pouring from its dismembered neck, staining everything as it spilled.

She closed her eyes, trying to forget the night's horror. Angel knew full well that Zared had had to do it; after all he was a vampire just like Zared, and if he had left him there, then he would have healed in a matter of hours and rejoined the hunting party. Angel just wished she hadn't had to have witnessed it.

Angel opened her eyes, letting go of the fence and dropping to her feet. She forgot to roll as Zared had instructed her, and landed heavily, twisting her ankle. Shooting pain went up her leg. She had also landed facing the fence, so when she looked up she saw blood-red eyes with fangs bared for all to see. She gasped, slamming a hand over her mouth, stopping herself from screaming as the dismembered head lay in the middle of blood-soaked earth. She hoped no one had heard them and were heading their way.

A loud thud landed next to her making her jump and knocking her off balance. It was Zared landing, ready to go on the attack, covered in blood.

"Come on." Helping her up, they began to move for the pier where there were small boats tied up. Tears were streaming down her face.

"They knew we were running. How?" she asked, hobbling beside him. The bag felt heavy on her shoulders. She could see the boats floating, bobbing up and down with the waves. "Leeda," was all he said as he raced off to sabotage the engines of the boats, except for the one that Angel was closest to.

Zared returned, picking her up with one arm wrapping around her waist and the other sliding under her legs. He leaned over the side of the chipped wooden boat, its old paint peeling, and dropped her in, nearly throwing the boat over to one side. The chains on the fence began to rattle behind them. They were coming.

Angel sat up front on a thin bench-style seat that went across the full width of the boat. Zared sat on the other at the rear next to the engine and pulled its cord. Hearing it roar to life and the boat moving away from the wooden pier, Angel's relief allowed her to relax briefly and inspect her wounds, which felt raw.

The boat was barely off the edge of the pier, when a large cat appeared, black as ink, racing towards them, and coming to a skidding stop at the pier's edge. The boat was only just too far for it to jump. Angel could hear sounds of rumbling anger coming through the air, mixed with a high-pitched sound coming from above. Angel looked up to see a large bird with silver wings spread wide, and reflecting glimmers of moonlight as it glided through midnight-blue sky.

Chapter Seventeen

The pain was so powerful that it knocked Angel back. She felt something hit her with such a force that she left her seat, unable to breathe. Angel could feel hands grabbing at her, pulling her, stopping her from leaving the moving boat. The burning pain in her chest left her upper body clamouring for release. She gasped breathlessly, trying to control her bubbling panic, to grasp some air as she tried to fill her lungs even if all she could take were shallow breaths.

Zared moved Angel lower into the boat. She looked up to see his golden eyes filled with fear as they looked down at her chest. His hands had moved so quickly that she could only just feel them brush over her as he opened her coat, moving it to one side. She fought the urge to look down at herself; she was too afraid of what she would see. Instead she looked towards the grassy bank. She felt the reality of it all shock her, hitting her hard. She could still die. Her future wasn't set in stone yet. Fear, terror, anger – all mixed as one, as a stab of unimaginable pain coursed through her chest, causing her body to arch suddenly. She screamed out in agony before dropping back. Tears flooded from Angel's eyes, running into her hair.

Angel saw him. He was there standing on the bank with a bow in one hand, smiling at them, satisfied with what he had just done. It was then Angel realised he was true to his word: she was going to die by her father's hand.

"Keep going. Get to the safe house," she gasped, her voice just a whisper, raw from her screams as tears caused it to break. She could feel herself suffocating slowly, tasting her own blood in her mouth, metallic on her tongue.

"We need to stop … I need to heal you!" Zared said ripping his T-shirt and pressing it around her wound, trying to stop it from bleeding so quickly, while he slowed the boat down smoothly. "No! Get to the safe house, then heal me. I'll be fine," she whispered, drawing on all her strength, bracing herself for their journey. "It's just a flesh wound."

"Angel, you're dying!" He knelt at her side, pushing his sleeve up to bare his wrist. "Zared do it! The sun's rising and you can't heal me if you're dead." She felt weak, sleepy, but she needed him to agree. "OK, but if you get worse then we stop, and I don't care if the sun comes up or not," he stated, returning to his seat. He gripped the handle to direct it as they sped up. Zared wished the little boat would go faster.

They docked at last. Zared jumped out, pulling the boat up the bank as quickly as he could. "OK we're here, but before we move, I need to break the arrow. If people see us and you have that sticking out, then there's going to be a big problem," he said, his voice strained as he bent down beside her. "OK," Angel breathed, "I'm ready, do it."

"I'm sorry but this is going to hurt so I'll make it really quick." Angel nodded in response, taking in quick shallow breaths, bracing herself. "One. Two." He grabbed the arrow's stick and snapped it.

Angel felt the pain go through every cell in her body, she couldn't stop herself from screaming out again in agony. She gripped the edge of the boat and dug her nails in as her body went into spasm with the aftermath. Silent tears rolled down her face as Zared picked her up. Angel began to feel like she was drowning. She could feel the air getting tighter in her lungs and bubbling in her chest as she gasped harder. "We have to move fast. I won't lie, it's going to hurt," he said. Her breath stopped as he held her in his arms. "It's OK. I'm ready." She spoke softly, passing out, allowing her body to drift into darkness, unable to cope with what had happened, and the amount of pain it had caused.

Angel opened her eyes at the sound of a woman's voice somewhere nearby. "Hi Angel. It's OK. I'm a friend of Zared. He's asked for my help." She looked young, in her early twenties, with light brown hair and eyes of the same colour. Her body was covered in bright colours as though someone had painted on her skin. She wasn't like any other she had seen so far. She had piercings in her lip, eyebrows, ears, and studs in her cheeks and chin. "My name is Sarha. I'm a healer." She smiled. Angel drifted again.

"Angel, you need to stay awake for me," Sarha shook her until she opened her eyes. "Can you hear me?" she asked, looking down at Angel. "Yes," Angel replied. Her vision blurred. Blinking to clear it, she saw a cracked ceiling with chipped paint. She noticed a smell of strong incense. "Where am I?" she asked, looking at Sarha. "You're in a safe house. You and Zared will be leaving in an hour, so we don't have much time," she replied, standing up. "Where is Zared?" Angel asked, feeling extremely calm considering what had just happened.

"I'm here," he said, coming into view. His coat was

stained red, his T-shirt ripped around the bottom, and his jeans had green patches on the knees. "What happened?" she asked, puzzled as to why she could only remember what had happened in the boat and nothing else that had followed. "You passed out when we got here, and you've lost a lot of blood. So Sarha here is helping to heal you. She's removed the arrow but it was lodged between your ribs. You were very lucky you didn't bleed to death." He sounded different; his eyes were blazing. Angel saw a touch of fear in them. "The arrow pierced your left lung, nicked your heart, and damaged muscles which she's stitched. Sarha's removed all the foreign bits, so you heal clean." He sounded clinical. His tone was raspy and distant.

Angel didn't feel lucky at this moment in time, she felt only pain. She held on to it, to keep it from escaping her dry lips. Zared put her hand in his. It gave her comfort to feel his warmth against her skin. Looking into his eyes, Angel focussed on fighting through the pain. Her fingers tightened around his hand, releasing their grip after each wave had passed.

"It's time we started," Sarha said from behind them. "S-start w-what?" Angel stammered, breathlessly, starting to feel coldness rattle through her. "You have to drink my blood until I tell you to stop. It will help you heal before we move again." Zared lifted her head up, seeing her flinch as he laid her gently in his lap. "C-could you leave us alone Sarha, p-please?" Angel stammered again, her body was shaking uncontrollably in Zared's lap. She felt guilty that Sarha had helped her and now she was asking her to leave.

Angel realised how much Zared influenced her life. How much stronger she felt when he was with her. How his presence took away her fear. How much she didn't want to leave him – she loved him too much. "Of course. I'll just be outside if you need me," Sarha replied, leaving the room.

"It was my f-father who did this," Angel said, looking into Zared's golden eyes. "I saw him when you looked over," he said, brushing the golden hair, which had stuck to her dried tears, off her face. "W-will he come after us again?" she asked, seeing that this was only the beginning. "Yes. But I don't want you to worry about that now." He gave her a wary smile. "W-when he comes, I-I want to kill him my- ... myself," she gasped. Her body arched with another wave of pain. She screamed, gasping for air. Her voice had sounded cold, detached. She felt so much hatred towards her father that she couldn't stop wishing he was dead.

"You will, my love. I promise you that." Zared smiled, bringing his wrist up to his mouth and sinking his teeth into his own skin, ripping his flesh apart. Blood drizzled into her mouth as he brought his open wrist to her lips.

"Drink," he told her. She obeyed, drinking its sweet taste, letting it smother her throat as it travelled down. She could feel it passing into her blood, mingling, making her burst with heat and pleasure, as she groaned, feeling its healing power tingling throughout her body, and letting her know everything was going to be OK.

She started to feel something else grow inside her. It was more powerful – a light burning like the sun. She felt herself drifting away, submerging into it. Shock waves of light pulsed through her, cascading over her organs, shocking them to keep them in working order.

"Angel, you must drink; you won't heal otherwise." He shook her, but she didn't respond. "*Angel?* Wake up!" he said, shaking her again. "*Angel!*" But there was nothing. Her head flopped to one side, her mouth still open; blood covered her dry lips, a reminder of what had happened. Zared watched as excess blood began to dribble out from the corner of her open mouth. Slowly, it started to get thicker, bubbling out from her flooded lungs. Its deep red air bubbles quickly bursting as they hovered over her lips, trickling its thick red liquid down her pale cheek.

Fear and panic hit Zared hard, knocking him off balance. He hated to feel these emotions; they made him feel weak, pathetic, as he sat there unable to do anything for her. He wanted it to be a dream, but it wasn't. Zared couldn't wake up from this nightmare. Their bond was getting weaker. He couldn't feel her fighting. She was quickly disappearing from their invisible connection, and he was receiving only its numbness – its lifeless strand.

"Sarha, get in here right now!" Zared yelled, holding on to Angel's limp body. "Something's gone wrong," he said, his voice sad and bitter as he picked Angel up in his arms, laying her down on the floor, ready for anything that Sarha could do. The door flew open seconds after he called. She ran towards them. "What happened?"

Zared looked up at her, his own eyes leaked with tears. "She just stopped drinking. She didn't take enough to heal." His voice came out in a calm rush. "The stitches must be broken. If it's not the stitches, then she has a bleed somewhere else. We'll have to open her up again. Zared I need you to help me," she said, rushing to grab things she needed and piling them beside Angel's still body, ready. "Hurry Sarha. I'm losing her. I can smell death on her and it's getting stronger." Sarha could hear the panic in his voice. He couldn't lose her again; he'd just got her back and now Leeda had nearly succeeded in killing her.

"I know … I'm moving as fast as I can," she said, grabbing a scalpel. She gave it to Zared. "Cut along the same path that I made, so she's ready when I am," Sarha said, as she rushed around. Zared nodded in reply, wiping his tears away.

Sarha grabbed a bowl of hot water and a cloth, while Zared removed Angel's bloodstained bandages, revealing neat stitches that had evidence of leaking blood around them. Slowly he put the knife to her skin, pressing it into the stitches and cutting them open. Angel's wound spread apart, opening easily. Blood spilled out, rushing at him with force as it escaped her body. He fought against tasting it, as it ran over her chest, landing in a puddle on the floor near his knees. Zared could feel ravenous hunger taking him over; the smell was driving his inner monster crazy, making his mouth water with delight at its strange fragrance. Angel had blood like no other. Its taste was as close to perfection as possible. The smell could be traced for miles. He knew that her blood was unique and alluring to every vampire's thirst.

"Sarha, get here now! You need to take over," Zared shouted, backing away slowly, trying not to breathe in its intoxicating scent. Sarha raced to him. He knew she saw his eyes changing, turning blood-red. His tongue felt thick in his mouth, as his fangs began to throb, begging him to quench his hunger, to just take a mouthful. "I can't stay. I won't be able to fight it much longer," Zared needed to leave. He needed to go and get a blood bag. His thirst was turning dangerous, famished. Just as he turned to leave, he heard Sarha's voice: "Did you cut Angel like

I asked you?" she asked puzzled, looking over Angel's lifeless body then up at Zared, who was standing in the doorway a safe distance from them. "Yes, why?" he said curious as to her question, and coming up behind her.

Angel had healed. Her skin had closed and was free from any marks, old or new. Zared couldn't believe his eyes. He had to touch her. He wanted to feel her, to make sure his eyes weren't deceiving him. Her skin was smooth, soft, hot to the touch. There were no red marks, no faint scarring, not a blemish. Her pale skin was the colour of cream, not white. He could feel her heartbeat strong and in perfect rhythm under his palm.

"I don't understand. She didn't drink enough to start healing. She only got a mouthful, if that," Zared said. His fingers stroked her heated face. Grabbing the wet cloth that sat in the bowl of water, he started to wipe away the blood that covered nearly half her body. "I don't understand it either. But I don't think it's just your blood healing her now," Sarha said, pushing herself back to give them space, letting out a sigh as she watched Zared clean Angel's skin, seeing the worry on his face disappearing with each stroke.

"Something different has happened. I can feel it." Zared finished and sat beside her, waiting for her to wake. "I think it might be the prophecy coming true," Sarha said, watching Angel as her skin gave off a faint glow as the healing continued. "What do you mean?" Zared asked, looking at Sarha curiously. "It is said that there is one that shall heal itself to prepare for a war that is to come," she replied, as if from memory. "This chosen soul will lead those to fight against the greatest of all evil."

"What can be more evil than demons?" Zared asked, glancing over at Angel. "There are many evils that are stronger than our demons," Sarha replied, watching him with Angel, sitting so closely to her, his protective energy radiating from him. "Like what?" Zared asked, looking at Sarha. "After demons, there are dragons, which everyone has heard of before. It's written in all the books that belong to our kind, but they're not as powerful as blood demons, and what comes out of their world," Sarha said shifting to get comfortable.

"I thought blood demons were a myth."

"No they're real. They come from another world. But their strongest demon, which is known as the *first*, can summon them through. Once they come into our world, they can call forth all kinds of evil. In 1973 a dead creature was found in Texas. It was like nothing they had seen before, but then a week later another appeared. It was hunting an element at the command of its master, a blood demon. Then an old witch from faraway lands wrote of them. She had seen them in a vision. She also wrote of a waste demon that ate the flesh and bones of the dead. She had seen them come through a doorway, called upon by a man that changed with black eyes," Sarha said, telling him the story of her people.

"That's impossible," Zared said in disbelief. "Is it? In the human world, we don't exist … and yet here we are. So what's to say in our world such things don't exist?" Sarha made sense. Humans had stopped believing in supernatural beings as their memories faded into legend. For the beings of the supernatural world it had become essential to become a secret, a myth, in order to be spared from the great witch hunts.

Chapter Eighteen

Angel felt the light travelling through her, helping his blood to heal her wounds. She felt it burning, heating her up. Everything around her disappeared. She no longer heard their voices. She was focussed on holding on to his hand, pulling the light to her, summoning all the energy around her, and calling it to heal her broken body. She could feel it flowing in and out of her, like a snake riding the waves, as it dived back into her body wrapping itself around her raw wounds, soothing them, healing them. Then, with one last explosion of bright hot light, it was gone. Everything had changed.

"Hello, my daughter." An old man came into view. His hair was pure white, along with his beard. He had eyes of an unnatural green that took her breath away.

"Do I know you?" she asked, frozen to the spot. "No, my child, you were born months after my departure. My name is Chaos and you are the third of my children. I had you sent away to keep you safe from your siblings as they fought; stripping you of all your powers until this life." He came closer. He was a solid man, who was inches taller than her. "Why now?" Angel asked. "I have watched their war go on for many lifetimes, and thought nothing of it. But there is a change now. Another power has entered the game and has shifted the balance completely … and now I feel the danger you are in. So I have decided to return your powers. Use them wisely and they will help you. But you must re-learn everything. The path you choose from this point forward, will decide the fate of your world."

He took her hands in his. "I'm sorry for not watching over you more closely. I hope that one day you will forgive me." The old man bowed his head and kissed her hands.

Angel felt herself suddenly jolted back to her body, flinging herself upright, as if she had just woken from a dream. Her skin was covered in a sticky sweat. Blinking madly, she rubbed her eyes with the palms of her hands, and then turned to see Zared, who was watching her carefully, his hands twitching with anxiety, momentarily driving away all memory of her experience with Chaos.

"*Zared.*" Angel saw his face relaxing. "Angel," he breathed, grabbing her, wrapping her up in his arms and kissing the top of her head. "Stop dying on me! And what the hell just happened?" Zared ranted, pulling away. Before she could answer, he put his hands on either side of her face crushing his lips to hers. "I have no idea," she replied, smiling when he pulled back. It was true; she didn't know. All she was aware of was the light healing her, along with Zared's blood, and of the man who called her 'daughter' – but was he real or did she just dream him up? Angel didn't know the answer, so she decided on not telling Zared.

"It's your powers Angel, they're growing … and with Zared so close, they're getting stronger a lot faster than could be expected," Sarha said, as Zared helped Angel to her feet. "Angel can't die, not with you alive Zared. It's foretold in one of the old books that there will be one that will return to stand by the chosen one – her mate and her warrior. So, in other words Angel, as long as Zared stays alive, so will you." Sarha smiled, standing beside them, rejoicing with the knowledge that the prophecies of the old book were coming true.

"What else does this old book say about us?" Zared asked, Angel still wrapped up in his arms as he kissed her head again and again, feeling relief that she was alive in his arms, and that her father had failed in his attempt to harm her. Now they had a new problem: his life was written for all to read, especially his enemies. He would be in their focus. Now he would become the bull's eye of all attacks aimed to kill her as well. This didn't settle too well with him.

"It does say something about angels from the gods that must battle the protectors of the four watch gates to keep the balance from falling. There shall be one of two, both able to slay with the sword made from blood. But that's all I remember. I'm sorry but it doesn't make any sense. To understand more you need to go to a witch called Jurisa Sand," Sarha said, giving Angel fresh clothes to wipe away any reminders of her ordeal. "That's who we were trying to find. She told me to go to her, but I have no idea where to find her," Angel said, stepping away to put on the clean jeans and top that Sarha had given her, not bothered that they could see her. After all she had only shreds of her old top left on anyway. Angel stayed as close as she could to Zared.

Sarha watched Zared move unconsciously, he followed her every movement. If she drifted away, he moved closer. If she came closer, he knew she would use him for balance.

"She lives in England. I will arrange flights and transport at the other end. I will tell her people that you are coming. She will be so pleased." Sarha clapped her hands with excitement, a look that was so at odds with her painted image.

"What about Leeda? She's here, and she knows about us," Zared announced, breaking Sarha's happy thoughts as reality came crashing down.

"Leeda is here?" Sarha cursed, running out the door, and returning a few minutes later with two chains that had some sort of coin dangling from them. "We have to move right now. She may already have seen the plan. Put these charms on, they will block her vision of both of you," she said, handing them the chains, saying nothing until they had put them on. "I have a driver outside. Follow me. Tell no one who you are, or what you're doing until you're in the safety of Jurisa's coven. If you see any of her people at the airport, then abort. Go a different route if you have to. Then head for a place call Scunthorpe, in the county of North Lincolnshire, when you get there, head for Normanby. There's a house behind closed gates. There are guards. Tell them you're there to see Jurisa Sand. Show them your charms, this will prove you are who you say you are."

Sarha opened the door to an alley, where a car was waiting. Sarha handed Angel an old coat that had been in the cupboard. Then, she grabbed a sheet off a hanger placing it over Zared as they took the few steps to the car and got in. "There are some bags of blood in there, if you're hungry," Sarha said, pulling up a divider that looked like an armrest. "Remember, Leeda has people everywhere, and they are all after you, so be very careful," she said, closing the door.

Zared wound the window down only so far. "Thank you." Zared meant it. "For everything," he said, smiling, showing that it came from a heart that wasn't yet cold and still. "It was my pleasure. I'm just happy I got to meet you at last. Please travel safely. I will inform those that need to know, that you are coming." Sarha smiled and backed away, giving them a small bow as the car pulled away.

Angel turned in her seat to see Sarha pull out her phone and begin talking, smiling, looking in their direction. Their car got to the end of the alley and was turning when Angel saw a shadow jumping above Sarha.

"Stop!" she shouted. The brakes squealed as the car came to a halt. Angel threw open the door. "Sarha. *Run!*" Angel looked up to see a creature descending and landing between their car and Sarha. It was hairy with a long misshaped head. Its eyes held pure evil. Its snarling mouth showed rows of sharp teeth. "Go!" Sarha shouted back. "Go now!"

A strong hand grabbed Angel pulling her back into the car. "Go!" Zared shouted at the driver. "There's nothing we can do. It's too late," he said, trying to calm Angel down, holding her, refusing to let her turn to see what was happening behind them. "Will she be OK?" Angel asked, knowing the answer. Zared didn't look at her, he didn't have to answer, she saw it in his eyes.

"What was that thing?"

"A wolf half-blood, or made-wolf by the look of it," Zared said, looking back at it briefly. Angel remembered the conversation she'd had with Barret: *Lycaon half-bloods ... a human that's only partly changed ... a whole new breed ... vicious, short-tempered, brainless – easy to control ... a deformed human, with coarse hair covering their bodies, the head of a beast, large feet, and hands with sharp thick claws.*

"What now? Do they know we're coming? Does Leeda know where we're heading?" Tears rolled down Angel's cheek before she wiped the warm wetness from her face. "We'll get there, don't worry." He pulled her into his arms, giving her comfort. "There are safe houses all over England, and with these charms, Leeda's not going to find us. We'll just take a different route, just in case she does know." Angel just nodded. She trusted him and if he had a plan, then she would follow. "Driver, did Sarha say which airport to go to?"

"Yes sir. Malboro Airport," he replied. "Then change it. Take us to Wiggins. We'll make our own arrangements from there," Zared told him, relieved that he had grabbed his wallet before they'd left Callie's. "Yes sir." The driver said no more for the rest of the drive.

Chapter Nineteen

It was a full day's drive to Wiggins, so by the time they got there it would be dark again. Angel fell asleep with her head on Zared's lap, while he propped himself up against the window. Angel began to dream.

Zared appeared in her dream, looking very confused. "Where are we?" he asked, looking around to see that they were in strange woodland. "I've seen this place before. It's where I got married," she smiled, racing off with Zared following behind. "You what?" He stopped. He couldn't believe what she had just said, and that they were at this strange place that she had obviously been to before. Somehow they had left the car behind, not remembering how.

"I dreamt of this place ages ago. I was stood right over

there." Angel pointed. "There was a priest reciting wedding vows. He asked me if I would take this man to be my husband … but it was strange I didn't see him. I knew he was there, but I couldn't see him … then everything changed, and you came to me."

"Great! So it could be me, or it could be someone else that marries you," Zared said with sarcasm in his voice.

"Come on. I'll show you." Angel grabbed his hand and walked towards the stone table. "This is where it all happens. Even Isis had her change here." She patted the cold smooth surface. "The table was put here when she was born." Angel sat on it, feeling its coldness through her clothes. "Can you feel it singing? It's like magic." She smiled, her face lighting up as she pushed her hair back behind her ear after the wind had caught it making it wild and untamed, showing the colour of copper mixed with golds, reds and browns as the moonlight shone. "This is our home! This is where we have to go!"

"OK, if that's what you want?" he said, watching her as she changed before his eyes. This place meant a lot to her. He could see the love she had for this place. He couldn't deny her that, not after everything they had gone through. "It is." Her smile beamed. "Now, if we only knew where this place was," Zared said, turning in a circle, trying to see if he recognised anything, or if there were any markings.

Isis suddenly walked into view. She was in her late teens or early twenties, and was wearing a long white dress which trailed along the ground, staining its edges. Her hair was straight, flowing down her back, the colour of deep rose against her creamy skin. Her eyes were liquid gold with rings of bright green that had had to have come from Angel.

Angel got up and walked over to Zared's side, entwining her fingers in his, and watching as Isis passed silently by. Angel kept still, even though she wanted to go over to touch her. They watched as she stalked, hunted something; her white wings rested flat against her back as she tiptoed around not making a sound. Angel pulled away, following Isis. Zared stayed close behind Angel, keeping an eye on their surroundings and remaining on high alert.

Something big moved in the shadows causing Angel to freeze. Zared wrapped his hands around her arms, pulling her back to him. Zared was getting ready to attack. "They're surrounding us," he whispered into Angel's ear. "Get ready to run. I'll hold them off," he hissed, crouching, ready to attack.

"No. I'm not leaving you this time," Angel said, taking in deep breaths, ready to summon all of her strength. "I'll stay and fight. I can't keep running Zared." Zared just nodded, but his mind was focussed on protecting her as well as himself.

A menacing growl came from behind them. Spinning around they saw something stepping slowly from the shadows. Angel's heart pounded against her ribcage. Its shadow was large. She feared this thing was going to kill them. Zared moved forward hissing as he protected her. The moonlight spotted the shadow attacker revealing to everyone what the beast was.

Angel's breath stopped; it was a made-wolf, or even a half-blood. It was standing tall, its body bulging, drool dripping from its razor-sharp teeth. Angel could smell its stench, burning her nose and throat. More sounds came from around them. Turning she saw more of the creatures emerging from the shadows.

"Well done! You created a trap. I should have seen it coming." Isis's voice sounded light, fearless, as she mimicked Zared's stance, her knees bending, ready to jump. "I guess it's proof you're not as stupid as you look," Isis laughed. It sounded musical. One of the beasts suddenly howled in anger, a signal for the horde to attack. They ran at their prey.

Zared leaped at one of the beasts, but nothing happened. Angel heard him hit the ground, and saw him spin around to check that she was OK. "I just went through him." Zared got to his feet, dusting himself down and looking around. He saw Isis fighting alone. "I don't think we're really here. I think it's a vision into her future and what's to happen," Angel said, walking to Zared's side.

Isis hissed. Her fangs were ready as she ran at the first one. Zared and Angel watched as she landed on the beast's chest, knocking it to the ground with the momentum. Isis quickly sank her teeth into its neck, pulling away, shaking her head as she ripped a chunk from its body. Angel saw blood pouring from its open wound. Its hands flew up to cover it, trying to stop the bleeding.

Isis turned, smiling, her teeth still clutching a huge chunk of flesh that pulsed out its last sliver of blood. Isis spat it out. Her eyes had turned deep red. She had the taste of blood and the ecstasy of the fight flowing through her body. Her nails had grown into weapons for her to use at will. Standing to her feet, she wiped her mouth with the back of her hand, smearing the liquid like war paint. Turning to the animals that surrounded her, she locked eyes with them, her lips arched wickedly as she stood ready for the next attack. Their eyes glanced at the gurgling body at Isis's feet. It had finished spamming and returned into its human form.

"Who is she?" Zared asked. He couldn't take his eyes off her. She looked familiar but he couldn't remember having seen her before. "*What* is she?"

"She is Isis," Angel said proudly, as she watched the battle. Zared looked at Angel. She could feel his shock as he watched her fight. "My daughter," Angel added. "No, it can't be," he said, moving to see her better. "That's impossible."

Angel watched as the thought of Isis being her daughter sank in. A smile touched his lips. It was then she saw just how amazed he was. "She has golden eyes. Is she mine?" Angel couldn't answer that question. "She reminds me so much of you." It was all she could say as Zared watched, fascinated with Isis's movements, as she mimicked his own.

Two half-bloods jumped her, their hands grabbing her from either side as another came forward; its muzzle snarling, wide, ready to rip into her.

Angel couldn't stop herself; she stepped forward, placing her hands on Isis's shoulders pulling her closer to her. "Summon the energy," Angel whispered into Isis's ear as Zared shouted for Angel to get back. "Fire I call to me!" Isis shouted out loud. Angel felt her body being pulled, merging with Isis. She pulled energy from all around her, it burned hotter and hotter. She could smell burning, not from her or Isis, but from something else.

Zared watched in shock as Angel entered Isis's body. She was only in there for a short time, but it was enough to worry him. He watched as her body became smothered in thick grey smoke, which started from her feet. It crawled up her body, igniting into hot red flames that danced just above the surface of her limbs. He could hear it crackling, deafening his ears. He watched it flicker wildly, growing stronger. The heat forced him to step back. The flames were so hot that they suddenly shot off, travelling so fast down Isis's arms, as if they had caught on gasoline, that there was no time for the creatures to let go. Flames hit their fur, lighting it like paper.

Zared watched the blaze move like a bushfire as it travelled across their bodies. He heard their screams of agony as they tried to put it out by beating themselves, before dropping to their knees as their life expired. He could hear the popping of their skin as it burst open. Some places were so hot they had melted, flesh falling from its bone. Death had claimed another two: returning them back to their human forms.

Angel felt the burning heat turn cold. She released the energy she had claimed, sending it back into the atmosphere. She stepped away. Isis was by herself again. Angel slowly backed up, seeing the two lumps of black mass, still feeling the heat sizzling from them.

"Angel!" Zared grabbed her and pulled her close, keeping a tight grip on her.

"Thank you, mum," Isis spoke softly. Angel felt her heart ache, she had known Angel was there, watching over her. "How does she know we're here?" Zared asked, but Angel just shrugged. She didn't have an answer for that either.

Isis went on the attack again, hitting one made-wolf which was stood in front of her, was still stunned by what he had just witnessed. Isis moved just as quickly as Zared, throwing her hand forward, sinking her claws into the beast's chest. It howled in pain as she closed her fingers into a fist and yanked her hand back; its flesh, covered in thick hair, was still in her grasp. An arm came at her.

Zared and Angel watched as Isis ducked, dropping the fleshy tissue, and springing back up to punch him with her fist repeatedly in the side of his large head. He moved back. Then, he punched her in the face using all of his weight behind him, sending her flying and landing beside Zared.

Zared bent down automatically to pick her up, touching her arm. Zared felt a sudden surge of energy rush at him, opening him up to her mind just the same as with Angel. Only Isis's mind was like silver mirrors, allowing only words to go through, stopping Zared from seeing into her thoughts. But it did allow Isis to enter his mind in a way that she could picture his thoughts. *Aim for the legs Isis! It's the weakest part of their bodies!* He sent her the image of what to do. She did as he said, bringing her foot in hard to its knee and breaking it. The beast cried out above the sound of cracking bone, and collapsed to the floor. *Now snap its neck! They can heal like vamps.* Isis listened to Zared's voice and jumped on its back, twisting its head quickly.

Behind you, jump now! he ordered, watching her follow his instruction, spinning around in the air and landing behind her attacker so that she was facing his back. Zared watched her move to his command as if this were a training exercise. She focussed on her surroundings as well as his voice. *Don't waste time. Kill it now.*

Angel watched Zared giving out orders, unaware that he was speaking silently to Isis too, just knowing that he was enjoying the fight as if he was part of it. *There's one left in the tree line behind you. You're doing great. Keep going.* He sounded like a proud father as he pulled away allowing her to enjoy this kill on her own. "Don't leave me!" She spoke out loud, turning towards the trees. *I'm not leaving. I'll be watching you, don't worry. You're doing great. I'm proud of you.* He pulled away, leaving her mind buzzing.

Isis was smiling at his last words, making herself move faster, using the trees to her advantage, and coming down on her attacker from above. She wrapped her legs around its waist and grabbed for its head. The beast hauled himself back to the tree, throwing her over and over again until she lost her grip. Isis fell to the ground rolling away from the fiend. She landed on her left leg. Reaching under her torn dirty dress, she grabbed a silver blade from her right leg. Standing slowly, she gripped the weapon tightly, pointing its double blade at the beast. "Do you know how to use that little girl?" It was male. Its voice was deep, old, and as he spoke the hint of a low growl was heard. Its beastly face was scarred from battle, and chunks of its right ear were missing. "My father is a good teacher," she smiled. "He told me to always carry a blade for when I meet your kind."

"Who's your father?" it asked, circling her. She followed its movements, keeping her senses open, her wings pressed flat to her back. Her dress was torn and stained. "Can't tell you that, but then you already know my mother," she smiled. "Then I'm going to enjoy killing you," he snarled. "You already tried that once, or don't you remember?" she snapped, jabbing at him. "You couldn't do it the first time. What makes you think you can do it now?"

"The first time you were lucky. I won't make the same mistake twice."

"I'll be sure to tell my mother that. She'll be pleased to know you're still alive. She will enjoy meeting up with you again," Isis returned, grinning as his eyes widened briefly before returning to their hard cold stare. "Your mother is Angel? She is highly wanted by Bay ... and bringing back her firstborn dead will make me rich."

He lunged at her, but she was quicker, moving out of his path and bringing her blade down, slicing his long hairy arm. He grunted in pain and turned quickly to face her again. "Tell me child. Is it true her mate is dead? It's been a long time since I've seen Zared. I guess it should be easy to kill her now," his lips curved up. "My father will kill every one of your kind before that happens," she snarled, as they circled, "He will never let you touch my mother, neither will her guards … and I'm sure you re-member the last time you attacked her, after all you still bear the scars."

Isis grinned as she saw the beast flinch. He touched his face absently; his fingers traced a long dark line. "He can't protect her forever, and with demons on our side one day he will lose, and when that day comes I have a score to settle with her," he snarled, saliva dripping. Zar-ed looked at Angel, but she just shrugged at him. "May-be I should keep you alive as bait. I'm sure Leeda would be pleased. You'll be her slave, passing your genes on to demon offspring," he grinned. "I don't think so," Isis snarled, watching his movements. "You've got to take me alive first," she hissed, lunging forward and striking him hard.

Shadows came over Angel from above. She looked up to see wings. They where large, black as the night with red tips. Angel pulled at Zared's arm pointing up. "Help's just arrived," she told him. *Isis help's coming! Hold him off, you're going to be safe.* He saw her nod slightly, and then he pulled out of her mind completely, watching her defend herself, relieved with the knowledge that she would be safe. Then Angel saw another set of wings approaching. The first of the shadows landed in the small gap between Isis and the wolf; his sword ready to strike as soon as he moved. The other winged man landed just in front of Zared and Angel, guarding them and blocking their view. "Zared! This isn't the end," the beast snapped at the winged man stood in front of Isis, running off into the shadows as a blade came at him.

"Zared?" Angel said, puzzled. Zared looked just as puzzled at hearing his name called out. Angel walked round to the guard in front of them, seeing a different man to the one she remembered having seen before – *Madoc!*

Madoc tried to stop her, but it was too late, she had seen him. "No, my Queen, Zared cannot see this. His future has changed once already. The Zared of your time must not come into contact with this Zared. It will change everything," he said, turning to face them, blocking Zared's view. Angel just nodded, but she had already seen him: the long velvet black coat with the Gaelic patterning on its high collar, which he wore over the tight black top that showed off the shape of his body; the black combats with their many pockets; and the chains and knives that hung from his belt. His heavy-duty boots were laced up, covering half of his calf muscles. To Angel, he looked like a warrior, fallen from the gods. His wings were as black as night with their blood-red tips. She saw a glimpse of the mark on his neck and she knew that he was her soulmate. Isis had turned to the right, and Angel saw she had the same marking on her arm, only red and bigger – a birthmark to say she was hers.

"Madoc." Angel smiled. "It's good to see you." Her eyes found his mark – it was in the same place as Zared's. She had known it was Madoc, recognising the voice, and his eyes. He had sun-kissed blonde hair that half covered his stunning eyes – still the colour of pure silver. His perfectly sculptured body showed under his tight-fitting clothes, indicating his strength. He was a warrior. It radiated from him. Their bond was evident instantly and embraced them both, pulling her to him.

Only this time, it didn't just stop at Madoc, it opened her soul up to both him and Zared. She felt everything at once, making her dizzy with its overload. "It's good to see you too, my Queen, but it's time for you both to return." He smiled. "I know," Angel replied, disappointed, but then she felt her future Zared walking towards her, Isis by his side. She felt him so strongly as his connection to Madoc amplified their three-way bond. Madoc lowered his head towards hers. Angel felt the warmth of his breath on her face, as his hand brushed over her cheek, causing her heart to beat faster. Her stomach somersaulted as his fingers touched her skin, tilting her chin up to him. He kissed her lips. She felt the warmth of his love go through her. She wanted to pull him closer. She fought the urge to put her arms around his neck and be drawn in to his smouldering fire.

Madoc touched Zared, placing a hand on his head. Angel watched as Zared's eyes became heavy. "He will wake with you," Madoc said, as Zared left their vision. Madoc embraced her again, wrapping her up in his wings so no one could see them, his kisses becoming more intense. She couldn't help but return them with just as much passion. Her fingers rested on his hard chest, pulling at soft cloth. Her breathing was heavy, matched with his. She could feel him within her, stroking her mind. His energy called to her, entwined with her own. She was losing herself, leaving everything around them, merging with him, as his hands studied her body. She quickly came to her senses, pulling away reluctantly. She knew he could feel her desire for more. Angel looked into Madoc's silver eyes, which were now tinted with violet. She was breathing heavily as her pulse raced at the sight of his smile. *If I had come to you first, then it might be different*, his voice whispered sadly in her head. *This might have turned out different.*

What do you mean? Angel replied, confused, still feeling like jelly in his embrace. *I am a part of Zared. Without me, he cannot live. I am the one that keeps him alive for you, and without you I can not ...* Madoc stroked her face. *He desires you just as strongly as I. Your bond with him is strong and I cannot stop this, but only he can protect you now.* Madoc brushed his lips against hers. *I don't understand. Will I hurt Zared?* Angel looked into the liquid silver eyes, watching the violet colour deepen as they swirled. His lips were inches from hers. *That is something I cannot tell you my Queen,* he said, kissing her, his fingers sweeping over her cheeks, warming her skin. *But the time is coming when he will have to step away.*

What's that meant to mean? Angel's voice was low, her heart pounding. *You will see,* he replied. *Will things change between us? Will he take a different path ... away from me? Will I hurt him?*

Madoc didn't answer at first. Her breath stopped. One of them was true. *Your bond will change he has no choice in that. Your future will not be as you thought.* He turned away from her. *Why?* Angel asked. Something bad was going to happen, she could feel it. *Your future is different now ... It wasn't meant to be, but something happened to change its course.*

Can it be changed back? Angel didn't want her future to have changed. "Soon you will call on me," he whispered to her. His voice sent shivers down her spine. Change of subject. *How do I call you?* Angel asked, suddenly wondering if she should trust him. Was the bond to him clouding her mind?

There will be someone that will be close to death that you shall heal, out of trust and love. When that time comes, I will join you. He kissed her again. His fingers combed her hair, making her skin tingle. His words worried her. She felt helpless to stop what was coming. *Zared must never know of our conversation. His future is not yet determined.* Madoc's words echoed in her mind as she faded away.

Both Zared and Angel woke together. "Well, that was new," Angel said, bolting upright. "You think," Zared said, sarcastically. "I don't like the way Madoc looks at you and I definitely don't like the way he kissed you," he blurted out.

"I can't control that. It's a vision, one that he controls. I can't stop him feeling the way he does, neither can you," Angel replied, feeling their bond vibrate with his anger, but compared to what she was feeling it was nothing. Angel could feel it – their time was running out.

"Are we there?" Zared asked, his teeth were clenched as he fought back the images of Madoc and Angel's kiss. "Yes sir. Just pulling in," the driver replied. "We'll talk about this later," Zared said, turning to Angel. His eyes were blazing. Angel just nodded. Her head was spinning and the feeling of loss wouldn't leave her.

It was dark when they reached the airport so the worries of how to get on a plane didn't matter so much, but getting off was going to be difficult if they didn't time it right.

Zared made calls to friends in England, giving them the details of the flight he and Angel were booked on and arranging for them to be picked up.

"OK, we land at Heathrow at about eight p.m. We have an eight-hour flight, so sleep if you can. From there we have a driver who'll take us to Paxton. The good news is, by then it will be completely dark. English nights are different to ours, so wear a coat when we leave. You never know what the weather is going to be like," he said, finding seats in the departure lounge as they waited to board.

"Is Madoc going to be a problem between us?" Zared asked suddenly, while he was watching a small TV screen that hung on a white wall. "No! Why would you ask me that?" Angel said, looking at him. His eyes remained fixed on the screen. Her palms were sweating. Zared could smell her nerves. Something was wrong. "Because I know how you felt when he kissed you," he replied acidly, looking over at her to see how she would react. Angel didn't want to discuss it, but she knew she had to and without giving away her conversation with Madoc. "I can't explain it. It's the bond. He can call me when he wants to. Only with him the bond is different somehow," she said, watching Zared carefully, as she tried to explain. "What do you mean?" He returned his attention to the screen. He was jealous that another man had kissed her and she had had a reaction to it. Now he felt cheated that he had to share her with this man who she also had a bond with.

"We have a connection that is separate from you and me. It's strong, really strong, but in the future it links all of us. You and Madoc both have the same mark in the same spot. You are both so alike in your actions, but there is a darkness … something goes wrong. I heard it in his voice … It was as if something has failed." She paused before she continued: "Madoc was the one who kissed me. He did it to stop me from seeing something that has happened, and it was used to wake me up. I was sent there to do what I had to for Isis, and we did that," she said, not knowing what he was thinking as she explained it to him, or if she was explaining it right.

A woman spoke over the intercom telling them their flight was ready to board and asking all passengers to make their way to the gates. Zared got up first, standing still, trying to take in everything she'd told him. Then, he turned to face her. "Next time, try not to kiss him back," Zared said coldly, looking past her before walking away, heading for their gate.

Angel was left trailing along behind him, feeling guilty that she had hurt him, that he was mad at her for Madoc kissing her, and he had every right to be. She hadn't stopped him. Instead, she'd returned the kiss. She knew that in the future things between her and Zared would change. It was coming, whether she liked it or not, and at this moment in time that scared her more than any of Leeda's people. Angel had no idea of what was going to happen to him, but she had to block it from her mind, to try not to worry about it until the time came when her mark appeared – because that's when she knew Madoc would appear and her world would be turned upside down.

Chapter Twenty

Nine hours later, they were getting into a car and heading for Paxton. "What is Paxton?" Angel asked, trying to get him to talk to her, after having spent the entire flight in silence, which had made her feel even worse. She fought back her tears. "It's a safe house for my kind," he said at last. "They know I'm with a human, so you'll be safe," he replied coolly, returning back to silence. His presence in their bond felt cold, sharp, untouchable. She turned back to look out the window.

Paxton was a large building made from mirrored glass, and filled with many rooms. All bookings had to be made by phone, as humans were forbidden to enter unless accompanied by a vampire. The reception desk was like any other, with staff dressed in burgundy uniforms with gold name badges and false smiles. "Hello. Welcome to Paxton. Do you have a reservation?" the women behind the desk asked. Her pale face was smooth. Her red lipstick and brown eyeshadow made her eyes look even bluer than they were. Her long straight glossy brown hair was tied up in a ponytail. "Yes," Zared replied dryly, stepping closer to the desk. Angel stayed at his side, still feeling his icy presence. His coolness was as obvious to everyone else around them.

"What name is it please, sir?" she said, her voice had a musical note to it. She looked Angel up and down, licking her upper lip, making Angel feel like lunch. "Cain Dedrick," Zared said. Angel remained expressionless. "Ah yes, with one human," she said, clicking at a keyboard, looking at her screen. "How will you be paying, sir?" she asked. "Cash," he replied coldly, pulling out his wallet. "Just for one night?" she asked. Zared nodded in agreement. "OK, that will be a hundred and fifty pounds. That includes everything that's in your fridge … and your safety of course," she said with a friendly smile. She took their money, exchanging it for a key that looked like a piece of card.

"Your room is on the second floor. If you go that way," she pointed behind them, "there is a lift. When you get out, there will be signs on the wall showing you where to go, and thank you for staying at Paxton!"

"What time do we have to vacate the room?" Zared asked. "Nine p.m. It will be completely dark by then," she replied with a plastered smile. "Thank you," he said, turning and heading for the lifts.

"Stay close to me," Zared told Angel in a low voice. Angel stayed by his side. In this environment, she noticed Zared looked more like a vampire; his look had changed, becoming more menacing, with strength and power resonating from him. His golden eyes blazed, looking cold, dangerous. He seemed like a stranger as he walked towards the nearest lift.

The doors to the lift slid open. People poured out, chatting among themselves. Angel saw a couple arm in arm. His dark hair was long past his waist. He wore heavy black eye make-up and rich red lipstick. His coat was long and made from leather, his tight black trousers made from what looked like the same material. His chunky boots were open, and his tight black top had holes and safety pins. He looked at her as they passed. His eyes were translucent, almost white. He gave her a chilling smile, licking one of his extended fangs. His eyes flashed with the temptation to taste her. The woman on his arm kept her eyes forward. She looked like she was dreaming, walking without seeing anything; she was dressed in thin shiny fabric that was tight around her body. Her leggings stopped above her heels. Her top only just covered her chest, showing off her tattoos and a ring hanging from her belly. Her hair was different to the man's; it was spiky, shaved at the sides with different colours that looked bright in this environment. Her ears were pierced from top to bottom and her eyebrow had a bolt through it, as did her nose.

"Angel," Zared hissed at her. She tore her eyes away from the couple when Zared grabbed her arm, pulling her in. "Don't look at them."

"Why?" she asked. "Because they're vampires, and if they choose to, they could snap your neck in a second," he snapped in her ear, stabbing at the button for their floor. "OK, I got it," she said coldly, pulling her arm away from him, trying to calm herself down. "No! That's just it … You don't get it. Any one of them could be working for Leeda, and with you staring at them, they're not likely to forget your face, are they?" he snarled. Angel felt darkness coming back. It was starting to grow, making her body feel thick, sticky and unfamiliar.

"Zared. I'm sorry, I didn't think," she said to him through clenched teeth. "No you didn't!" Zared snapped back, following the signs to their room.

Entering the room, Angel was fighting her anger. The darkness inside her was now causing her pain. It felt hot as it stabbed at her organs. She tried to force herself to calm down. Closing her eyes briefly, she thought of the quiet woods that she loved so much, and the gentle breeze ruffling her hair. "Tomorrow we leave. Until then, we have to stay low," he said, switching on the TV set and throwing himself on the bed. "Get some sleep. You're going to need it," he said, his anger was still raw in his voice. "Just try not to dream. I'm too tired to be dragged into your head," he yawned, "And if you do have any more surprises for me, just make sure he's not there." His tone was sharp. He turned away from her; his jealousy still eating at him.

"For your information, it wasn't a dream." She breathed, taking in deep slow breaths. "And it's not something I can control!"

"So I'm likely to see him again?" He tried to stop this emotion but the more he fought it the stronger it became. "More than you realise," she replied absently.

"I'll kill him if he comes near you again," he hissed with anger. "The only way you can kill him, is if you kill me," Angel said, taking a deep breath and rubbing her damp hands down the blue jeans Sarha had given her. "Madoc's the reason you're here, so think yourself lucky."

"What's that suppose to mean?" He bolted upright.

"You figure it out … And it was Madoc who kissed me, so get over it … and it's not like I can control these things, they happen if I like it or not!" Angel snapped.

Zared's eyes had turned deep red with anger. "... And another thing, Madoc *will* come. Soon he'll be by my side, in flesh and blood, living and breathing, and bonded to us both. But if you don't deal with that, and pretty soon, then he'll remove you from my life ... and if you become a danger to me he'll kill you! And that's something I don't want ... and neither do you. So when he does turn up, you're going to have to get over it, one way or another ..." She stormed into the bathroom, slamming the door shut behind her.

The darkness was so strong now that it started to rattle her bones, begging to break free. Angel gripped the sink, her knuckles turning white. The darkness inside her started to become visible. Her aura turned as black as night. A mist swirled around her, spanning the open space of the bathroom.

Angel looked into the mirror. Her eyes had turned pure white. She tightened her jaw, trying hard not to scream. Everything around her that wasn't fixed in place began to rise up. Stepping back from the sink, she felt heat touch her skin before it burst out, hovering in front of her, flickering, crackling, turning different shades of red, orange and blue. *Stop, calm down,* she told herself over and over. Her hands were holding the sides of her head just above her eyebrows. She started to rub in circles, trying to relax the tension that had built there from the day.

"Well, I don't trust him with you. He gives me the creeps," Zared was saying, as he opened the door, his face brooding. "Angel, I don't want him …" He came to a stop when he saw the flames lashing out, licking the mirror, causing it to turn black.

"Angel, calm down," he spoke softly to her, watching as the flames pulsed at the sound of his voice. "Get out!" She gritted her teeth. "And close the door!" Zared didn't argue with her. It was too risky for him to make her any angrier, especially when she had no control over the darkness that had manifested in full sight – and with enemies everywhere, waiting for a sign to lead them to their whereabouts.

Angel focussed on her breathing. The heat was burning so close to her, she was afraid her skin would blister red-raw. She concentrated on the blaze, picturing it cooling with each breath; its heat was slowly smothered as she pictured ice forming, cool pale-blue water absorbing the heat of its flames, turning them solid, while cool translucent colours travelled through the inferno's veins, forming a wall and devouring its fiery centre, trapping the smoke before it could fill her lungs.

Angel opened her eyes to see the burning wall in front of her had died, turned to a wall of ice, just as she had imagined. Angel let her built-up emotions go, screaming out as loud as she could. The wall of ice exploded, pieces shattered to the floor along with exploding soap and tubes of liquid.

Zared rushed in to see if she was OK, stopping in the open doorway. He burst into laughter, stopping her breath; its sound was rich and deep, coming from a place hidden inside him. She was covered in shampoo, conditioner and some hand moisturiser. She looked like someone had come up behind her and played a prank, pouring the concoction over her head like custard.

"Do you feel better now?" he sniggered, trying to hold on to the rest of his laughter. Angel looked at him, her eyes narrowed. "No, I'm covered in gunk!" She hid a smiled when she saw a glimpse of herself in the mirror. "But at least there was less damage this time," she said, lifting her hands up to catch the drips. "That's because you're learning to control it," Zared said, running the shower for her. "Come on, get in. I'll grab you some towels." He smiled, walking away as she peeled off her clothes, dropping them into the sink so they didn't drip everywhere.

Angel came out an hour later, clean with a towel wrapped around her body. She grabbed a black T-shirt that hugged her, stopping just above her waist, and a pair of striped blue shorts to sleep in. Angel returned to the bathroom to put them on, before coming back into the room and sitting on the edge of the bed next to Zared. Angel saw a tray filled with food on the counter. As soon as she saw it, her stomach grumbled. She suddenly felt so hungry. It had been far too long since she had last eaten. "Eat, you need to keep your strength up," he said, watching her eye it up, licking her lower lip, fingers wanting to grab something.

Angel ate what she could, a mix of chips, sandwiches and apple crumble in custard. She saw fruit, wrapped biscuits, and other packets of snacks. She stuffed them in her bag, saving them for later. Zared watched with interest. She knew how to save food, an instinct developed from her father not feeding her much. His neglect had also trained her to survive on as little food as possible.

"Have you eaten?" Angel asked, looking at him, feeling rather full. "I will in a minute. There's something I need to say first," he said, smiling. "OK," Angel said, with caution. "Look, I know Madoc is a part of your life. It's just hard for me to share you with another man, even if he is bonded to the pair of us. I just got really pissed when I saw him touching you."

"I know it can't be easy for you, but there is a lot more to it than just what you saw," she said, not really knowing what she could and couldn't tell him. "What else is there? I know he wants you like I do, I could see it in him," Zared said, studying her. "There are some things I can't tell you, it's forbidden … just in case our paths go their separate ways," she said, combing her hair so she didn't have to think of him. "I have a bad feeling about this. If we get to the witches, they can tell us more about him," he said, turning on his side, propping himself up by his elbow. "OK, when we get to the witches, we'll ask them," Angel said, looking at Zared, knowing he was satisfied with this at least.

The phone rang on the counter next to an old white kettle. "Hello?" Zared said, picking up the receiver. "OK, thank you," he said, putting it down quickly, grabbing the bag and zipping it up.

"Put your shoes on, we have to leave right now," he said with one rush of breath, grabbing his stained brown coat off the chair, and making her put it on as she slid her feet into her caramel trainers pushing them on. "Zared, what's going on?" Angel said, as he grabbed her hand, pulling her out the door, and heading for the stairway opposite a vending machine filled with blood bags of different types.

Angel heard the door close behind them, just as a ping of a bell indicated the lift doors were about to open. "Leeda's people are here. That was the girl from the reception desk. There are vamps covering the front, so we have to go out the back through the staff entrance," he said, taking two steps at a time, reaching the first-floor stairway door. Pulling it open quietly, he stuck his head out, looking in both directions to check it was clear.

Zared grabbed her hand, holding it tightly, and pulled Angel across to another door with a sign reading: staff only. He opened it, staying on high alert as they ran through it, dodging people coming in and out of the kitchens and other areas, and watching for Leeda's people as they ran for the rear exit. "This way." He headed for a door with 'Exit' lit up on a bright green sign, dragging her behind him, pushing the door open.

They landed in an alley that smelled of rotting food and stagnant water. They ran for the exit that led to a main road when someone jumped out at them. Zared released Angel's hand so he could fight but she jumped with surprise; her hands flew up, pushing her pent-up energy out. It hit the attacker causing him to fly through the air, hitting the wall behind him, and knocking him out. Zared grabbed her wrist. His grip sent sparks through her body, making her aware of him, bringing Angel out of the daze of her shock, as they took off down the street.

Six blocks away, they slowed down to a fast walk, checking behind them to see if anyone was following. They barged through people dressed in sparkly tops and short skirts, shirts and trousers, short tops and jeans. They all looked different. They were giggling, shouting and swaying as they chatted to each other, flocking together.

The mix of heavy perfume and aftershave covered their scent, as they swarmed, blocking the path in front of Zared and Angel.

"In here." Zared turned to an old fenced-off building that had been tagged by local gangs over its rust metal sheets. Angel followed him, squeezing through a gap only just big enough. They ran to the far east of the building, where there was what was left of a doorway – the top half of it was still boarded up. The exterior of the building was crumbling in places that had been badly affected by the weather. The windows were black holes.

"Down here. It'll keep us safe for now. I can't smell any trace of humans. It must have been a while since a human has entered this building, so I don't think they'll be coming any time soon," he said, helping her through doorways and over holes that she wasn't able to see with her own eyes.

Zared found a small room at the blackest part of the building. She felt steps beneath her feet, as Zared guided her. They entered a small room that smelled of dust with no signs of a window.

"No one's going to come in here, and we have to get out of the sun," he said, his voice sounding clipped, as he pushed an old dusty wall cabinet over to block the entrance, blocking their scent from leaving the room.

Angel opened the bag after Zared put it in a corner.

She pulled out the packets of food she'd put in there earlier. Then she found combats and pulled them on over her shorts, figuring she would need the extra warmth. Angel also pulled out a jumper, slipping it on after removing Zared's coat.

"There's no blood!" Angel examined the bag. Her hands rummaged, feeling what was inside. Panic tinted her voice, as she sifted through – there were definitely no bags of blood. "I know. I didn't grab any," he said, his voice was low, worried himself about his bloodthirst. "Then, you're going to have to take some of mine," Angel said, putting everything back into the bag and fastening it closed. "No. I'll get some tomorrow," Zared said, coming to sit beside her. "I'll be fine until then."

"But you need some now," she replied, seeing only thick darkness. "It can wait." His voice was demanding her to listen, but their bond was telling her how hungry he was. "No, it can't. You forget I can feel it too," she said, edging closer in the direction of his voice. "Where do you want it from?" she asked.

"Want what?" Zared's voice was distant. "You know what. Now where do you want the blood from?" she sounded irritated with him. "Fine. I can only take a little for now, then I have to go get something when we wake up," he said, making it sound as though he just had to pop to the shop. "That sounds good to me," Angel said, just happy that he had submitted to her. "Give me your arm. It's less intimate," he said, not really wanting them to get up close and personal on a cold dirty floor in an abandoned building. Angel rolled up her sleeve and held out her arm. Zared held her wrist, gripping it with both hands and turning it so her palm was up, showing him her map of blue rivers running just under its surface. He tightened his grip, bringing it to his lips; pausing briefly, not really wanting to hurt her, but knowing right now he had to – to stop the bloodthirst taking over his senses, making him the heartless monster he tried so hard to keep her from seeing.

Sinking his teeth in, rich life exploded into his parched mouth. She felt them pierce her skin, burning as they sank in, feeling strange as he drank. Her free hand rubbed his back out of comfort. Her hormones started to heat up, kicking in a familiar sensation.

Angel trusted Zared as he drank from her, but there was something that was holding her back now, and it was all thanks to Madoc's words. Zared pulled away before their bond could get any stronger and her soul be opened up to him again.

"That's enough for now," he said, watching her wound seal as he spoke. He wiped the remainder of her blood from his lips. "We need to sleep, tomorrow is going to be a long day," he told her, lying down and using the bag as a pillow. "We'll take a car after I've eaten," he said, pulling her into his arms, letting her head rest on his chest.

"How far do you think it is to Jurisa's?" Angel asked, her eyelids getting heavy. "I'm not sure, but we'll get there soon," he replied, as they both drifted off to sleep.

Chapter Twenty-One

Angel woke to feel his brown coat covering her, keeping her warm. Her head rested uncomfortably on their bag. Zared was gone. The cabinet had been removed from the door, leaving her alone and scared in the pitch blackness. The sound of her breathing echoed around her. She could hear the beating of her frightened heart in her ears. Angel sat up and focussed on her breathing, calming herself down. She pushed out her aura to feel for Zared, but he was gone, which meant he wasn't in the building or anywhere near it.

Eat, her body was telling her, so while she waited for him to return, she ate a packet of dry shortbread biscuits and a cereal bar that she'd kept from yesterday. It didn't fill her, but it took the edge off her hunger, which still rumbled. Angel felt coldness grow inside her. The room had trapped it there, making her lonelier. The bare concrete floor assisted her body to shake even more from the missing heat – and the fear of not being able to see what was around her, or if anything was in the room with her, silently hiding in a dark corner.

You can't be scared any more. Your powers are stronger. Everything has changed. You must become fearless to protect your future. Use this power. Concentrate. Call the fire to keep you warm. You're alone now, so practise controlling it. Use this time to your advantage. Chaos's voice spoke to her from the shadows. Angel nodded into the darkness, closed her eyes and pulled the energy that waited inside her.

She felt her energy grow, as she drew it from around her. She imagined heat dancing on the ground in front of her, warming the room, stopping her shaking. Energy twisted inside her, ready to burst out, making her flesh tingle in anticipation. Then she was ready. Angel pushed it out. It burst from her like a balloon popping. Opening her eyes, she saw the flames dancing on the floor in a pyramid shape. She couldn't help but smile at her triumph, as she put her hands out to warm them. She felt the heat on her skin glowing, as her body pulsed with pleasure from the warmth. She sat watching the flames sway, controlling them with her excited mind, and using her hands as a magnet to do her bidding.

She waited for Zared to return, lifting the flames then lowering them. Then, she lifted the fire from the ground altogether, letting it hang in the room before she settled it back down. She had waited for what felt like hours for Zared to return, but she felt happy; she had another power under control.

"You're getting better," a voice spoke from the darkness, making her ears throb at the sound, as her body jumped, making the ball of fire fly across the air towards the voice. Angel saw his face light up in an orange glow. She made a quick movement with both her mind and her hand, closing the latter into a fist so the flames extinguished into black smoke and disappeared into the shadows.

"Zared! You scared the living daylights out of me," Angel gasped as her hand flattened over her fast-beating chest, feeling ribs under the thin layer of skin.

"Sorry." His voice sounded wrong – it was his, but not his, which didn't make sense to her, but something told her to trust her intuition.

"Come on, I've got us a car outside," he said, coming closer, her body aware of how close he was to her now. "Did you eat?" she asked, wondering if the strange feeling was from lack of food, or maybe overindulgence. She didn't know, but her mind was going through the options. "Yes. We have to go now!" He grabbed her left wrist. His hand was cold – another thing that was wrong. Even though Zared was a vampire, his skin was warm against hers, but this vampire, his touch was cold – very cold. *This isn't Zared!* Warning signs went off like an alarm bell, telling her to fight or run. *It's a trick. He looks like Zared, but it's not!*

"Wait, I have to get the bag," Angel said, pulling her wrist away. "Leave it!" he said, grabbing her again, forcing her to move with him.

"Who are you?" It came out as a whisper. She dug her feet down, her heels scraping along concrete, trying to stop him from dragging her out. Only it didn't work, he was a lot stronger than she was. "It's me, who do you think it is?" He sounded cold. Her insides were going crazy with the threat. "No you're not! You're not Zared. You're something else," she said, focussing on his hand, heating it up, burning his grip.

She pictured it getting hotter and hotter, blisters bubbling. "Ouch!" He released her, swinging around on the spot, and hitting her across the face. She could feel the back of his hand scalding her skin and exploding under her left eye; stinging, shooting pain rang around her jaw and inner ear. The contact almost spun her right round, knocking her off balance, and turning her legs to jelly. She reached out to find something to steady herself with.

"You'll pay for that bitch," he hissed. Angel regained her composure. She refused to cry. She could hear him coming closer; she could feel her space being invaded. Backing away, she hit a wall behind her. He'd trapped her. She could almost see him smile in glory over his domination.

"How did you find us?" she asked, feeling coldness seep through her skin; her brain trying to think. "Leeda pays well. And those that back her ... you could say, they are very persuasive." He sounded smug. He was getting closer. "She also has humans that will do anything for her, just in the hope of getting turned. Then whaddya know? One of them found a footprint in one of the rooms above. She had a shifter check it for your scent, and well ... what did we find? You both shacked up. We had to wait of course for Zared to leave before we could make our move ... it would be a bit strange seeing two of him. But I was hoping you would tell, because I just love the scent of fear in the morning," he chuckled near her ear. Angel froze.

"How did you? How can you look like him?" she questioned, her mind still trying to wrap itself around him looking identical to Zared. Angel opened her senses to feel where this vampire was, closing her eyes to picture him as he spoke to her. "A witch. It's what you call a glimmer spell. Thank god it only lasts an hour, his body is repulsive," he snarled, coming closer, smelling the air around her: "I hope Leeda doesn't mind me having a little taste, you smell exquisite." She could almost see him licking his lips with the temptation.

Angel's paralysis broke. *I'm stronger than them,* she told herself, pulling at the energy around her. *They can't hurt me any more.* She felt stronger, more confident. She focussed on him flying through the air, pinning him to the wall, holding him there, far away from her and her teasing scent of blood.

"Where is he?" she demanded, feeling tension growing inside her, ready to explode. At that moment, she knew she was ready to release it. "Don't worry about him. It's being taken care of." He went to grab her. Angel pushed out, feeling the force hit his body as it rushed out of her, knocking her off balance, making her light-headed, almost floating on air.

The impostor hurled through the air, just as she had imagined it. The sound of his voice slammed out with the impact. She could hear him hit something solid, his skull bouncing back, his spine cracking, hands pinned. He raged at her, screaming for his release.

"Fire!" She summoned it to her so easily now, power hovering around her like static electricity, brushing against her skin, letting her know it was by her side. She held her right hand out, palm facing up. She watched as the flames grew brighter and brighter, lighting up the darkness that surrounded them. "Where is he?" she asked, her fear gone. Power filled her aura as she walked towards the pinned struggling body.

"You're too late. He'll be dead soon." He laughed out loudly, as she approached. The pressure from her presence built up against him. He hissed at her, fangs bare, wanting to rip her throat out.

"Answer my question, or this will hurt a lot." She smiled, feeling the power flowing through her, making her more and more confident as she used it. He laughed at her. This didn't go down too well with Angel. She raised her left hand touching his wrist lightly.

"Don't say I didn't warn you." She smiled and pushed her energy out slowly, touching his skin. Angel's hand lit up like lightning, sparks flew off her fingertips. She forced them to give him pain by going into his wrist, flowing up his arm and into his shoulder. He screamed out, saliva drooling from his mouth. She called her power back to her, returning it to the hand it had left, watching as his head dropped forward from exhaustion.

"Where is he?" She was calm as she drank in more energy from around her. He started to laugh again, raising his head. Angel waited for him to speak, but instead of speaking he spat at her then swore. Angel grabbed his wrist; her fingers tightened. "You will speak."

Blue sparks of pulsing lightning snaked over her body, they dived in and out of her skin like fish in water. Vines of electricity curled around her arm, twisting and humming, heading to wherever she commanded. Angel looked into his eyes and smiled cruelly. Sparks hit his skin, wrapping around his arm as if it were a pole in stormy weather. She watched smiling, knowing that she could do this, that she felt no pain, that she was finally fighting back.

His scream pierced her ears. Her electric vines were leaving singe marks on his pale skin. "Tell me where he is, and I'll stop." Angel let go of his wrist, keeping him firmly crucified to the wall, pacing in front of him as he regained some of his strength. Silence.

"Tell me and you won't feel any more pain." Angel ran a finger down his chest, listening to him scream out again as sparks entered his skin, burning, blackening flesh as it followed her finger. His body arched as he tried to pull away from the invisible chains that held him so firmly to the wall. "You think you can torture me, and I will tell you everything? You're going to have to do better than that bitch!" He spat on her again. "That suits me just fine." She grinned, wiping his spit away with her sleeve.

Angel placed a hand on his forehead and closed her eyes. She pulled at his energy. She felt herself drinking as she asked the question: *What would make you talk?*

What is your weakness? She pushed her thoughts into his mind, connecting to it, sifting through it, seeing his darkest thoughts, murderous visions, and thirst so strong that she could taste it. *So this is what it's like for your kind?* she said silently, opening her eyes, smiling, releasing him before she drained his energy completely.

"So that's your weakness." She smiled. "What did you do?" he snapped, snarling, looking at her with dangerous eyes, threatening to rip her apart if she got closer. "The thirst for blood is so strong it drives your kind insane. Just the smell of it makes you crazy. To be so close that you can taste it …" She watched him squirm. He was right, torture would not get her the answer she needed, but a mindless monster would give it up just to get a taste of life.

"It won't work … what you're thinking … I'm an old vampire with more control," he grinned. "Maybe so, but you forget, my blood is different from a normal human's. I'm a rare power … otherwise you wouldn't want me so bad." Angel stepped closer. She was feet away from him. "So … I think we should see how much control you have. After all, if Zared can't fight it, I'm sure you can't."

"I'm three hundred years older than him," he said, watching her return to her bag. "Yes, but you're still a vampire …" She grabbed one of the buckles, opening it up, using its prong to dig into her flesh, dragging it along her arm. Blood dribbled down, dripping off her fingertips, leaving a trail across the floor as she returned. "Let's see if your monster will talk?"

Zared's clone hissed at her. His jaw tightened, trying to fight the smell. Angel stepped closer, fire still burning bright; she had it hovering above her now so her hands were free. "You can't fight it. It's only a matter of time," Angel said, watching him tremble with the effort. "You won't win," he hissed, "You're as good as dead. It's just a matter of time," his voice trembled. Angel laughed, placing her bloody fingers on his lips, watching him lick then, ravenous for more. His eyes turned ruby-red. He shook his head, his eyes returning to the same colour as Zared's.

"Tell me where Zared is." Her voice was soft, cold. "*No.*" He was struggling. "*Yes,*" she whispered, rubbing her hand over her wound. "Tell me." She came closer, placing her bloodstained hand on his neck. Her fingers running up his skin, tracing his jaw line until she saw his eyes had changed completely. Now there was no amount of shaking his head that would save him. The monster inside had come to the surface.

"Tell me." She placed her other bloody hand on his covered chest, rubbing her hand over it, spreading her own blood, intensifying the smell, enticing him to speak. She moved her other hand down his neck. Her blood-smeared finger tracing his artery, travelling over his Adam's apple, her blood covering every inch of his neck and chest. She could hear him panting, his fangs at the ready to enter flesh.

Angel gripped under his chin pushing his head up holding him firmly there, not just with her physical strength, which didn't match his by a long shot. She could feel him tensing. He was slowly surrendering to her.

She moved up close to him, whispering into his ear. "Do you desire my blood?" she asked him, brushing her nose across his cheek, letting him smell her skin, feel how soft she was to touch. "*Yes,*" he replied, his voice raspy, tense, not able to withstand her. He wanted to drain her of the blood that called to him so loudly.

"Do you want to taste me again?" she asked, moving his face to hers, keeping him pinned. "*Yes!*" He looked at her, his eyes hungry, the colour of pure red blazing under golden light. "Feel my skin against your lips? Have my pulse beating against your mouth?" she said seductively, brushing a finger over his lower lip. His mouth opened, fangs just showing.

"Just tell me and I'm yours," she whispered, her body so close to his that he could feel her heart pounding against his chest.

"He's two blocks north from here," he replied eagerly. "Who is with him?" she asked. "Vampires." He tried to move, staring at her neck. "You can't help him. He's dead already." Angel stepped back, releasing only his head, stroking her bloody hand down her neck, teasing his eyes. "How many?" she asked, tilting her head to one side. "Six," he groaned, his eyes transfixed, his chest panting for the taste. "Is there anyone outside?" Her voice remained forcibly soft. "No."

Angel took another step back. "Give me what you offered!" He looked at her with eyes of ice. Angel smiled; she had what she wanted. Looking at the fire that hovered above her, she pushed it at him with her mind and her hand, watching it hit him, bursting like a lava bomb. He screamed, swearing at her treachery. Flames spread in all directions, burning brightly as they engulfed his body. His screams faded as the inferno's roar echoed through the room.

Chapter Twenty-Two

Angel grabbed her bag. Her stomach heaved as she ran for the exit. Adrenaline was pumping through her system. She had to get to Zared before it was too late. She ran as fast as she could, feeling for him through their bond, looking for signs as to what direction to go in. She turned right. It felt stronger. She ran one block, passing side streets. She was getting closer. Her chest heaved as her lungs fought for air. Second block. She wasn't far now. She turned a corner to see Zared covered in blood and on his knees. He was out in the open, under a streetlamp, and only feet away from her.

Angel saw a vampire stood behind him with a thick, heavy, silver chain wrapped around Zared's neck. The vampire pulled it tight, his knee pushing hard into Zared's spine. Zared's fingers wrapped around the chain's large links, trying to pry it loose. His neck was turning red where the links were imprinted, burying into his throat. Another vampire punched him repeatedly, aiming at his face.

"Hey!" Angel shouted, coming to a quick halt, waving her bloody arm breathlessly – droplets hitting the wall, some scattering on the footpath around her. One of the vampires turned to face her. His skin was dark, but paler than it would have been in his human form. His dark eyes were evil, chilling. He smiled dangerously. His fangs were bright under the streetlight.

"*Angel,* run," Zared choked out. "Get her. Leeda wants her dead or alive," the vampire commanded, his deep voice shattered through the night, filling the air with menace. His cold finger pointed at Angel, blood was smeared across his knuckles. Two more vampires stepped out from the shadows of hidden doorways, smiling, ready for the hunt, rubbing their hands in excitement, and laughing like hyenas, rocking from one foot to the other.

"*Run!*" Zared yelled out, loud enough for her to hear before the vampire tightened the chain around his neck. Chilling laughter filled her ears. "Run little girl, run!" one shouted, as it charged for her. Angel turned and ran. She knew she couldn't out run them, but she needed a place where she could see them coming – somewhere she could defend herself during their attack. She ran past closed shops. She could hear them behind her, shouting and making war noises before a kill, howling like crazy animals.

An alley; it's the only place close enough. She suddenly saw one across the street. She turned towards it as she ran, passing empty cars. She hit darkness. She ran deeper and deeper into the alley. Her palms were outstretched in front of her to stop herself. She slammed against a wall, touching cold damp brick with moss creeping over its surface.

Angel turned. She tried to slow down her breathing, leaning against the wall, hoping her legs would stop shaking. Angel was trapped. There was only one way in and one way out, and they where already halfway to reaching her. "Trapped now, little girl." He laughed. Moonlight shone on his face. He was about her age with shaggy brown hair and crazy hazel eyes. He was dressed entirely in black, blending in with the night. "You're a pretty one. Maybe we should take our time with you?" His voice was cruel. He made it obvious to his partner what he meant as he crept closer.

You need to kill them. Use your power to keep yourself safe. It was Madoc's voice this time. *I know that,* she told him, pushing her fear away, summoning everything she could.

"He did say Leeda wanted her dead or alive. I'm sure it doesn't matter what condition she's returned in." His partner smiled, walking slowly towards her. He was dressed the same way. His hair was lighter, with frosty blue eyes. "As long as Leeda gets what she wants."

"I don't think so." Angel smiled, bringing her hands up, putting one in front of the other. She pushed. It burst out of her, hitting them hard and throwing them to the wall; she heard them slide down, clothes scraping against brick.

"The little bitch has picked up some tricks," the first one said, snarling. "It won't save you," he hissed, leaping at her. She closed her eyes, pulling more energy, getting her body ready to release it as he struck. He landed on her knocking her down. She opened her eyes to see his fangs; his mouth inches from her face. She could feel his lips brush her skin. Her hands tucked under his body. Angel smiled and placed a hand on his chest just over his still beating heart. She pushed her pent-up energy, forcing it to explode from her, and slam into him with every ounce of her might. It went through him like lightning, throwing him off her. He landed on concrete.

Angel's eyes widened when she saw his chest. His black top was ripped in half and blackened by the impact. "Shit!" she heard from behind him. His friend backed up, watching in amazement. The lightning had removed his heart, leaving a gaping bloody hole in his back. Thick dark liquid poured from it, draining his carcass. He slumped to his knees, hands grabbing for the hole in his chest as blood flowed freely. He pressed down hard, not realising that the hole in his back was bigger. Blood seeped through the gap. He fell forward on his face, looking almost mummified, before he burst into a flash flame, turning the remainder of him to ash.

Angel scrambled to her feet ready for her second attacker, when she noticed he was gone. She could smell the vampire now, it was the smell of old blood. Blood that was rotten. She had smelled it many times before coming from her own body. She watched as the puddle evaporated, erasing all signs of his existence.

Zared! she thought, running back to where he was. Angel turned the corner to find the scenario had changed. Zared had managed to kill the vampire that had been holding the chain around his neck. Now he was fighting the dark-skinned vampire.

Angel ran towards them, summoning energy to her. Both vampires turned to see her running at them, screaming like a banshee.

Zared watched Angel thundering towards them, her body flashed. He watched as her skin changed. Vines of bright blue light snaked around her, making her physical body flicker as electricity slithered in and out of her flesh.

As she got closer, the current started to pulse, throwing out strands like claws, trying to grab the air, crackling as it touched objects, sending them flying before it dived back into her body.

"What are you?" Zared heard his attacker say, shocked at what he was seeing. Angel screamed as she ran faster. She was getting ready to jump at him when he turned from them and ran, heading in the opposite direction. Angel slowed down, releasing the energy, sending it back to the earth, with a silent thank you for those helping her.

"Are you OK?" Angel asked, exhausted as she stopped next to him, bending over with her hands on her knees, trying to breathe; her lungs were tight, causing sharp pains in her chest. "Yes, and you?" he asked, smiling at her, feeling their bond humming with excitement and joy that they were both still alive. Angel was still gasping, unable to speak, so she stuck a thumb up.

"How the hell did you do that?" he asked, amazed. "I learned to control some of it at last," she panted. "You left me. I got bored," she panted, her breath slowly returning. "So I started practising, concentrating on how it felt inside me, and how to use it." Her breathing was deeper, she was able to stand up straight now. "Plus, it helped that I was freezing my butt off!" Her breathing eased, almost back to normal. She pushed strands of hair behind her right ear.

"How did you find me?" he asked. "I had a visit from someone that looked like you. He tried to get me to go with him. He said he had a car waiting for us, but I knew he wasn't you … he felt wrong. Our bond wasn't there … and then when he grabbed me, he was like ice," she said looking at him. "Another vampire like me?" Zared couldn't believe it. Leeda wanted her that much, but why? It couldn't just be the power she had, there was more to it than that. Maybe whatever she was planning had more to do with Angel herself; whatever it was he needed to find out.

"He said it was a spell. An illusion," Angel said, feeling his shock disappear. "He also told me where to find you."

"He just told you?" Sarcasm was in his voice. "There was a little persuasion involved, but I got there in the end," Angel admitted. "I can see that!" Zared looked at her. His eyebrows arched as his golden eyes travelled up and down, seeing the remainder of dried blood on her neck and her open wound that still leaked blood – unable to heal, Zared guessed, due to the amount of power she had used tonight.

"Where is he now?" Zared asked, wondering how she had gotten away, as the smell of her caught in the breeze. "On the wall," she said, looking at him, his eyes turning the colour of rubies. "Dead!" It wasn't a question, more of an understanding. She nodded. "Yes, he's extra crispy," she replied with a faint grin. "Good!"

Zared looked very pale. His scar was more defined against his eyes, which were getting redder and redder. "Over here," Angel ordered as they left the streetlight to loiter in a shadowy doorway. "I need to close that wound." His voice was hoarse. He turned away from her, ashamed of how he looked, of how hungry he felt. "You can't. You've lost too much blood already," Angel said. "You're going to have to take some of mine until you can get some more."

"No!" Zared shouted. Angel looked around to see if anyone had heard. "I need to heal you. When you're healed, I'll get some blood, but I'm not taking it from you."

"Why not?" she demanded. "Because I need more than just a little, and I'm afraid if I taste your blood then I might not be able to stop." They heard people walking towards them. Angel could see them getting closer. *They can't see us, not yet.* She felt her stomach twisting. She grabbed Zared, pulling him close. Her body brushed against his. Angel couldn't take the chance of anyone seeing Zared as he was right now, so she did the only thing that came to mind: she leaned against the locked door, keeping Zared's back to the streets and the rowdy drunks, and she kissed him hard.

This kiss was different from their first one. It wasn't fast and furious. It was hard, faked, but it wasn't long before it became passionate, gentle and loving. Her fingers glided through his soft hair, tugging it with pleasure. She could feel his hands gripping her waist, holding her tight. His fingers began clawing at her top. He was trying to keep himself under control.

Bright light flashed between them. His mind filled with her presence. She was the colour of greens and golds. Zared heard groans of pleasure whispering in his mind. Angel had lost herself inside him, waiting for him to take her. Zared couldn't fight her any longer. Her skin was like honey to a bee. Her heart sang like a siren. His lips followed her delicate curved line; his tongue licked at the spot, savouring her sweet skin, feeling her heart jump as she held him there, wanting to explore more of their desires. Zared could almost taste what was just hidden out of sight. His hands glided around her, pulling her closer; her body arched under his weight as he leaned forward.

Yes. Her voice was a seductive whisper. Her breath trembled with the need to have him. Zared held her wild hair to one side; his tongue traced the spot slowly one last time.

Angel felt his fangs extending, touching the spot, causing shuddering pressure, heart-stopping agony of a different kind, as she waited for him to enter her again.

Then, she felt the burst of sensual pleasure. He was inside her, tapping her veins. She felt the searing heat flowing from her to him. Her heart pounded with excitement; her fingers tightening in his hair, listening to him groan in her ear.

Zared could feel her body trembling. Her breath filled his lungs, awakening his still heart. She had pulled him so close that he felt every curve. He saw images in his mind of them being together, mating under the light of the moon. This aroused him again, feeling the press-ure against his jeans crushing against her pelvis, as he cupped her leg, lifting it, allowing her slender body to move against him, bringing his erection to its fullness.

Giggles came from behind them. The sound of wom-en's heels coming to a stop. "Hey!" one yelled, giggling with her friend, "Get a room." They both burst into laughter, staggering away, starting to sing out of tune.

Zared stopped suddenly, dropping her leg and pull-ing away slightly. His hunger was still present, but the pain of it had gone. Zared looked up into Angel's eyes. There was a look of frustration in them. "Take some of my blood, so you can heal. When you've done that, we move." *What's wrong?* Angel asked, feeling him pulling away from her body and mind. *I can't do this any more.* He stepped back, looking at the wall behind her, his head bowed, his breathing still heavy. *Do what?*

This ... with you! I can't keep taking your blood, Angel. Every time I do, I want you, and it's getting harder. Zared pushed strands of hair away from her face, tucking them behind her ear. *There will be a time when I won't want to stop ... when I don't want to. If that happens, then I could kill you.*

So what are you saying? That you'll find blood elsewhere from now on? Angel felt hurt. She wanted to be the only one to feel this with him. *That's what I'm saying! Taking blood from others doesn't feel like that. It's only with you. I'm guessing it's the link we share.*

Zared felt her ease, at least she knew he didn't feel the same way with others. *If I take some blood will you be OK?* She needed to know. She could feel weakness inside him and pain in his right arm. *I'll be fine,* he replied, re-opening one of his healing wounds. Angel placed her warm lips over it and drank. She could feel it travelling down her throat, thick sweet liquid, making her hot and dizzy. Angel clung to him for support, feeling his arms take her full weight. Something was happening to their bond; it was growing stronger, brighter, changing again. Angel felt herself being engulfed by it. She could see Zared standing in front of her, only this was different. She watched her body from the outside, drinking his blood and Zared too stood, watching his own body holding on to Angel. He was in his astral form, just like her.

What just happened? He was puzzled, studying their bodies, and how they reacted to each other. *Well, you have just left your body for a bit, like I did when I met you the first day.* She was smiling, moving to touch him. *How?*

It must be from you drinking my blood. It has given you some of my power. Angel touched him. She was surprised, it was like touching his solid form. *Will it last long?*

I have no idea. But this is great! I can still touch you in this form and if you practise it long enough, you can go anywhere.

It's not right. A vampire is not meant to do this. Zared was uncomfortable with the idea of leaving his body. *Well, a vampire is not meant to be bonded to a human, but guess what? ... you're not exactly a normal vampire,* she stated. *True, but you're not exactly a normal human either. Now, how do I get back to my body?* he demanded. *You concentrate on it. See yourself returning to it. You'll feel it pulling at you, so just go with it.* Zared closed his eyes, focussing on returning, then he felt the pull. It was like falling from a great height. Angel had already returned and was waiting, watching him coming back, whispering in his ear calm, soothing words as he returned. "How do you feel?" she smiled. "Off," was all he could say. "How's your cut?" he continued, gathering himself together. "Healed!"

"Good." He still felt strange, but at least his facial wounds were healing steadily, the red marks almost faded. "We have to go. One of them escaped, which means he's gone back to Leeda, telling her everything, which puts her in the knowledge of your power … and by what we've just seen, she will try to bind it, using the power of her coven." He looked around, seeing silhouettes in the distance.

"Actually, two. One got away earlier," she corrected. Zared swore, then took her hand and started to walk towards a black ford.

As they walked, Angel noticed his black T-shirt had been ripped. The blood stains were still wet from the attack. The bruises on his arms had slowly begun to disappear, as the cuts to his flesh started to close, healing themselves. He was still cradling his right arm, hugging it close to his body. Angel could see flesh missing below his elbow, looking jagged and raw. His upper arm muscle looked almost twisted, ripped away from the bone. "You lost a lot of blood. We have to get you more." Angel was just as hungry. It was his hunger that gripped her, telling her to eat so much so that it was suffocating her lungs. She fought against its painful cramps.

Crowds gathered around a small doorway. "Stay here," Angel ordered, as she watched them enter. "Where a you going?" he said, reaching for her wrist. "To get you blood." She looked at him, pulling her arm from his weak grip, a sign that he needed to feed soon. "Now stay here," she said, walking towards girls her age and older.

Standing close to them, she watched the way they moved, the way they flirted, wearing short skirts, tight tops and heels. Nothing that she was wearing. She listened to what they said to the person guarding the door, how the girls giggled. Some even ran their fingers down his jacket. This is how she needed to be to get in. Angel removed her torn stained jumper, jumping when Zared appeared at her side, taking it from her.

What are you doing? he asked in silence. *What does it look like?* She was pleased that her black top looked tight and was still in one piece. Angel used her slim figure to her advantage, pulling the top up half way, and tucking it under so that it hugged her above her flat stomach, showing off her cream skin – that looked untouched after the night's events. She pushed her combats down so they rested low on her hips. She tipped her head upside down, fluffing her hair up with her fingers, and straightening up fast, letting her head fly back, allowing her golden curls to bounce past her shoulders. She looked into a car's wing mirror to see her face. It was stained. She turned to Zared who looked very pale, his face was strained. He ripped a piece of cloth off his T-shirt and used it to take as much dirt off her face and neck as she could. She turned round to face him. "How do I look?" Zared didn't say anything. He just stared at her, fascinated by how different she looked. "Will I get in?" she asked him. "Yes," was all he replied. "But your arm looks a mess."

"I'll have to hide it until I get in, and then wash it in the toilets," she replied. "I'll stay close, just in case something goes wrong, then I'll wait for you across the road," he said. Angel nodded. "Just be careful, OK?" He pulled her close. His lips touched hers, brushing together over and over, turning into something deeper as he held her tight. *I'll be back soon. Don't worry. If anything happens, I'll call you.* She pulled away, smiling. She ran a hand over his hair, then she walked away. *Don't be too long, or I'm coming in. I don't like the fact you're out of sight ... my sight, not while Leeda's people are around.*

I wont be long. I promise.

She smiled as she reached the doorman, talking to him, acting like the girls she had watched. The doorman smiled, speaking to her briefly before stepping aside. Angel sent loving thoughts to Zared through their bond, feeling it pulse as he received it. Zared watched as she disappeared out of sight. Crossing the street, he leaned up against a wall and waited.

Ten minutes had passed and Zared was getting antsy. *I have two eyeing me up. What do you want a thi one, or a tall big one?* her voice asked him, making Zared jump, after their period of silence. *One with lots of blood!* he returned, feeling hungry just at the thought. *Big one it is,* she said, the sound of a smile in her tone. *I'll get him when we leave. I'll call you!*

Don't be long, he warned her, anxiously, thinking that this was a bad plan. Or maybe it was him being over-protective, either way he didn't like it. He couldn't defend her from this far away. Thirty minutes had passed since she'd entered the building. *We're coming out,* she told him.

Zared watched the door anxiously, waiting for her to come out, pacing in the shadows. Angel walked with a large man looming over her. He had long slick dark hair tied back, and stubble on his round face. He was about Zared's height, six-foot-odd, and dressed as an overweight biker. His large hand wrapped around her waist. They walked towards him. Zared watched with anger building as this stranger touched her in a wanting way, his gut spilling over his dark jeans as he pulled her closer.

Is he good enough for a big meal? she asked, while giggling at the man's words every now and then. They walked past Zared. Angel glanced over at Zared quickly. *Oh, he's perfect! But if he keeps touching you like that, ‌en I'm going to take my sweet time with him,* Zared snarled, following them. The excitement of the hunt was building inside of him. *You can take as long as you wish. As long as you feed and heal fast,* she replied. *It will have to be soon though, he's making me feel sick.*

"I can't wait till we get to your place," Angel spoke to the man softly, smiling up at him. "Is it far?" *Get him to the ally, it's coming up soon,* Zared said quickly from across the road, eager to strike now. "It's another block away," the man replied, his fingers running up and down her back. "You know, John. I can't wait that long. I have no patience. When I want something, it has to be now." She smiled, coming to a stop as she spoke, and moving in front of him to make it clear as to what she meant.

She ran her fingers down his leather waistcoat coaxingly. *Don't over do it, will you,* Zared's voice echoed acidly in her head. *I'm getting him to change his mind. Don't worry, I know what I'm doing.* She was still smiling at the stranger. *That's what I'm afraid of!* Zared couldn't help but smile despite his jealousy. Angel was learning fast about human nature and how to get things done, manipulating the mind to what she wanted. Even after all those years of terror, there was still courage inside her.

"How about we take a detour?" the stranger offered, pulling her closer to him. "You read my mind," Angel giggled, batting her eyes at him. They continued to wal'

The dark alleyway came into sight. "This looks good to me," he said, as they reached it. Angel fought back her fear. She knew Zared was close and he would keep her safe, but there was still a chance that he wouldn't get there in time. "Perfect," Angel smiled, letting him pull her into the shadows. *He's ready for you,* she told him, as he crossed the road, sneaking towards them.

Big John pushed her against the wall, hovering over her, placing a large meaty paw on her breast, and groping at her with a force that caused only pain. "Now, John," she made her voice sound calm, and as sexy as she could, as she forced him to spin around so he was the one with his back against the wall. "What's the rush? No one can see us," she said, running a finger over his lips. He pulled her to him. Her body pressed against his. He made a movement with his hip, thrusting it against her. She could feel something hard on her leg. Angel stopped herself from cringing.

Zared, move your backside and get here right now! she screamed at him silently. "Oh yes baby! Show big daddy what you got," he smiled, reaching down, trying to undo her button. Fear gripped her, she was losing her calm.

I'm here get back from him. Zared's voice spoke to her with anger, giving her the strength she needed. *I would, t he's a little stronger than me,* she replied with sarcasm. "John," she pushed on his chest, "there's something else I want to do first," she smiled seductively at him. He let her go eagerly. "Oh yes?" he said with excitement, unfastening his trousers, ready to pull them down. "Take it in deep baby, all the way, just how I like it," he continued. This comment puzzled Angel, but at the same time made her feel sick. "I want you to meet Zared."

Angel smiled with relief as he appeared from the shadows, fangs extended, eyes red as blood, snarling and hissing as his nature took over, feeling anger against this stranger for touching his mate, from being attacked by so many, not being able to fight them all off, not being able to protect her when she needed him, and bloodlust, a thirst so overpowering that he was in his most dangerous state.

John's skin smelled of Old Spice, stale tobacco, and the strong stench of bitter ale. Zared drank. Gulping. Knowing that Angel was watching the streets in case someone saw them. The blood tasted metallic, plain like everyone else's, except for Angel's, which always aroused him. But this was just hunger, filling him up, satisfying a day of starvation. The breathing became fainter, as the heart slowed; this stranger that she had brought for him was dying. Zared released him on the verge of death, satisfied for now. He dropped the dead weight, which collapsed behind a pile of boxes. Zared wiped his mouth clean.

Are you OK? he asked, returning to her. *Yes, but that man freaked the hell out of me, and what did he mean by taking it in deep all the way?* she asked, not sure she really wanted to know. Zared laughed out loud. *Maybe one day you'll find out, but for now we have to go before some one comes past and sees us here.* His silent voice still had traces of laughter.

Chapter Twenty-Three

Four hours later, they finally reached Scunthorpe. They drove past the McDonalds and Burger King, and carried straight on, until they reached a set of traffic lights. Turning left, then right at the next set, Zared passed a takeaway. He pulled up and dashed inside, grabbing a bag of chips for Angel.

He kept driving, passing buildings, all with life, until he smelled one that had no trace of human activity. "The sun will rise soon." He looked at the sky, it was showing signs of sunrise as pinks and purples laced the clouds. He parked the car outside a pub opposite the empty building. Zared could feel the air around him heating up.

"We'll have to stay there for now." He pointed to a building that had a clock. It looked like a small chur from a distance, only the church was a few block from it. Zared broke a window at the back of the building, helping Angel through it.

They noticed then that it wasn't a church but an old library. Abandoned bookcases lined the walls, with a dusty counter that faced the locked doors. They saw steps behind the counter that led to the next floor. They both climbed over the counter and wandered up the stairs, curious to see where they went. They were mindful to be quiet as they checked the rooms upstairs. Some had been used for storage, with smaller rooms for the staff. "This will do for now," Zared said, leading Angel to the larger room and getting ready to settle in for the day.

Angel woke to hear Zared on the phone, only catching the end of his conversation. "Who was that?" she asked, sitting up, rubbing sleep from her eyes, and stretching away stiffness. "Jason. He told me about this club and how to get there. He said that if we head there, someone will know where Normanby is," he replied, putting his phone back in his pocket. "Can we trust him?" she asked. "It's just that we've had a lot of people after us so far, and I'm kind of hoping that no one will find us yet."

"I know, but we have to go there. We need information on how to find Jurisa," he said, helping her to her feet. "When we go, stay alert. It's not exactly a human club," told her, pushing a strand of hair behind her ear. "It ldn't matter if it was a human club or not, this will be the first time I've been to a club." She smiled, feeling her skin smothered in dirt that made her itch. "Come on. Let's get it over with," he said, holding her hand, keeping her close as they exited the building and returned to their parked car.

They headed back to the main road, turning left towards a supermarket. They passed closed shops and a large building with 'LINK' lit up in big letters across its steel exterior. Turning right they headed for the town centre.

"We're here," Zared said, getting out of the car, followed by Angel. "That's where we need to go." He pointed; Angel followed his finger to a building that looked like a museum. "The entrance is round the back." He didn't move from his spot next to the driver's side door.

"But first, I think we should clean up. We'll go in there. It's a public toilet, but at least it has hot water you can use." Zared walked round the car and took Angel's hand. "When you've finished, meet me here. And don't move until I come out." He stopped in front of a building that had a parking area with different levels. Angel could see the dark stairs leading up to each floor, causing shivers to go down her spine. It wasn't a place to venture alone in the dark; there was an eerie presence to it. "OK." Her voice sounded weak. She looked at the two doors tucked away in a corner, both had pictures on them, on representing a man; one a woman.

It was cleaner than she'd expected. The toilets didn't look dirty, the sinks weren't blocked, and the soap dispensers were in one piece. Angel looked in the mirror and saw how shocking she looked. Taking a handful of soap, she washed her face, neck and arms, drying off using tissue that was still in a cubicle. She ran her fingers through her hair like a comb, pulling knots loose, making it look half-decent. Then she used the facilities provided, washing her hands before leaving.

Zared was already waiting for her, leaning against the wall, hands in pocket. "You ready?" he asked, as she wiped the last of the dampness from her hands down her trousers. "Ready." She felt her fried nerves making her edgy. She wasn't sure what to expect and who would be there, or who might attack them this time.

Round the back of the building was a grey fence with a guard by it. "Good evening sir," he said, sniffing the air around them. "Leech right?" he said, moving on to Angel, trying to smell her but only detecting a mixture of dirt, cheap soap and vampire, which made it hard for him to tell what she was. "Yes. A friend told us we had to check this place out," Zared said coolly, one hand shoved in his pocket; the other holding hers. "Who's your friend?" he asked, eyeing Angel, still trying to smell out what kind she was. "No names. He comes here regularly." Zared managed a half-grin, pulling Angel close. "OK, you can go in. But she …" He didn't finish. "Is safe with me," Zared said quickly, smiling, his fangs showing pure white and dangerous. "OK. But if anything happens to her in there, then it's on you," the guard pointed out, opening the gate and letting them both through.

Angel said nothing as they passed, keeping her eyes turned from him, but she could smell the musky scent of wet fur coming off his skin, reminding her of the beasts Isis had fought.

"Say, you don't know if Jurisa Sand is here?" Zared asked. "No why?" the guard asked. "Nothing, it's just someone said she comes to this club a lot." Zared smiled wickedly. "See the bartender. He might know if she's in tonight; he knows everyone that comes here," the guard said, locking the gate behind them. "Thanks," Zared replied, walking away, holding Angel's hand tightly, keeping her behind him.

Entering the building, Angel got a shock. She'd never seen anything like it. It was dark with walls covered in painted art that glowed under fluorescent lights. There were people everywhere, all dressed differently. She watched as a woman walked by them, holding a chain that was clipped to a collar that went round another woman's neck. Both were wearing Lycra and knee-high boots, and had lots of tattoos, earrings and studs. The woman wearing the collar wore a mask, which covered her whole face, except for small slits over her eyes.

A strange-looking band played in a sealed cage made from chains, which was centred in front of the far wall. She couldn't help herself from staring as they played the loud music like nothing that she had heard before, and threw their heads back and forth, their long hair thrashing around them as they jumped to their heavy beat. The gathered crowd facing them jumped along, arms raised up, screaming with a few singing along to the songs.

Heading towards the bar, Zared and Angel passed part of the dance floor where poles were scattered in various places. Women and men danced, using the cold steel in their moves. Angel had to avert her eyes from some scenes, as the dancers gained a small crowd of hypnotised onlookers.

The walls that surrounded the room had a medieval feel to them, with heavy chains that hung from large steel hoops and had thick cuffs on the end of them. Some were in use. She passed one man in his early thirties, handcuffed, with his hands hanging just above his head. His long blonde hair was brushed to one side, as his female partner sank her teeth into his neck. Blood dripped down his tanned skin. Another woman licked traces of blood from his bare muscled body. The man was clearly enjoying every moment as he moaned out loud, pulling at his chains, begging them for more.

Zared continued towards the bar, still holding Angel's hand, and guiding her past the strangers. Angel found herself wondering how it would feel to be restricted in that way, allowing Zared to do as he wished to her. Angel felt a sudden ping in her chest wishing that he would. The thought brought a grin to her lips as she bit one corner of her lower lip, holding onto her smile as Zared turned to look at her, a smile on his face. Angel wondered if he had read her mind, or if she had sent her desire to him through their bond.

Quickly their path changed towards the dance floor. Zared had seen someone that batted for both sides, and right now he didn't know which side he was playing for. The only solution he could see was to take her out of view and become lost in the sea of dancers.

Angel watched as a couple swayed in front of them. She could feel the beat moving through her, pulling at her, urging her to go with it, to let it flow through her limbs and bring them to life. She watched the couple while Zared scanned faces. Angel began copying their moves, swaying to the music until her own rhythm took over. Zared took her in his arms, swaying in time with her. Their bodies brushed against each other, their legs slightly parted; they moved like the others around them, which made her feel sexy as his hands glided over her.

His hands rested on her hips as she moved his leg in between hers, as hers was with him.

Angel closed her eyes as they lowered their bodies, grinding up to each other. She moved the way her body told her to. Zared watched her eyes close. He could feel their bond. He moved, swaying to the music along with Angel. In that moment they forgot everything that was happening to them. Her shoulders rolling, her hands slowly rising, she slid her fingers into her hair, pulling it back and exposing her neck. Her head tilted to one side. His hands glided smoothly up her arched back, reaching her shoulders, pulling her closer and letting her tip back; his hands wrapping around her, as her chest crushed against him. He leaned forward, kissing her bare collarbone and slowly moving up to her lips. Her arms wrapped around his back and gripped his top, pulling it tight across his skin. His lips reached hers; light exploded. He could see her thoughts in his head pleading for more, enjoying their night, not wanting it to end just yet.

The music filled her, numbing her troubles, filling her with the joy of just hearing it. Angel could feel Zared's lips gliding down her neck. She felt his sharp fangs brush against her skin teasingly, as he tipped her back, grabbing her hair and tugging it lightly, making their movements feel erotic as he brought her back up. Spinning in his arms, she pressed her back to him, one hand entwined in his hair; the other gripping his firm buttock. Feeling his warm lips kissing her neck, she moved, twisting slowly down, almost sitting on his lap, grinding together.

Angel imagined him chaining her to the wall in their own private room. Doing to her what the women were doing to the stranger. Tasting her, dominating her, seeing her clothes ripped from her body by his strong sculptured hands as they roamed her body tenderly, playfully wanting her to suffer, to long for more as her body burned, sparking at his touch, until he gave her divine pleasure.

Angel stop! I won't be able to control myself if you keep thinking like this. His voice raged in her head. He gripped her waist, pulling her closer. His warm breath was heavy in her ear; she was melting in his arms. She felt hardness against her pulsing wet body. He turned her to face him.

She opened her eyes to see his blood-red eyes looking at her with a burning hunger. Gripping one wrist with such speed, he spun it behind her back, pulling her close. Her heart jumped into her throat at the feeling of his skin on her. An image flashed in her mind of his cool perfect naked body with his washboard stomach, soft smooth skin touching her, brushing against each other slowly, knowing each other's rhythm, their breaths entwining, heat rising, savouring every moment, every touch, every feeling, every spot that gave them ecstasy.

Angel's heart pounded. She felt the lust intensify as he held her. His jaw clenched as her fantasy overcame him, willing him to obey. He was fighting against himself to take her, to lead her to a private room that was rented hourly, and devour her completely. He leaned in, breathing quickly on her neck, feeling her tremble, his face buried by her hair, hidden from view. Her breathing deepened as she gripped his hair with her free hand; her cells alive and praying he would take her.

Yes, her voice whispered in his head as she tilted her head back further, tugging him closer, teasing him. His fangs scraped her lower neckline, making her groan with excitement. He entered. The warm sweet taste of her filled his mouth as he swallowed, letting her enter his soul.

Light crackled. Their bond was merging them together once again. He felt her desire for him, her longing for him to go further, to join them as one, to give her everything. He wanted it too, now more than ever. Releasing her trapped wrist, he placed it around her waist, moving slowly. She imagined him taking her over to the dungeon's walls and locking her in its thick chains, forgetting every person that was around them, seeing them all slowly disappearing.

Stop. We have to stop, it's not safe. He spoke to her silently, still tasting her. His hands studied her shape as they moved over her body, caressing her breasts. She hoped her images would entice them to roam further. *Sorry ... I'm trying. You're so close ... it's hard, I want you more and more,* she replied, her fingers gripping his clothes, pulling him as close as she could, ready to remove them as her hormone levels reached a new high, making her feel strange, dreamlike, a feeling she fought her own body against.

Why do I feel so intense? I don't understand. I want more, it makes me ache, she said, feeling his lips brushing against hers, over and over, filled with a passion that told her he felt it too. *I want to remove everything,* she hissed, stopping the impulse to rip his clothes off. *It's because you belong to me and your body knows it, and fighting it just makes your body want me more ... just like I want you,* he replied, pulling his fingers away, tugging at her golden curls, her emerald eyes burning for his touch. *I want you now.* She smiled. Her eyes looked at him with raw passion, lust of the night. *I want you before it's too late.*

And I want you, but for now we have to wait, when we are safe, then we can go further. He smiled back at her, kissing her, taking her hand, leading her off the dance floor; returning to the task in hand.

Tables blocked a clear path to the bartender. They passed one mixed with vampires, shifters and a couple of witches. One woman had the group's full attention. She had drinking glasses in front of her containing a clear liquid. "I bet you I can do it like she did," the witch said to her guests. "I'll take that bet," one of the men said, placing money on the tabletop. The three clear drinks belonged to the vampires; Angel could see their fangs as they watched eagerly. The witch was older than Angel, in her late twenties or early thirties, with short dark hair, brown eyes, and dark tanned skin. She spoke in a light teasing tone to them, as she leaned forward, blowing over the three misshapen glasses, turning them dark, almost black.

One of the vampires took a glass. Taking a small sip, he smiled and clapped lightly, daring others to take a taste. "Turn mine into a bulldog twist!" her other guest said eagerly. He was one of two shifters; she could tell by their eyes, they reflected just like Barret's. Angel and Zared continued to the bar, just seeing her turn the liquid electric-blue with mist frothing over the glass. Her friends cheered and slapped the vamp on the back.

Reaching the bar, Zared asked the bartender about Jurisa. The bartender said nothing; that he didn't know who Zared was talking about. Angel heard Zared mention the word 'Normanby' during a gap in the pounding music. She watched as the bartender shook his head, saying something unheard by Angel. Zared replied with 'a thanks' and stood up. He turned to Angel, shaking his head.

Disappointment filled her. What were they going to do now? Angel grabbed the chain from around her neck and started to play with the coin between her fingers. "So, what do we do now?" She was at a loss. They had gotten this far for nothing. No one could tell them where this place was, and they couldn't stay up to ask a human. "I don't know yet," was all he could give her. "I need a drink," she shouted over more loud heavy music. Zared just nodded. "I'll get you a soft drink," Zared said, needing them both sober and alert, just in case. Angel leaned on the bar as Zared called the bartender over.

"One coke and one bottled blood," Zared yelled into his ear. The bartender nodded then froze. "Where did you get that?" he demanded, looking at Angel. "A friend of ours gave it to me," she replied. "What's your friend's name?" he asked, reaching for the chain that she had left hanging. "Sarha Wand," Zared replied, as the bartender turned the chain over in his hand. "This is a powerful amulet. It protects those that wear it from any visions or spell casting. It's only given to those that are of great importance," he said, looking up into Angel's green eyes, searching for something he should know.

"Who's after you?"

"Why do you ask?" Zared stepped closer to Angel.

"Well if it's one of Leeda's people, then we don't have much time, she'll be here soon," he replied, looking around. "How do you know that?" Angel was curious to know. "Because her witches are here … there in the back room." He pointed to a dark mirrored glass wall. Zared swore under his breath. "Meet me outside. I'll be there in five minutes," he told them, removing the towel from his waistband.

Zared took Angel's hand and led her back towards the exit. "Keep alert. If it's true that Leeda's people are here, then there'll be more coming soon." They were nearly out the door, when it hit her again: it was a feeling of time running out. She had forgotten that it was there, but now it was shouting at her, and she didn't know if it was because of what the bartender had said, or if it was just tucked away somewhere at the back of her mind waiting for the opportunity to rear up again – but it was for certain a change was coming.

"Can we trust him?" Angel asked, wondering if they were walking into a trap. "No. But we have to take a chance. We're running out of options and Leeda is getting closer to finding us." They stood outside the gates of the club, waiting, looking around and getting more on edge the longer they waited.

"Where's your car?" the bartender asked. He was young, college-age, with spiky multicoloured hair and dark eyes. He had dark stubble, a sign of him growing a beard. In the relative light after the darkness of the club, Angel could see he had changed his clothes, and was now wearing a dark – 'no fear' – T-shirt and black jeans that hung round his hips and had lots of pockets. A few chains hung down his legs. She saw tattoos on his arms of faces and shapes that were black and grey. He also had a hoop in his eyebrow.

"Over there." Zared pointed. "Good. You drive, I'll point the way." All three walked to the car, both males looking around on high alert, while Angel walked in the middle, pushed along by Zared's hand on her lower back.

Chapter Twenty-Four

They reached Normanby and parked in front of an old building that used to hold wild animals. Zared had followed the bartender's instructions, all the while looking in the rear-view mirror to see if anyone was following.

"This way," the bartender said, climbing out of the car. He walked quickly down a stony white path. Zared and Angel followed, keeping a few steps behind. They walked past more buildings, which looked like stables. Angel looked up to see if she could see any animals, but there was nothing, just empty buildings with open doors.

Angel noticed something odd; they faced in all directions some looking straight at them. Angel tugged at Zared and pointed up at the strange-looking objects that stood out from their surroundings. "Security cameras," Zared whispered, looking into one.

The bartender took them further away from the buildings, past a park and a large pond. Angel was looking around, trying to memorise the surroundings, and focus on where they were heading, but all she could concentrate on were the cameras. They were everywhere she looked: on walls, signposts, even on sculptures of art.

"How far is it?" Angel asked. Something was wrong. "Not far. See that building behind the gate?" He pointed. "Yes."

Angel started to feel strange; she felt like she had just lost, like something was coming, only she didn't know what it was. "That's where we need to go," he replied. Angel started to slow down; the feeling was too strong to ignore.

"Angel, what's wrong?" Zared asked, turning to look at her. She looked very pale and was staring off into the distance. She felt millions of eyes on them. "What's up?" the lad asked, coming back to meet them. Angel's stomach twisted. She could hear a voice calling to her. She had this intense desire to turn around, to look into the trees. "I don't know," Zared replied, studying Angel's face, probing at their bond. She was worried. Something bad was going to happen and she was projecting the warning to him.

Angel had the sense that time had just run out. She forced herself to turn around slowly, looking in the same direction they had come from. "Angel?" Zared looked up too, scanning the vast tree lines.

"Run," Angel whispered, fear overwhelmed her, twisting inside of her, forming a tight knot, making her feel sick. "*Run!*" she said louder, as the fear grew stronger, telling her to go, to go as fast as she could. "*RUN!*" she yelled at them, turning on her heels. She ran. She ran as quickly as she could, her lungs burning in her chest. Zared and their companion ran beside her. They were only feet away from the gate. The bartender was screaming at its guard to open up.

A large strong hand with an iron grip wrapped round the top of Angel's left arm, swinging her around straight into Zared's arms. He cocooned her against his chest, feeling her heart pounding against him, her breathing fast as she fought against the panic that hammered through their bond. She'd felt something whistle past her ear and brush through her untamed hair.

Zared had saved her again, removing her from the path of another deadly arrow that was travelling at high speed, determined to pierce through anything it could. A sound of gasped air rushed out in front of her, making her jump. Then, she heard a thump right next to her; the crack of bone on hard surface played loudly in her ears.

Angel unravelled herself from Zared's arms to see that the arrow had just missed her and hit a new target: the bartender who had been helping them. Angel just stared at him, feeling numb with shock.

The arrow that was lodged in his back, buried in deep, had been meant for her. Blood was oozing out, covering the ground beneath them. This time the arrow had been intended to be lethal. It had ripped right through him. Sadness filled her. She didn't even know his name. She wondered if it was better that way. The young, college-aged, male with spiky multicoloured hair now lay still on the cold surface. His dark eyes wide open, with no one to tell his family what had happened to him.

"*Run!* Just keep running!" Zared pushed her forward, leaving behind their fallen friend.

They had only gotten a few feet away when the gate opened, and bodies burst out. They ran at her in a crazed mob. Angel fell to the ground and curled up into a small ball. She could hear them passing over her and around her; loud war cries echoed through the charged air.

Angel looked up when they had all passed. Her heart pounded in her chest and her body was shaking violently. She watched wide-eyed as shapes ran from everywhere. She heard the clash as both sides hit each other with such force that sounds of cold metal crackled.

Zared! Angel scanned the strange faces when she realised he wasn't at her side. He had held back, watching her run for the gate, while he stayed to fight, to make sure she had gotten there safely – prepared to give up his own life for hers.

Standing to her feet Angel turned to watch both sides battle, hypnotised by bodies shifting from human to animal, screaming out in hatred, and the defenders attacking their intruders in mid change. Angel had never seen so many animals in one place at one time. All different, all large, and all beautiful in their own right.

A gentle hand grabbed Angel's shoulder, making her jump. Squealing out in surprise, she turned slowly, not knowing if she should run, or use what she had learned of her powers along the way. "Sarha!" Angel breathed a sigh of relief, and pulled Sarha into her arms, hugging her hard, extremely glad to see that she had survived the attack in Boston.

Sarha Wand's glittering brown eyes looked into Angel's. Angel took in the familiar brightly-inked patterns on Sarha's creamy skin. Sarha was unique to Angel. She had never seen anyone like her before. She had been her healer, a kindred spirit, her saviour after the ordeal at Callie's house. Sarha had returned to the safety of Jurisa's coven. She had saved Angel less than a week ago after her father's arrow had pierced her lung and nicked her heart. Angel owed her life to this woman; a debt that she could never pay. She remembered the last time she had seen her, in the alley, being attacked by the half-blood wolf. "You're alive!" Angel cheered throwing her arms around Sarha again.

"It's good to see you too, but you have to come with me now. You're not safe out here." Sarha took Angel's hand and guided her through the gates. "I can't. Not without Zared." Angel pulled Sarha to a stop. Her eyes began to search the crowds. Bodies had fallen to the ground, bloody. She couldn't see any of their faces, only blood, which painted everything it touched. Angel took a deep breath, closed her eyes briefly, and focussed on their bond. Relief slammed into her, hitting her like a brick wall. He was alive and enjoying the battle. It gave Angel an odd sense of comfort to know he was close, feeling his happiness within the heat of war.

A young boy with mousy hair ran past them, almost forcing Angel aside. He was no older than sixteen, average height, skinny, and wearing blue jeans and a white T-shirt. He ran at a stranger. The stranger's broad back was facing them, but Angel knew this stranger was a vampire. Angel had learned over the past week that shifters' auras pulsed, as did wolves', and that with witches and humans it was just one solid energy – right up until a witch used magic. Vampires had no aura at all; just pure black energy, which she guessed is why she had dark energy, being linked to a vampire through an invisible bond.

"Simon, no!" Sarha shouted after him, releasing Angel and running in the same direction as the boy, trying to catch his top. "*Simon!* Get back here!"

Angel followed her, as she raced after the young boy.

The stranger turned on them, his eyes red as rubies, yellowed fangs bared. He hissed as he crouched ready to lunge at them.

"Simon." Sarha grabbed the boy's T-shirt from behind, pulling at it, trying to get him to stop. The vampire moved with incredible speed and placed a strong hand around the young boy's throat, squeezing the windpipe slowly. His stone gaze watched with pleasure as the boy choked. A bitter smile touched the vampire's cold lips. Sarha was screaming at the vampire, hitting his chest as hard as she could with her fists, kicking him over and over again, trying to get a reflex reaction so he would drop the boy.

He's going to kill them! Angel panicked. She frantically looked around for something that could help her. She spotted a sharp-looking stone, and swooped down to grab it. "Hey!" Angel dragged the sharpest point along her palm, digging it in as deep as she could. She heard her own breath whistle as she sucked it in quickly – knowing now instinctively how to get a vampire's attention.

The vampire pushed Sarha away, drawing Simon closer to him. His lips were peeled back, ready to quench his thrust.

"*HEY!*" Angel yelled at him as loudly as she could, causing her throat to sting, and making her cough and wheeze. She stretched out her hand so he could see the long gash in her palm. She rolled her fingers into a tight fist, squeezing them as hard as she could and making blood pour from the wound that she'd created. The blood dripped from the crease her little finger made. It was working; she'd gotten his full attention. Only now Angel didn't have a clue what she was going to do next; it hadn't occurred to her to think that far ahead.

Fire! Madoc spoke to her silently. Images of the last vampire who had attacked her popped into her head; heat had killed the last vampire. "You want this? Come get it." Angel started to circle around them, hoping he would drop Simon's struggling body and come after her.

The vampire was tall, oriental, with hair as black as ink and spiked into place with strong gel. His head followed her. His burning eyes hungry to feed. Angel kept her breathing calm as her heart rampaged in her chest. She forced her blood to drip off her hand. His arched mouth could taste her delicious scent. His tongue licked his lips as his fangs extended to their full length, throbbing with desire.

Suddenly, everything happened so fast. Sarha had made a grab for Simon while the vampire was focussed on Angel, but this had only brought his attention back to Sarha. He grabbed her by the hair and hauled her through the air. Angel watched wide-eyed as she twisted in flight, hitting a shifter still in her human form, and landing on top of it, knocking the shifter out and taking the air out of Sarha's lungs.

Angel's eyes moved back to Simon who had turned another colour under the vampire's grip; his air had run out. Then she saw blood on the vampire's lips. He had sunk his fangs into Simon's tender neck, ripping it open, drinking mouthfuls like it was water in a desert. Angel watched as excess blood covered Simon's T-shirt.

Angel had no idea what she was doing, only aware that she was suddenly running at the vampire instead of away from him like any normal person would do. Forgetting all her fears and anxieties, she heard laughter coming from Simon's attacker, causing anger to rumble inside her, making her blood boil.

Fire come to me now! Angel shouted silently to the night. She felt the pressure twisting under her skin; the air around her hummed with electricity. She reached out, grabbing the vampire's arm which was free from Simon. Angel pushed her restless energy out. She felt it burst free, leaving her body, seeking out a new source to invade. The force knocked her back a step as it hit him, lighting him up like a dry bonfire.

Simon fell free from the scorched blackened hand. Angel caught him as his legs buckled under his own weight. Both of them went down. Angel landed on her knees, keeping a firm hold on Simon's weak body, making sure he didn't hit the ground hard causing him more pain. Simon was ghostly pale with skin cold beneath her touch. His white T-shirt was covered in his own blood, with some of her own smeared across his arm.

"Stay with me Simon, everything's going to be OK." Angel's voice broke. Tears threatened her eyes; she had to blink them away. Simon was getting paler as his breaths became short and shallow. "*Sarha!*" Angel yelled for her but she didn't move. Simon was now gasping; she could hear each inhale. His eyes where light brown just like his hair. There was no fear in them, just an eerie calm.

Simon was just looking at her: the chosen child had finally come like his family had said she would. Her hair was a mixture of bright golds, her skin pale, and her green eyes looked like gem stones. *Gasp. Gasp. Gasp.* Stillness. Angel shook him in her arms but he was gone. His eyes were still wide but empty and hollow. His lips had turned light blue, and his skin a chalky grey. She heard no breath; felt no warmth from his bloodless body. Simon had died in her arms. He passed with peace and not in fear. A tear fell from her eyes, landing on his stone face.

"Simon?" It was a voice from a distance; it sounded like a question waiting to be answered. "*Simon!*" Sarha had raced over to them and took the boy gently into her own arms. Tears covered her face as she rocked with him, whispering under her breath. "I'm … sorry." Angel was lost for words as she slowly backed away, giving Sarha time alone to grieve.

Slowly standing, Angel wiped her damp hands down her legs, which felt wet from the ground. She turned quickly, heading for Zared. She didn't want to be alone. She didn't want to be away from him. It scared her that it could have been him lying there in her arms.

Angel spotted Zared. Relief flooded her. A light smile touched her lips even if it was just for a brief moment. She knew he was alive, but even though their bond had told her this, she had needed to see him with her own eyes, just to confirm it to her racing heart. She saw he was fighting with one of his own kind; she was just as quick, just as strong, and she had a weapon, whereas Zared had nothing but speed, and a history of being in many battles.

In front of Angel, a woman was spun around, causing Angel to turn her attention away from Zared. Blood sprayed from the woman's mouth as she was hit with such a force by her attacker that it knocked her off balance and caused her sun-kissed skin to turn slightly purple. She stumbled over the rough ground, landing on her knees, shattered. Her long blonde hair covered her beaten face. Angel watched as the woman tried to get up. Angel wanted to help but she couldn't; her legs wouldn't move, she was frozen to the spot, helpless. The woman's solid aura began to shiver, getting stronger and stronger, pulsing, becoming brighter and brighter. She was a witch using her powers. Feeling them intensify, Angel could see her whispering words under her breath. She was casting a spell, recalling it from memory, making her attacker scream and grab at air.

Angel felt her legs release. She kept moving, heading for Zared. She saw a wolf, grey and white, snarling as it jumped, changing into human form and revealing a slender woman with long blonde hair and ice-blue eyes. Her skin was covered in a thin suit that had changed with her. Angel watched with shock as the shifter jumped onto a man's back who was twice her size. The shifter grabbed his head between her hands and yanked it around. Without taking a breath, she returned to her wolf form, running into the thick trees, howling in the distance.

Another shifter suddenly came at Angel. His aura pulsed against her skin; she felt its rate speed up as his body began to change: thick brown coarse hair burst from his skin. His suit disappeared as his figure grew two sizes bigger. His head got wider covering itself in the same thick brown mass of hair. She watched in horror as his face disappeared, turning into a muzzle filled with long yellow sharp teeth. He was now snarling and growling at her, standing on his hind legs, towering over her. His paws were the size of shovels with his claws ready, like razors, to tear through her flesh.

Angel stopped herself from screaming, but she couldn't stop herself from cowering before him. Fear overwhelmed her. Her breathing was shaky as she began to hyperventilate.

Angel tripped over something lying on the ground. It was the abnormally twisted body of a man. He had a gaping big wound that went from his mid chest down to his abdomen. His shredded flesh was curled back. Thin red strings of veins and muscles spaghetti-ed over the stained grass. His lifeless eyes were still open, frozen in time, wide with terror, as blood still dripped from his partially open mouth. Angel scrambled over his rubbery body as the large creature came closer; her hand landed on something cold smooth and slimy. She wondered what it could be as it squashed under her touch. Angel's fingers had wrapped around it. It felt wrong; it wasn't meant to be there, she wasn't meant to be holding it. It was tube-like – large, bumpy – in her shaky grip. Fear twisted her stomach making her feel sick. She had to look; she had to know what it was. Her head twisted slowly. Her breaths came faster as she tried holding on to her panic. Bringing her hand up, still gripping the tube-like mass that was squeezable in her palm, her eyes slowly focussed on it.

Angel couldn't stop herself from screaming this time. Her eyes were wide with shock. Her hand was covered in blood, thick dark liquid that was turning colder by the second. It dripped from her skin as some of it trailed down her elbow. Her mind suddenly realised she was holding a long organ: his intestines. They had spilled out of this fallen stranger who had battled, costing him his life. Angel fell into the pile in front of his body, which she had unfortunately scrambled into.

Angel quickly dropped the man's organs. She kept on hearing her own screams echoing in her ears. Her body was shaking so violently that she could no longer move. Looking up at the beast, she knew he was going to kill her. He came at her, lips peeled back, growling. Angel felt its loud rumble go through her. It went to grab for her with his teeth. Angel threw her hands up in protection, knowing it was of little use against the huge beast that was three-times her size and inhumanly strong, with a mouth full of sharp teeth. Just as the beast went to grab Angel, she felt her fear burst out in an adrenalin rush that hit the shifter hard, forcing him far enough back for her to get up and start running. *Get up,* she told herself, turning onto her hands and knees, and pushing herself onto her unsteady feet, being careful not to trip over the stranger's body parts, or slip on his blood, which had now covered the soil around him turning it to slime.

Breathing fast, Angel swallowed hard and ran. She didn't know where to run, only that she had to run; she had to put distance between her and it. Angel heard it behind her, pounding against the dry earth as it ran. Its breathing was heavy, grunting as it moved faster.

Turn around, she told herself. *Face him!* Angel commanded her disobedient limbs, but her fear was too powerful. She kept running, dodging people, ducking her head as animals jumped, barely missing her but for a few inches; others thudded into her in the scramble, but not forceful enough to knock her off her feet. *I can't out run him. If I don't fight him now, then what's this all for? Everything I want will be gone.* Angel slowed down. She realised she needed to face the fight, that the freedom she wanted depended on her staying out of Leeda's hands, and on keeping Zared alive.

Everything began to happen in slow motion. Angel skidded to a halt, turning on the beast that still charged at her. Taking a deep breath to clear her mind, Angel saw light surrounding her. Calling it to her, drawing it in, she felt it filling her soul, wrapping her body like a blanket.

She closed her eyes, blocking out the noise and chaos all around her: the sounds of the battle that still raged on, the heavy breathing of her oncoming attacker, and the smell of its damp musky fur. Angel relaxed telling her body to stay calm, to go with it. She felt her soul release, as her body fell to the ground – still protected by the force field that she and Barret had discovered the first time she'd met Callie.

Angel stood at the feet of her collapsed body, while the animal slowed, changing back to his human form. His thick brown hair was loose, hanging long down his back. His suit was black against his tanned muscled body. Angel stepped forward coming up to him, stopping inches away. "What's a ghost like you going to do?" He grinned – his breathless voice was deep – as he looked over at her lifeless body; his eyes revealed his cruel intentions if he managed to get at her. "Fight? It's kind of hard to when your body is left vulnerable." He looked at Angel, his hazel eyes fearless, "it just makes things a lot easier for me." He stepped forward confident of an easy kill. Angel reached out, placing a hand on his chest, and pulled the pulsing energy that surrounded him. She felt it tear out of him, uprooting with force, causing him to shout out in agonising pain. She pushed her own energy at him, forcing his to entwine with hers; it seeped in, finding its core of power. She finally drew it back; now it was flowing freely, giving her pleasure as she drank it up, knowing that his energy gave her strength. His hand went over hers; it was the source of his pain. She was slowly killing him. His eyes widened, looking into hers, as he fell to his knees. "What are you?" he asked weakly, as his body became weaker and weaker. "A ghost. Remember?"

She kept her hand on his chest as he went down, his aura was turning black, his breathing was slow and shallow, like the boy's who had lain in her arms; then, she heard his last exhale. His energy was gone. Nothing more came from his body. She had killed him.

Angel thought of Zared. She felt herself move, hovering over a carpet of air, but it was finding him? Then, she spotted him fighting with the same woman she had seen earlier. The woman had a sword made of silver and was thrusting it at Zared, who ducked as she swang for his head. *She's trying to behead him!*

Angel flew past bodies. Coming up behind his opponent, Angel saw Zared's eyes find her briefly before returning his full attention to the woman with the sword. Angel could see his jet-black hair messy around his face; his golden eyes blazing – he was excited by the fight but not hungry.

Zared was still wearing his black T-shirt, which had been ripped and stained with blood in their last attack.

His jeans were still covered in dirt from sleeping rough in abandoned buildings, as well as fighting off Leeda's people.

Angel felt darkness rise. This woman was another vampire; she had no aura for Angel to take. It was the easiest way to kill, but this time she had to think of something else. Closing her eyes, Angel allowed darkness to rise inside of her: getting darker and darker, more powerful. She could feel it burn her skin. She envisioned wood. Everything wooden around her – fallen branches, solitary benches, rotten stall doors – she called to her, pushing her energy out to them, claiming them all. She needed more energy; it wasn't enough to stop them all.

Zared watched as her ghostly form set itself alight; blue and orange flames covered every inch of her body, crackling loudly behind the woman, causing her to turn around. Zared backed up. He knew the power of her darkness; he had felt it rise inside her as she found herself unable to help him.

Now Angel was standing there, flames licking the air, as snakes of lightning leaped out, making contact with all the shifters and witches, linking each of them to her. Zared caught sight of vibrations of energy pulsing from her feet as they moved out, expanding: a puddle of power rippling out. Zared watched as it grew stronger and stronger. Bodies that had auras dropped around him, leaving only vampires standing who looked around, puzzled as mini-earthquakes shook their balance.

Angel opened her eyes. It was ready; it itched inside of her, twisting at her soul to be released. Only Zared would be in danger if that happened. She called to his soul. He had her blood inside of him giving him the power to leave his body like she could. Angel watched as the light grew around him, filling him. It was like hers, shielding him from everything around him, before he fell. Zared felt himself becoming lighter, falling into darkness.

"What happened?" he was standing beside Angel seeing his body lying on the ground, protected by a bubble of light that was a mixture of white and blue, flashing, pulsing with its own heartbeat. "I called you," she replied, "it's the only way I could protect you from what I'm going to do next," she said, releasing the energy that had been raging to be let loose. Zared said nothing. He watched her body arch.

Power, seen as pure light, blasted out of her, circling the vampires that stood, confused. The ground beneath them let out a thunderous roar as a cloud of wood rose.

Zared turned to see Angel's arms extended out in front of her, commanding the cloud of twigs and branches that hovered, ready. Zared watched them smother in smoke before orange flames leaped from their bark.

Angel held the vision of the vampires surrounded by

light that linked them together, bound and glued to the spot, unable to run.

With a final powerful quiver of energy, she released the cloud of burning wood; her hands guiding the blazing debris to its terrified targets. Zared heard their anguished cries meld into one, before their screams finally died into silence.

Chapter Twenty-Five

Zared and Angel returned to their own bodies. Others remained still; some were alive, though barely. Zared saw his attacker lying in front of him: mummified, drained and blackened, with patches of broken flesh where heat had expanded her blood, forcing it out and oozing in a thick mass that burned his lungs with its ghastly smell. A thick charred branch still remained where it had pierced her chest, emerging from her back, twisted within her ribcage.

"Angel!" he called out, looking past bodies. "I'm here." He heard her voice; relief filled him at the soft sound. Even though their bond told him she was fine, her voice was the confirmation he needed. Zared saw her move, slowly getting to her feet. She had been lying next to a half-blood shape-shifter named Andrew. Zared had been on jobs with him before; he had been good for crowd-control, considering he was huge and shifted into a grizzly bear – a bad tempered one at that, and full of himself. But he was vain, enjoying the sound of his own voice. Zared had hated being on jobs with him, and refused them when he could, but for the high-priced ones when he had had to put up with Andrew's constant ranting.

Angel moved slowly towards Zared, gingerly stepping over strewn bodies, aware that some were still alive. They were all strangers to her. "Are you alright?" she asked him, her hands stretched out, ready to grab him when she was close enough, and giving her the extra balance she needed as she tried to avoid standing on spread limbs, or falling into the organs that had spilled from gaping holes. "Yes, are you?" Zared asked, coming to meet her. He stretched out his hand when he got close enough. "Yes," she nodded, "is it over now?"

"For now. But we still need to get inside, out of danger." Zared touched Angel's fingertips. Then, he doubled over. Wide-eyed, Angel watched in slow motion, as he went down. An arrow was driven through his thigh, causing red-hot pain to shoot through their connection. Angel whipped her head round to see a beautiful Indian-looking woman with long silky jet-black hair and smooth milky-coffee skin: Leeda. Her large eyes, the colour of rich chocolate, displayed her joy as her target fell to his knees. Standing at Leeda's side was a woman who looked like a ghost in the shadows of the moonlight. Her skin was lily-white; her hair white as chalk. Her black clothes blended into the darkness around her; a hood was just visible, ready to cover her head.

Angel watched in shock as the woman raised her left hand which was holding a bow. With her right hand, she gripped an arrow, pulling the string back to her face and pointing it in their direction. Angel's breath stopped. Leeda flashed her a dazzling half-smile; her eyes travelled from Angel to Zared. The arrow was released. Angel could hear screaming, not realising it was coming from her, as she threw herself at Zared. She was too late. It hit him hard in the chest, knocking him flat to the floor. His body jerked. Angel landed across his stomach. She pushed herself off him, tears running down her face as she watched him fighting to stay calm. *"Hold on! You'll be OK! Just hold on!"* Her voice cracked as she sniffled. *Please don't let him die!*

"Take it out," Zared whispered, his body convulsing with spasms of pain. "I can't," Angel sobbed, looking around, shouting for help. "Yes you can. I know you can." His hand grabbed the arrow. "Angel you have to, because I can't. Just get a good grip on it then take a deep breath and pull it as hard as you can." Angel nodded;

everything was speeding up around her. She was losing him fast. Angel wiped her face, took a couple of breaths and pulled herself together. She grabbed the thin wood and pulled as hard as she could until it broke free, causing her to fly back landing hard on her buttocks.

Zared's wound wasn't healing. It was mean to, but it wasn't. Angel watched as it kept bleeding, blood bubbling up around the hole. His skin turned black. The web of poison had spread quickly to his chest. Something had been put on the arrow's head; something lethal to vampires, causing them to bleed. She put her hands over the wound, pushing down, trying to stop the poison's progress, or at least slow it down.

"*Zared ...*" She didn't know what to say. "What do I do?" she said at last. "There's nothing you can do. It's been poisoned; there's no way to stop it." His body arched in pain; his golden eyes glazed. "There must be something?" His blood was turning her skin red, but his answer was written in his eyes: there was nothing.

"*No!* You can't die on me. I won't let you!" She took a deep breath, looking around for any ideas. Then she saw something flash in the corner of her eye: a blade. Grabbing the blade that lay next to the female vampire, she picked it up. She sliced her arm, gasping at the stinging pain, squeezing it to encourage the blood to flow faster and thicker. "Drink, it will help," Angel ordered, placing her arm over Zared's mouth so he couldn't stop her. She felt Zared suck at her wound, drinking in gulps before he went still. *No! He can't die ... not for me.* She grabbed his shoulders and started to shake him. "Zared!" *All these people who died to help me!* She felt daggers of pain slicing her into a thousand pieces. "Zared!" she screamed, "don't you dare leave me!" Anger rose inside her. She was helpless; she was losing him. If he left her, then she would be alone again; she would be the person he had found weeks ago. Leeda would have won.

Angel screamed as loud as she could. Everything around her crackled and sparked; her skin was alive, tears still running down her face. Angel screamed again as loud as she could, releasing energy; she felt it explode out of her, driving into the earth, hitting hard, providing a wall of dirt. Its earthy musk filled the air as a blanket fell over both of them, concealing them from the outside world, protecting them.

Her grief still burned, ripping her apart, growing in strength, turning dark and hateful, and filling her with rage; a rage that wanted to strike out at those that had taken him from her. She wanted to cause damage; she wanted to save Zared; she wanted to give life back to those that had lost it, to save them the way they had saved her. The air around her began to spin, entwining with her blanket of dirt, and howling around her ears as it circled them. Her heart began to beat faster, helping the vortex around her to speed up. Feeling her own body linked to it, Angel felt it begin picking them up. She was off her knees; Zared was floating in front of her, hovering inches off the ground, along with loose foliage spinning around them. Their tunnel of energy raised them higher and higher.

Angel, looking up to the night sky, could see no stars, only clouds that had formed above her, erupting with grumbles of a storm approaching. Angel screamed again, feeling the sound slice through every other noise, commanding silence. The sky lit up, lightning flashed streaks across the vast sky, before circling them, striking down with blue light that hit the ground, throwing up more mud and grass. Angel could smell it burn.

She put her arms out wide. Her skin felt raw; every sense was awakened. Dark energy licked her skin, weaving in and out of her, pulsing, sparking, waiting for her command. Angel wanted more energy; more than any she had taken before. Lightning struck her. Energy that surrounded the earth joined her. She wasn't Angel any more. At that moment Angel had gone; replaced with pure energy, a power so strong that it lit up the night sky.

Angel screamed one last time, thinking of those that had helped her, of Zared lying still, lifeless. How she wanted him to be alive. She placed her hands on his chest over his open wound. Her skin was hot, pulsing, vibrating with pure energy. Her eyes no longer seeing; she was blind, only white light filled her vision.

Suddenly, it seemed that everything exploded, the force knocking her back. Waves of energy pulsed over and over in the night air, turning the sky into golds, pinks and purples, colours of the sunset and the -rise, which she had long forgotten as her tears continued to fall. She could feel the power punching through them, through their bond as well, hitting his lifeless body, making it arch with each intense blow.

A dark silhouette looked down on her: his eyes burned silver, a colour that was pure with no taint or hint of another colour – just pure silver that reflected light, a mirror of truth. "Hello my Queen. Everything's going to be alright now." He smiled, lifting her into his strong arms. "Madoc?" Angel managed to whisper before passing out.

Angel opened her eyes to see a bed to her left. Zared was lying on his back, his dark hair ruffled, his pale skin looking even whiter against the hospital-like sheets. Angel felt a smile tug at her dry lips; he was alive and sleeping next to her, safe within the four walls. She turned in her bed. Her bond to Zared had changed slightly, breaking off in another direction. She could feel another presence inside her, a strong safe sense came from this bond. *Madoc!* She remembered having seen him before the darkness had taken her. She had wondered if he was really there, or if she had just dreamt it.

A warm hand touched her skin causing her to jump, yelping at the same time in surprise. She saw Madoc sitting to her right on a padded stool. Madoc was the same height as Zared, with skin just touched by the sun. Unlike hers, his features were flawless, model worthy. His straight golden blonde hair half covered his perfect eyes, which were still the colour of pure silver, with a marble of darker steel that circled their centre – a colour that appeared then disappeared. His perfectly sculptured body showed under his tight black shirt. His strong large hands touched her gently.

An energy of 'warrior' radiated from him, making Angel feel safer than ever before. Something secretive deep inside her soul drew her to him. Their bond was intense, wrapping around them both, masking her from

Zared and every other person that was suddenly linked to them. Madoc moved closer. She could see the mark on the left side of his neck, in the same place as Zared's. He hovered over her, watching her, carefully studying her. He could hear her heartbeat picking up speed the closer he came. Her breath trembled, not with fear, but desire. Their link burned, heating up his own emotions, which he had forced himself to forget. Angel lay there, frozen, staring into his eyes, which had now turned violet. His skin smelled perfect. She wanted to inhale deeply, to take his scent inside her and remember it forever.

"Madoc?" Angel said breathlessly, her fingers kneading the sheets at her side, wondering what he was to her. "Hello, my Queen." He smiled. His voice sounded husky, making her chest ache, her stomach twist, her face flush.